END OF
EVER AFTER

AN
END OF EVER AFTER
NOVEL

E. L. TENENBAUM

ISBN: 978-1-68046-689-8

Fire & Ice Young Adult Books
An Imprint of Melange Books, LLC
White Bear Lake, MN 55110
www.fireandiceya.com

Published in the United States of America.

Cover Design by Caroline Andrus

LH"U

EVER AFTER

Once upon a time, the palace wasn't my prison.

Not that kind of prison; there are no bars upon the windows and I can stand in the sun whenever I choose. My power is almost unlimited, I am free to go where and when I want. This is a different type of prison, one of half-truths and warbled perceptions; a prison I unwittingly stepped into the day all my dreams came true.

For what can a sheltered girl of sixteen know about reality when her life plays out like a faery tale? I had never wondered about Snow White once her prince kissed and whisked her away. I had imagined a similarly happy fate for the Sleeping Beauty, for the Beauty and her Beast. Would either have warned me had I asked for the truth? That "happily ever after" doesn't last?

Because I wasn't a princess, not at first. I wasn't anything but a dusty servant girl, and for a while, it really seemed like my story would be different from the others. Maybe I was only playing my part, embracing the destiny I believed was mine because it had rolled out before me like a soft red carpet spilling from a royal carriage the day that sealed my fate.

And wasn't my faery godmother part of all this, too? Hadn't she displayed the best and brightest magic, dressed me like a princess so I could win a prince? She wouldn't have done so if this wasn't supposed to be good.

Yet I would never go back to the way my life was before. It's taken me five years to soften the skin on my hands, to undo the callouses marring my palms and knuckles that marked me as a servant. Now, I have servants of my own to get me whatever, whenever, however I want. Any request of my stepmother or stepsisters could be irrational, unwarranted, unworthy of my time, but a queen's requests are never foolish, never too simple to ignore or sweep under the rug until she goes to sleep.

Every princess learns that life goes on after happily ever after, and my life is better than it ever was. But often I wonder what would've happened if I'd kept dreaming in my own little corner instead of going to that wretched, wretched ball.

BEFORE

My father was often away on business, far back as I can remember. Each time he went, Mother took me to the study, pulled out his large spinning globe and a pile of maps, then showed me exactly what route he would take. I would think that being adept at direction so early in life would have made me a better navigator of my future.

"Father always stops through this inn when he travels this way." Mother guided my hand, pointing with me to a little square sitting just off the main road.

"Because they have the best ale," I chimed in.

Mother smiled and stroked my hair. "Because they have the best ale," she repeated.

I walked the route with my little fingers. "Why can't Father sleep at home if it's so close?" I wondered out loud.

"The map shows how all this land looks from Heaven," Mother explained. "Down here, everything is much farther apart."

"Will Father leap across this river?" I asked, tracing a blue line from its origin in the mountains to its end in the sea.

"Father will take a ferry across and when he does, he'll be thinking of you," Mother said. She traced the route then came back round again toward our little slice of paradise. "And from here he'll already be counting the steps back home to us."

My knack for maps can be traced to those early days. Even after Mother was gone, I would sneak into Father's study to trace his route on the maps. Perhaps I did it more to reconnect with my mother than my father. By that point, he hardly remembered the daughter from his first wife.

I suppose Father was successful, because we lived on a fairly large piece of land though we weren't titled gentry. During spring and summer, the green lawns were hardly visible beneath the most wonderful shades of blue, pink, purple, yellow, and white flowers. They cozied up to tree trunks and popped out between blades of grass, their petals radiating in the sunlight in a way quite befitting a faerytale land.

Our home was tucked back beside a clear, bubbling stream and a small orchard that gave us all the fruit we needed. The path leading up to our property was lined on either side by a low stone wall which guided it through the bramble and drooping willows until our house emerged behind a sharp bend where the path yielded to a circular drive. I never thought much of that drive, but Madame was to later teach me that having a circular drive was very important for a person of means. We were never allowed to descend any of the twelve steps that climbed to our front door until the horses of a visitor's carriage were already slightly turned to align his door with ours. I thought that rule the most unbearable whenever Father returned home.

Before Madame came, we were happy, as happy as any family can be, and it's odd to think now that the time when our family was only Father, Mother, and me was my true happily ever after. Those days, a square of grass could hold an entire kingdom, a full plot held an entire world. Those days, sunshine was proof of

Heaven smiling down on me, the clear sky a window thrown open above to light up a world waiting to be discovered. Those days are frozen in the colors of memory that never fade.

Thinking back on the house that was once my home, what stands out most to me is not the oil-painting tranquility I left behind, but rather the constant trilling of birds. Snow white pigeons and turtledoves, blue robins and startling red cardinals all made their homes in our gardens at one point or another. At times, it felt as if every bird stopped for a visit during their migrations, as if we were their inn of choice for their travels. And those birds were always singing, always the chariots of faeries in my childhood games.

My mother was beautiful, dainty, and gentle. From the moment I could walk, it was quite clear that I was formed in her image, a fact I used to wear with pride until it would come to haunt me. I was born small and stayed so. I have a small waist, small hands, tiny feet, and when made up, the heart-shaped face my mother bequeathed me very much resembles that of a fragile porcelain doll. Before I came to the palace, my looks were the cause of much ridicule by my stepfamily whom I'm sure would have been glad to crack me underfoot.

From what I can remember, I don't think my mother was as small as I am. She may have seemed bigger to me because I was so little, but I don't think so. However, there was something about her that was larger than life, and I think it was largely part of the reason why she was well respected. She was kind and generous, pious and sweet, and never lost her temper. She tried hard to pass those traits on to me, and I think she must have because kindness, generosity, and sweetness, while much lauded by bards and minstrels, have also been the bane of my existence. They are the root of my naiveté, my blind trust, my acceptance of whatever I'm given, and my perverse instinct to always rationalize a person's behavior for the good. I've been working on changing some of those things. I certainly didn't get Mother's unshakeable temperament.

My mother and I were best friends for as long as she was alive, our delight in each other's company a wonderful buoy to help us through Father's long absences.

"What shall we feast on today, Ella?" was the question I would wake up to the first morning after Father left.

"Corn cakes!" I'd jump on my bed so I couldn't be tripped by the ends of my white nightgown. "White powdered confections! And chocolate roses! Lemon tarts and strawberry cream cake!"

Mother would giggle and grab my hands to jump beside me on the floor.

"And roast goose!"

"We shall have all those things and more, dear princess!" Mother cried. "And no amount of sweets shall be too much!"

Mother didn't know then, as I know now, what my life would be like as a princess. She never would have called me that if she had.

Mother would dress me herself, in little dresses of navy blue dotted with pearl-colored flowers, leaf-colored greens decorated with bows of orange ribbons, lavender layers embroidered with pastel yellow beadings. And always a bonnet pulled tight over my head to keep my skin milky white beneath my rosy cheeks.

We'd spend all day outside, or inside, whichever suited our fancy. Together, we traveled the world and were it not for those early years, I would have grown up with an imagination as painfully dull as my stepsisters'. Like most good things from my past, I cursed my imagination when I understood how it distorted the truth of palace life, but I am learning.

Once a week, Mother bundled me up, ordered up the cart, and took me on her rounds to visit the peasants who rented the King's land surrounding ours. Mother remembered everyone's name and the little details of their lives that were so important to them. We would visit homes too small for the families they were supposed to shelter and women whose husbands couldn't care for them after childbirth because they couldn't miss a day in the fields. At all these places, Mother's arrival was like a ray of sunshine on a cold and cloudy day, a momentary whisper of heavenly trumpets sending away the drudgery of the world.

Mother always made me hold the basket of fruit I'd helped her pick from our orchard. She insisted that I give out the fruit and made sure I did so with a warm smile.

"Ella, remember, there is always, always someone more unfortunate than yourself," she would tell me in the time it took to ride from one house to another.

"What if I keep giving and then there's nothing left?" I wanted to know.

"Kindness does not run out." Mother smiled and lovingly tapped my nose with her finger. "There are too many people in need of an open ear and an accepting heart."

Madame had Mother's cart smashed to kindling the day she arrived.

Father always brought back something from his travels, no matter where he'd gone or for how long. Treats and confections, laces and beads, something for Mother and something for me. One time, he brought back a life-size doll, or perhaps it only seemed that way because I was so small. That doll frightened me away from its room for two months, and I only went near it when Mother finally tricked me.

"Ella, you must come quickly," she woke me one morning.

"What is it, Mama?" I was instantly wide awake at her urgency.

"A little girl is in trouble," she hurried to explain. "She's being held captive by a giant!"

I clambered out of bed. "We must save her at once, Mama!"

"This way."

She took my little hand and led me to the playroom where

she'd barricaded one of my favorite dolls behind a fortress of blocks and pillows. Before all that loomed the giant, that scary life-size doll I was afraid would crush me should it topple over. Mother must have felt my hesitation, because she wouldn't let my hand go.

"We cannot abandon the girl!" she insisted.

I tried to pull away. "Surely there is some other brave knight who can rescue her."

As part of his contribution to our games of pretend, Father gave me fencing lessons whenever he was home. I can't say that I was an expert, but I was proficient at holding my own against him with my little wooden sword. Now, Mother pushed the sword into my hand and set me firmly forward. "You are the only one left. The little girl needs you."

"Perhaps there's a way to trick the giant?" I suggested hopefully.

Mother softened at that. "Perhaps," she agreed.

We rescued the girl and I was no longer frightened of the doll, but it would always be the terrible giant thereafter.

Usually, Father's gifts were darling like the small, bright orange goldfish he once brought me on a whim. I have no idea how it survived the journey and am even less certain how such a tiny creature persevered through all the changes over the years. Father bought it for me a few months before Mother died, and when Madame came, the first thing she said upon seeing it happily chasing its tail around its tiny bowl in the study was, "Get that animal out of here."

It moved into the attic with me and the boxes of other unwanted and forgotten items. Many of those things were Mother's, the remains of her clothing, bits of inexpensive jewelry, and a faery-dusted sword with an unbreakable blade sharp enough to cut stone inherited from Mother's father from a time when magic was easier to come by. Sometimes, I'd take it out for a few thrusts and parries, gaining a feel for the blade as I reminisced about the wooden swords Father and I used to play with. I snuck it upstairs when I was thirteen, the age I finally acknowledged that I no longer trusted Father to protect anything that once belonged to Mother, not even me.

I also received a wonderful, cream colored pony with brown socks above its hooves, which Madame would soon pronounce me underserving of owning. A mosaic topped jewelry box, a kaleidoscope of color in the light, with a false bottom, which I've since lost to one of my stepsister's whims. Real jade earrings and a little ivory princess charm carved from the rare tusk of an elephant, which, again, are no longer mine. Then, one day, about a year after Mother passed from this world, three months after my ninth birthday, Father brought home the gift he thought would outdo all the others: a new mother.

My new mother brought with her the title of Baroness, a fact she flaunted with pride, though she'd earned her rank through her first marriage. She must have thought the commotion over her station was enough to hide the fact that her blood didn't really run blue at all. While my father was allowed to change his stationery to accept the new title, such privileges were not extended to me. From the beginning, it was quite clear that I was not, and never would be, the baroness's daughter. She already had two of her own and didn't want any more.

"You'll call me Madame," were the first words she said to me after a few, long, agonizing moments under her disapproving scrutiny.

"Yes, Madame," I replied willingly, eager to please this proud, aristocratic woman, who Father said would take care of me. It wouldn't take long for me to know that if I'd ever had a thought to change that title it would never have been to "Ma" but "Mad."

Madame was not horrible at first, but she was never very good to me either. In the beginning, however begrudgingly, she allowed me to join all the lessons in the finer arts she arranged for her daughters to mold them into the ladies of quality she dreamed them to be. Thusly, I learned how to dance, how to paint, how to play piano, how to sing, how to dress, how to eat, how to stand, and how to faint convincingly for the purpose of gaining a gentleman's attentions.

Despite what she later did to me, I have to give her credit for unknowingly training me into princess caliber material.

Madame's two daughters, Maybelle and Calliope, carried themselves with no less airs than their mother. They were beautiful, talented, and unhelpful to a young girl trying to exercise patience. Calliope sang with the heart of a fallen angel; Maybelle played the piano like a favored muse. Even after they'd banished me to the cinders, I could still enjoy listening to them practice together.

Etiquette was overbearingly high on Madame's list of musts for a proper lady. Here too, she included me in the tedious and insufferable lessons with her daughters, often forcing us to eat soup with books balanced on our heads so as to maintain perfect posture throughout. She took away our food if she saw us leaning toward it instead of bringing it up to our mouths.

"Remember, girls, a straight back comes from your ribs," she'd shrilly command. "Lift them and the rest will follow. Good, now chins up and follow me. One, two, three, step and one, two, three and step. Up. Up."

At this point, we were expected to gracefully float behind her, twisting around furniture and stepping over any amount of obstacles she'd shove off nearby tables and into our path. The trick was to never flinch, never falter, never lose poise.

"Carriage up, Calliope, up."

"Your neck is a swan, Maybelle, but only your neck. We have no use for the rest of its body."

"Keep up, Ella, and try not to get underfoot."

"She really is small, isn't she Mother?"

"She could fit into my pocket!"

"Calliope, smile coyly when you have something witty to say. Grace, modesty, and suggestion."

"That's a good effort, Maybelle dear, but lift your chin more so you only have the one."

"Ella, how can a mouse like you make noise like an elephant?"

"An Ella-mouse!" Maybelle chirruped.

"An Ella-phant," Calliope corrected with a carefully coy smile.

My stepsisters were quick to teach me that Ella was a name easily paired with almost any term of ridicule.

"Quite right, girls. Now, to the drawing room for tea. Ella, be a dear and clean this up."

On cold nights, when the fires burn too low to warm me, and the sky's too dark to let the stars shine through, the echo of her voice still haunts me.

I'm not sure how Father viewed these lessons the few times he stumbled upon us as we glided along the bottom floor of the house, up the stairs, down the stairs then to the gardens, keeping pace, changing pace, but always with a coy smile and perfect posture. The first few months after he brought Madame home, it really seemed as if he would allow himself to be happy, even if he would never be the same. Then he started traveling again and staying away for longer and longer periods of time. He withdrew into himself only a year or two before I was completely left to the whims of Madame. By then, Father couldn't save me, even if he had wanted to. I may have too well reflected my mother's image for him to ever look upon me without reliving the pain of her loss.

During that time, he brought a macaw parrot home with him from one of his trips, and considering Madame's reaction to my goldfish, I was surprised she let him keep it. The macaw was usually confined to his study, however, and I wonder now if wasn't there just to keep her out. Despite the macaw's bright red body and yellow-and-blue wings, he named it Iris, I assumed after my mother, though he'd never admit as much to Madame. She only every referred to it as "that beast" anyway. I supposed Father simply felt he needed someone to talk to. Looking back now, it pains me to wonder why that someone was never me.

The last kindness I ever received from him, or anyone in that house, was a short while before the bold colors of my soaring imagination were buried under the soot of my stepfamily's dulled one. I was almost eleven then, going on three years into my life with the woman who would never be a mother to me. Father was preparing to leave on yet another trip and like a proper family, we all stood at the top of those twelve steps to wish him farewell.

In the last moment—perhaps as an afterthought or, as I like to believe it, a moment of clarity—Father stopped somewhere around the seventh or eighth step, turned around, and with a genuine smile asked each of his daughters what gift we wished him to bring back for us.

"Beautiful dresses in the latest fashion of all the high courts!" Maybelle immediately exclaimed.

"Pearls and, and," Calliope stuttered in her excitement and Madame hit her accordingly, "and jewels!" she managed to finish.

"And you, Ella?" Father turned his sunken, once warm and peaceful eyes upon me. "What would you like?"

I kept my gaze on the steps unsure of what to ask for considering my stepsisters' requests. All I really wanted was the Father from before, the one who'd never asked but always perfectly surprised, whose smile began at his lips and ended in his eyes, the one who readily joined my mother and myself in our sheltered world of pretend. But he was gone and I, the mirror image, the spectral of my mother, could do nothing to bring him back.

I searched his face for the whisper of the man who used to

delight in me. "Please bring me the first twig that brushes your hat on your way home, Father," I finally said. "That's all I want."

My stepsisters snickered beside me, but I focused on the way my father's eyes softened for just a brief moment before they distanced back to vacancy.

"Of course, dear Ella," he replied, and with that he descended the last of the steps and swung himself onto his horse.

My father was as good as his word. When he returned, Maybelle was given three dresses: one a golden yellow to match her bottle curls, one a cobalt blue with silver trimming on the bodice to match her startling blue eyes, and one a pastel pink to match her rosy, well-fed cheeks.

Calliope was brought jewelry as she'd been promised. A string of white pearls to adorn her swan-like neck, a pair of tear-shaped emerald earrings to match her forested eyes, and a bracelet of rubies to bring attention to her delicate white hands.

As my stepsisters reveled in their finery, I was granted my one simple request, a thin, leafy branch, unnaturally healthy despite being removed from its source since it brushed my father's hat. It did not match my oddly colored lavender eyes, for which my stepsisters often mockingly suggested that I was not a small human but an overgrown faery, it was too big for my small white arms, and overshadowed my reddened auburn hair. Yet it was exactly what I wanted.

The fleeting spark in my father's eye told me that perhaps he'd chosen which tree would brush his hat first, and so I took the twig out to the end of our estate, near the low stone wall where my mother was buried, dug a hole and planted it. Two years I watered and cared for it, despite unaccountable amounts of teasing, then I trekked out one day to find that the thin twig had taken root and blossomed. Within months, a sturdy tree had spread its unnaturally green branches over that small corner, my small corner, of the estate.

Of course, by then, it was too late for me, and the tree's emergence, quickly followed by its production of succulent green pears, sealed my oncoming fate.

"Ella dear, how marvelous!" Madame beamed at me one day not long after the first pear peeked out. "To think you could turn a dead stick into a pear tree."

"Faery," Maybelle smirked, but for once Madame ignored her.

"A green thumb in the family," Madame mused to herself without moving her cunning gaze from me. "Perhaps you could help Cook sometime in the garden?"

Despite the suggestion in her words, the tone of her voice said it would be done.

"Yes, Madame," I answered dutifully, and turned toward the garden as expected.

It wasn't just the tone that compelled me to listen to her, nor the misguided thought that she might still replace the mother I lost. I thought, naively I realize now, that perhaps if I would just do right in this one thing, if I would help Cook with my green thumb and coax the garden to produce the most delicious vegetables, then, finally then, Madame would notice me and treat me like a true daughter of the house.

But green is the color of envy and illness, not love.

"Oh Ella," Madame cooed after me.

"Yes, Madame?"

"Do change your dress before you begin," she innocently suggested. "So it doesn't ruin."

"Yes, Madame."

That is how it began. Helping Cook in the garden turned into feeding the chickens, which turned into drawing water to wash the windows and the hardworking ladies-to-be after their strenuous lessons in etiquette. Then it was sweeping the floors, polishing the silver, and setting out tea, then serving the others breakfast...in bed.

It came to a point where I had so many responsibilities about the house that Madame announced, "I simply don't know what I would do without Ella. It would be such a waste of time to bring in someone new and start from the beginning."

Why was I ever kind to her? Perhaps I was weak or dimwitted. Perhaps I thought it could win her favor or was too desperate for her kindness to think of anything but. That same mistaken mindset would follow me to the palace where it would mislead me there as well. For, though my mother had done her best to teach me how to be kind, I needed more than that in my life. Kindness is not a currency many people trade in.

That time felt like the end but was really only the beginning for me. Each night, as the pile of work grew larger and the nights grew too because of it, I would recede into my small kitchen corner and work by the light of the fire. My back grew stiff from sitting too long on a hard, broken wicker chair and my hands cramped as I scrubbed and mended and swept and cleaned. I no longer had time for books or lessons, could scarce afford a moment to paint or wander around outside at my leisure. Yet neither Madame nor Maybelle nor Calliope, who in bursts of goodwill would sometimes sneak me some of the treats from the table that I was no longer allowed to have, could manage to take away nor dull my imagination. As a young girl, I had traveled the world with my mother, and as I grew older I traveled it again, not to explore, but to escape.

As I worked, I dreamed of many things, of exploring jungles and befriending exotic animals, of singing and dancing on the world's greatest stages, of wearing the finest clothes made from the softest silks, and even, perhaps, of being the kind of girl tall enough and pretty enough to make others take notice. I foolishly thought then that looks were all I needed.

Above all else, my favorite and most recurring dream was that one day someone would rescue and carry me away from that now-wretched place. For my part, I would never look back, never regret what my life would become. And who better to rescue a maiden in distress than a prince? I put so much hope, so much faith into that dream that when reality came, I mistook it for the other.

Overall, the adventures I managed in those days were too few and far between for my liking. Late at night, when I was sure the house was asleep, I would gather some of the pears from my magical tree and sneak away to the homes of the poor that I used to visit with Mother. I didn't dare take anything from the vegetable garden, orchard, or even leftovers from the kitchen as I was certain Madame kept track of it all. The pear tree was too close to Mother's grave for her to ever go near, so they were one of the few things I still genuinely owned. Unfortunately, my chores at home kept me from visiting at a more appropriate hour, so I didn't speak with any of the people anymore. Instead, I would quietly hang a few pears from the door latch and pray the gesture brought some comfort when they were found in the morning. Those nights taught me a thing or two about sneaking about silently, certainly more Ella-mouse than Ella-phant.

Because of the brief time I was allowed to paint, it was discovered that I not only had a green thumb, but also a keen eye for arranging colors and patterns. So it was only natural that I soon be tasked with helping my stepsisters with their makeup, then somehow hair, and even dresses for the innumerable balls they were soon being whisked off to at the homes of the surrounding nobility.

"It sounds so wonderful," I made the mistake of murmuring one day, while helping Calliope out of the mounds of material it seemed I'd only just swathed her in.

Maybelle let out a cruel giggle. "Wonderful!" she crowed. "Oh dear, you don't actually wish to come with us?"

I kept my eyes down, a habit I'd unfortunately overdeveloped of late. When Mother was alive, my eyes couldn't look far enough past the skies, now I was noticing every shade of earth, every warble of wood in the floor beneath my feet.

Calliope, who was usually more tolerant of me—well, more than the others—couldn't hold back her shriek of laughter. "Could you imagine?"

"A cinder maiden at a ball?" Maybelle passed a finger over my soot-stained cheek without quite touching it. "A cinder wench!"

"A Cinderwench!" Calliope parroted, then collapsed on her bed in giggles.

The name stuck, as cruel and silly names often will. And after a while, that's what I became. No longer was I petite Ella, rescuer of damsels in distress, commander of the stage, captain of the swiftest ship, a human in a faery land. With the name came the reality, and only later did I wonder that none of the other servants ever said a word at my sudden fall from mistress to maid. Most of them had come to our house with Madame, but surely, they knew, surely, they saw what was happening. The only thing I could think to say for them is that perhaps, when someone repeats that my life is nothing for long enough, then everyone else believes it, too. So I was, and believed myself to be, nothing more than Cinderwench, with only a goldfish, a faery sprinkled sword, and a pear-bearing tree for company.

BEGINNING OF THE END

*N*othing ominous dawned on the first day that changed my life forever. More precisely, it was a warm and lovely day, a hint of spring in the last days of winter, the perfect kind of day for pretending in the garden with Mother when she was still alive. Now, the perfect day would be put to good use like all other perfect days are by adolescent girls; shopping.

Madame only allowed my sixteen-year old self into town with my stepsisters because someone had to carry the packages. Anything large was taken back to the carriage by the footman, but anything small or delicate was placed in my care. Especially because it was to be a full day venture, we would be going into the streets of Camallea, the capital, where, no matter what time of day or year, anything could be bought. Thus, we were under strict orders to stay tight together with unbending carriages and upheld chins. Even Father, uninterested and removed as always, was dragged along to complete the image of the baroness's perfect circumstances.

After helping my stepsisters choose new colors for their spring dresses, which of course I would be tasked with designing, after choosing the right feathers, beads, and other bits to accessorize them with, which of course I was charged with carrying, I wandered a few feet behind the others as they strolled through the market stalls piled high with shiny red apples, sun-kissed oranges, tart yellow lemons, and mouth-watering chocolates. I wasn't too far behind them on purpose, my short legs could hardly keep up, especially with the packages weighing me down.

A handful of the little shops behind the stalls, the ones not dedicated to mundane trades, boasted mounds of white and pastel-colored confections in their windows and it was only a matter of time before Maybelle had successfully maneuvered us all over to one.

"Just a little something, Mama," she pleaded, and Madame, who almost never refused her daughters, gave in.

"Ella, please stay here with the packages. We can't risk them getting ruined inside," Madame said too sweetly, sweeping Father into the store with her and her girls. "Really, she is just so dear," I heard her say to him as they went by.

"Cinderwench the gutterwench," Maybelle mouthed, as she gleefully brushed past me.

Looking away to force back tears, I spotted a well in a small piazza down a short alley beside the shop and figured to rest my feet there while I waited.

I do not think coincidence, blind fate, or fickle destiny led me to that very spot. Rather, I firmly believe a hand reached down from Heaven itself to guide me to what would be the beginning of the end. What I didn't, and still don't, understand is why it chose me.

Although nestled just one row behind the bustling marketplace, the piazza was somehow quiet, secluded, becomingly illuminated by glittering rays of sunlight with nothing marring the smooth cobblestones but a simple well. Wanting to take everything in, I turned around even before I entered and ended up backing straight into someone, whereupon I promptly tripped and let all my packages fly.

"I'm terribly sorry," I stuttered, then immediately dropped to the floor and scrambled to pull everything together.

"I beg your pardon, miss," a deep voice rumbled over me. I looked up to see the gentleman I had bumped into kneeling on the floor with me and trying as best he could to help.

"It's no matter." I dropped my eyes and focused too hard on the task at hand.

The man's large hands were protected from the chaff of horses' reins, bows, and swords, with black leather gloves which flew in and out of my vision as he adamantly set to putting things right.

"There," he reassured me once all the packages were carefully stacked against the stone well.

"Thank you." I dared glance up only then, but quickly looked away when I caught the man studying me closely.

He was dressed in a very fine, royal purple uniform that fit neatly over his broad frame. He had thick brown hair and soft brown eyes, which though puppy-like, were alert and chilling as a lion's. His voice though deep was gentle toward me and his actions confirmed his nobility. He wore his uniform with unstated pride and respect, and a sparkling sword hilt jutted up from the belt around his hips.

"Your eyes are—"

Till then the shadows must have blocked their color. I lowered my head so he could not look anymore.

I have been called beautiful, but if it's true, then I believe it to be of an ethereal sort. Some men can't look away and others can't get away quick enough. The purple hue of my eyes only compounds the matter, their rarity considered unnatural, a trait of faeries and not man. I have been called delicate and fragile, enough so that men feel an urge to protect me like a child. I wish they did not.

"I only came for some water," I blurted, then clamped my mouth shut before I could say anything more, or more foolish.

The man immediately jumped forward. "Allow me, miss."

"It's no bother—" I began just as the sound of hoof beats stomped over the silence of the piazza.

"There you are, Captain!" a melodious voice called out, and in an instant the captain's leathered hand shot out and stopped the nose of the horse that was about to trample me.

"Whoa," he rumbled, grabbing the magnificent horse's bridle, trying to keep from frightening the glorious creature.

The rider of the horse must have peered around then, because he suddenly exclaimed, "I didn't see you there, little girl! Take care, or you'll easily be trampled underfoot."

I was too flabbergasted to correct him. "I was only getting some water," I said dumbly, turning back to the well so neither man could see the blush of shame burning across my cheeks.

"As are we," the rider sang out.

Then and forever his voice was a melody, a rich, rolling symphony; a lone, fragile violin. In the beginning, especially, I heard the songs of angels in the very lilt of that man's voice.

I already had the bucket halfway up, and the words that would begin my downward spiral tumbled out, "Please take," I offered him the bucket, "and perhaps some for your horse as well?"

"Yes, yes, of course," the rider agreed. "How thoughtful."

It wasn't until I was pouring water into his metal cup that I snuck a glance at the rider.

My breath stopped. My world turned upside down.

Before me was the most handsome man I had ever seen. Even within the abruptly realized limited confines of my imagination, I could never dream up a man so wonderful to simply look at. He had sandy hair that curled at the too-long ends. A short straight nose, chiseled jaw, and eyes deeper than the oceans and bluer than the skies. His clothes were specifically tailored not in style, but not out of style either. I was to later learn this was because this was a man who set the fashion, as that's one of the many things princes do.

I was suddenly embarrassed to be standing before these two finely dressed gentlemen, the very accent of their voices belying their superior education and upper class. My sisters had new dresses made at each turn of the season, but I had been wearing the same two for years. I fingered the material that had been washed so many times the color fled back into the earth it came from. The hem had been taken out and adjusted until it could be no longer, and the sleeves had finally been cut short so my adolescent arms wouldn't give away their odd length. And this was my nicer dress.

Still, the man inexplicably grinned at me as I filled his cup, once for him and then once again for his fine white horse to clumsily spill over his shiny leather boots as it tried to lap it up. After, he effortlessly raised himself back onto his horse, and flicked over a gold coin "for your trouble."

Years of swordsmanship helped me catch it easily, and I dropped a short, flawless curtsy in thanks. The man leaned forward in his saddle as if to say something more, but it was then that I heard the sharp beginnings of "Ell—!"

"I must go," I apologized and grabbed the parcels even as the captain called out behind me, "But your drink!"

I scurried down the alley and fell into step behind my stepsisters before Madame could rebuke me. I prayed we'd be well on our way before either of the men on horseback saw me like this.

I didn't look back as I obediently followed behind my sisters, past farmers selling livestock and travelers selling exotic animals, past watchmakers and glassblowers, blacksmiths and taverns, until we came upon the end of the street. There, it spilled into a large promenade bordered by the river that scurried past the city before snaking around the palace and catching up with the sea. The palace sat on a large rocky outcropping that overlooked the capital. It was accessible only by water and the large main bridge that was carefully guarded from every angle.

We found some shade to wait under as Father was sent to track down our footman and carriage. We weren't waiting long before the loud ringing of a hand bell interrupted our rest. Looking up, we were greeted by the sight of a castle crier perched upon a hastily positioned wooden crate. Behind him, close enough to watch the proceedings but not enough to be part of them, was the handsome man from the well and the captain. They had been joined by a half dozen other men wearing the same purple uniform as the captain's, sans the gold epaulets on his shoulders.

Slowly, the little bits and pieces started sorting themselves out. Their manner of dress, the refinement of their speech, their beautiful horses, their presence here now...

The captain surveyed the crowd from his position atop his horse, his ever-watchful eyes missing nothing. I didn't know if he could see me, or would recognize me if he did, but even so I shrank down, mild and meek as a mouse in the shadow of a hawk.

One last ring of the bell—what I would later know as my death knell—silenced the growing crowd and the crier cleared his throat and began the proclamation that would end my current life.

"Hear ye, good people! So shall it be announced throughout the streets of Camallea, so shall it be proclaimed across Laurendale. In the name of His Royal Majesty, King William Robert Alexander, fair and just, defender of all, His Royal Highness, Prince Henri Christopher Charles Alexander, slayer of dragons, protector of the realm, will be hosting a masquerade in two weeks' time."

A soft tittering began at the edges of the crowd, and I glanced to the men on horseback. The way the handsome one sat, the way the captain's face never changed... could it be?

"The purpose of this event is to find, in a manner unbiased to standing, a wife for His Royal Highness, Prince Henri Christopher Charles Alexander."

"Do they have to say his whole bloody name every time?" a man muttered somewhere beside me.

The captain's head pivoted in our direction, making me certain he'd heard. At that moment it didn't matter to me, because it was then that I realized that the man beside him was the prince, whose full name I would definitely never tire of hearing. And I didn't, for over three years at least.

The prince, beautiful and handsome, tall, and valiant. He'd been away from Camallea for years to attend Laurendale's prestigious finishing school and military academy, from whence he'd been plucked when war broke out and sent straight to our eastern borders to ward off an invading army of ogres and gargoyles. He'd then headed south to fight against a hoard of dragons attacking the villages there. The prince had defeated all with a relatively swift and completely victorious hand. So it seemed he was allowed to return home to celebrate the newfound peace and share his victory with the people.

"All eligible maidens are invited to attend," the crier's voice continued to ring out, "all with proper attire," he raised his hand with a flourish, brandishing a parchment overhead, "and all with an invitation."

The crowd erupted as people shoved past each other to grab one of the coveted invitations still clutched in the crier's hand. They swarmed the poor man who tried as best he could to hand them out with the speed necessary to preserve his life, no easy feat considering as he'd just announced that almost anyone could one day be queen.

"Girls, we must keep our composure," Madame proclaimed just seconds before she lost hers to lunge for the precious paper.

Very few people were not swallowed in the ensuing frenzy: the prince and his cadre of guards, and myself, who was pushed to the fringes of the crowd to protect my stepfamily's packages as best I could. With my head ducked and my feet stepping high to keep from being trampled upon, it was no wonder I missed the man who approached me and shoved an invitation into my already full hands. I looked up in time to catch the back of a soldier's uniform skirting the melee and raised my gaze still higher to catch sight of the prince as he turned to leave. Behind him was the captain, who followed after the prince just as my eyes landed on him.

I couldn't say for certain, but I was almost sure that he had made sure the invitation found its way to me. Then, I couldn't say why. Now, I have my suspicions.

Carefully setting aside the packages, I hurriedly folded up the invitation and pocketed it before the step-women in my family found me again. Over the next two weeks, I endured their teasing as they proudly waved their tickets to royalty as if they were the only ones in the entire kingdom to have them.

"It's going to be marvelous," Calliope squealed. "Wouldn't you so love to come?"

I kept my lips tight, knowing that any answer would be to my peril. At the moment, I was trying my best to sweep the floor despite the two vultures circling me.

"And what would she wear?" Maybelle queried, pinching the edges of my rags with the tips of her fingers. "This?"

"It is a rather fitting costume," Calliope pointed out.

"Imagine a Cinderwench on display!"

"A Cinderwench on display!" Calliope echoed, then grabbed Maybelle's hands and danced with her in a circle, trapping me inside.

"A Cinderwench at a masquerade!" they continued to sing, as they twirled merrily about me.

I swept the same spot for ten minutes before they finally tired of their game and went to examine the progress of their butterfly gowns for the fiftieth time that day.

Foolish as it may seem, I did think that perhaps I would be allowed to go to the masquerade. If anything, faery tales I heard from my mother proved that even the miserable and wretched could possibly find happiness one day. Perhaps, Father, the real Father, would poke his head out of his study long enough to demand that Madame allow me to join. Perhaps, if I was perfect, absolutely perfect in everything I did, Madame would allow it in one brief moment of compassion. I could sew my own dress. I had my own jewelry. Madame needn't dress me; she need simply allow me to ride in the carriage. Besides, the prince himself had decreed that anyone with an invitation could come. It wasn't as if he would notice me. I was no threat to Madame or her daughters.

How shortsighted the present can be.

It took both weeks to build up the courage to ask Madame if I could go. Even then, the matter didn't come up by my own doing. Rather, since I'd received the invitation from the soldier, I had kept it in my pocket, sometimes running a finger over its soft, rich surface during the day, but otherwise never allowing myself to take it out until I was sure all had gone to bed. Then I would sit in my little corner by the fire and smooth out the creases, reading and rereading the words that promised the reality of all my faery tales. Unfolding the paper unfurled my imagination and there was no limit to how brightly my dress would shine, no shortage of suitors begging a dance from me.

It was one such night, lost in my dreams, that I missed the footsteps coming into the kitchen and was abruptly caught.

"Ella," Calliope's voice was suddenly alert. "What is that?"

I was too off-guard to hide the guilty look. "I was just finishing up."

Calliope's astute eyes saw right through me. "What's in your hand?"

"It isn't anything," I mumbled, grabbing for something near me to show that I had been busy at work.

"Let me see it," she demanded.

"There's nothing to see," I persisted.

"Let me see it now or I will scream and wake up the whole house." Calliope sucked in her breath to make good on her threat.

I doubted she would actually do it, not after all those times I'd told her fantastical stories to take her mind off of why Madame had shamed her enough so she cried into her pillow at night, but I'd come to the point where I wouldn't put anything past the people who had come to control my life. Those stories should have been a respite for me, a return to years long gone, but after the first few times I'd spoken on impulse because I was too young to bear her whimpering, too young to know we would never be friends, they quickly became just another means to command me. Some days Calliope remembered those handfuls of moments in goodwill, most others she turned her shame of them against me in spite. But even then, with my fragile future in her hands, I did not regret helping her.

"Here." I shoved the invitation at her and hurriedly looked away so she couldn't see how my cheeks burned with shame and longing.

Calliope had to have seen how worn, yet how carefully kept, the invitation was. However brief, a surge of pity must have washed through her.

"Would you like to go to the party, Ella?" she asked in a voice too kind, too at odds with her behavior just moments before.

I refused to answer.

"Answer me, Ella," she demanded.

Still looking away, I nodded my head.

"Then I shall ask Mama for you," she decided.

"Really?" I asked in a small voice, not trusting that she would actually extend this level of kindness to me.

"You're too small for anyone to notice anyway," she said, "and if someone accidentally does, you'll only make the rest of us look better."

She returned the invitation and I carefully put it away, vowing not to take it out again in a place where I could be so easily caught. I was too grateful then to care about what kind of wrapping she'd put on the invaluable gift she'd given me. The next morning, true to her word, Calliope spoke to Madame, in the most humiliating way possible.

The three women were sitting around the table in the small sunlit nook where they took breakfast when there was no one around to impress. I was serving, of course, the teapot raised to top off Madame's cup when Calliope made her announcement.

"Mama, the Cinderwench would like to go to the masquerade."

I blanched and spilled some of the tea into the saucer, from which it promptly slid out onto the tablecloth. I hurriedly grabbed a rag and tried to blot it out.

"Is this true?" Madame demanded of me.

I was forced to look up. "I thought if I could finish my chores on time," I began meekly, then stopped, unsure how to continue. "And everyone was invited," I finished lamely.

Maybelle choked into her napkin, but to my surprise, Madame didn't answer immediately. She rapped her fingers thoughtfully on the table, and till today I cannot claim to know what she was thinking.

"You will need to get that stain out of the tablecloth."

"Yes, Madame."

"And you have your regular chores, in addition to helping with the girls' costumes."

"Yes, Madame."

"It's soon spring, so there is much to be done ridding the house of winter."

"Yes, Madame."

"And there is the matter of finding something suitable to wear."

"Perhaps, something of my mama's?"

"Perhaps."

"Then I can go?"

"We'll see."

That was enough for me. For the next week, I hardly slept. True to her word and her style, Madame loaded me down with chores, many of which were unnecessary or could be taken care of after the masquerade. She demanded that all winter cloaks and blankets be thoroughly cleaned and packed away, even though the nights were still cool enough to keep them out a bit longer. She wanted all curtains washed, all rugs beaten, all floors scrubbed to an unnatural shine as if the party would be taking place in her home.

And that was without my sisters' incessant harping, their constant teasing, their obsessive and tedious changes to their dresses.

I went about it all dutifully, never once complaining, the mere promise of attending enough to deafen my ears to the commands, the mocking, the constant battering of what was left of my mind and self. For once, I was able to ignore it all completely, the wide wings of my imagination raising me above it all.

Most of what my mother left behind had been erased by Madame when she came, but I managed to find a soft yellow dress I thought suitable enough to work with. After my long, long days were over, I worked well into the night to fix up the dress with bits and scraps I had gathered about the house. I would have loved to take my scissors to any one of my sisters' old dresses that, though only a few months old, had already been deemed unwearably out of fashion, but I knew that wasn't an option.

The masquerade was, ostensibly, so the prince could find a wonderful girl without the distraction of physical beauty or some such nonsense. It was supposed to be a move to level the playing field, but anyone could determine half a girl's background simply by her manner of bearing and richness of dress. As I would later learn, it wasn't as if every girl received an invitation. Only those lucky enough, only those in certain suitable areas when the announcement was made. I only knew that the idea of wearing a mask simply lent intrigue to a night in which I wanted to disappear into a world of silks and succulence, a world that I had only thought possible to tread on in the streets of my fancy. I never thought the prince would pay me any heed. The farthest I allowed my hopes to take me was a duke. We would share one dance before I would twirl away into the night, leaving him forever broken, a piece of his heart missing, stolen away by the mystery girl in the soft yellow dress.

Having nothing else at my disposal, I chose to make my mask out of the leftover greens from Calliope's gown and cascading blues snipped away from Maybelle's. Their masks hid part of their faces, but their chosen colors would highlight their eyes in a way that would render the masks irrelevant. I was hoping that, if done right, the interlocked patches of blues and greens would help dilute the color of mine.

The day of the masquerade couldn't come soon enough, then all at once it was there too soon. Father was conveniently away on one of his travels, so he was spared the agony of the full day of preparations. The morning began late, and although Madame harped about conserving energy, I was only allowed to serve them half the food they usually ate. Soon after lunch, I hauled bucket after bucket of water to the house so my sisters could soak in relaxing salts and wash with sweet smelling soaps.

"You'll help your sisters put up their hair whenever they are ready."

"Yes, Madame."

"Then you will help them dress and make up their faces."

"Yes, Madame."

"This will not excuse you from any of your regular chores, and you will be expected to complete them if you are to come with us tonight."

"Yes, Madame."

"Today is a very busy day."

"Yes, Madame."

"Then why are you still standing here?"

I allowed myself to think of nothing but the promise of the night ahead as I scrambled to keep up with my stepsisters and the chores that seemed to multiply as the day wore on. I focused my mind and stilled my heart so I could work quickly and efficiently, seeking to complete everything in so perfect a manner that even Madame with her irrationally high expectations could not fault me. Not today, at least.

Thankfully, the young ladies were too caught up in the whirlwind of their preparations to grate on my life. They spent the whole day reviewing every aspect of the masquerade, from the entrance hall, to the size of the fruits on the table, to the number of guests in attendance, to the prince himself. Much time was dedicated to the host of the night and they wagered between themselves how many times he would dance with each of them.

And they had cause to be confident. By the time they were ready to leave, Maybelle and Calliope had been transformed into two very beautiful butterflies. They were both rather pretty to begin with, but a day's worth of primping had turned them irresistible.

I had precious few moments to change by the time the others were ready and waiting for the carriage that would whisk them away to the palace. I didn't have time to bathe, so I splashed water on my face and hands as best I could. The blackened cloth I dried them with made me believe that most of the dirt and soot had come off.

Ever so carefully, I stepped into the neatly ironed, altered yellow dress, and slipped on my jade earrings. Cradling it like an eggshell, I pressed my mask to my face and securely fastened it behind my head. Only then did I let out my stifled breath. Only then did I let a small smile sneak past my lips. I felt like a lady. I could be anyone.

I took up my invitation, lifted my skirts, and left my cramped attic room, making my way to the front door with quiet, demure steps. I smoothed my dress down once in the entry and waited patiently behind my stepsisters for the carriage to pull up just past the front door.

For one peaceful, blissful second, I believed in the magic of the night.

Then Madame turned her head and shattered it all.

"Why, Ella," Madame exclaimed innocently, "what are you doing here?"

Maybelle and Calliope turned to stare bug-eyed at me, but I fixed my gaze ahead.

"I've finished my chores, Madame," I replied with more courage than I felt.

"Have you really?" she asked, with what sounded like genuine shock.

"Yes, Madame."

"Let's have a look," she declared, sweeping back into the house with the three of us following close behind her.

Madame ran a finger along every windowsill and shelf, but I knew she would find nothing. I had made sure to banish every speck of dust from the house, fix every wayward scratch, every chip and dent. I had this one chance and I would not lose it to the whims of Madame.

Her inspection finally led us to the kitchen, where even the kettle had been shined hard enough to no longer be called black. Madame spun around slowly, taking in the stark neatness of her house, her mind no doubt unaccepting of the possibility that I had indeed met and exceeded her standards. There was one lone bowl on the kitchen table, one lone bowl ready for the morrow that I should have had the foresight to hide away. But, even after all the years, I couldn't have foreseen the extent of Madame's hatred of me.

Suddenly, Madame took the bowl and flung it toward the fireplace, scattering the carefully cleaned lentils into the ashes.

"Oops," Maybelle giggled.

Madame turned to me with a malicious smile. "Please clean that up."

I must have hesitated.

"Now!"

I grabbed the apron hanging neatly in my corner and forced myself to put it atop my yellow dress. Against my will, I let go of my invitation, leaving it on the table beside the now empty bowl. Iris, who had been moved to the kitchen for me to tend to while Father was away, squawked fiercely from his perch.

Calliope unhooked the pin from the door of his cage, no doubt hoping to free him into the chaos Madame was causing for me. "Oops," she deadpanned as he flew free.

But the macaw was the only one in the room that still liked me. He glided toward me and made his new perch on my shoulder, squawking and bobbing his head in time to my calming breaths.

Madame leveled me with an expectant gaze and I winced as I knelt in my beautiful sun-colored dress to gather the lentils from the fireplace, already seeing the darkened clouds the soot would scatter across it if I wasn't careful enough. The macaw took the liberty of helping me too, though with less care than I to leave behind the ashes.

With Madame's gaze boring into me and my stepsisters' snickering behind me, I picked up bit after bit of lentil, the whole while willing my stinging eyes not to cry. The mask over my eyes felt fake, not a mask of silk, but of shame that spread over my face and plunged down my neck to encompass all of me. It didn't take more than a few puffs of soot to make the dress I had once loved ugly, the night I had so much anticipated ruined.

All the while they stood behind me and watched.

When we were done, I poured some water from a pitcher and tried as best I could to wash the lentils clean. I presented the bowl to Madame, an unworthy offering, even to someone so undeserving.

"A Cinderwench at the masquerade?" she hissed.

Then she lifted my invitation from the table and tore it, and the remains of my heart, in half right before my eyes. She swept out of the room without a backward glance.

Before following in her wake, my stepsisters took the cue from their mother and each heaped one final humiliation upon me before leaving for the waiting carriage.

Calliope snapped the ties of my mask, mockingly took a green feather from her hair and awkwardly placed it in my mine. "Cinderwench at the masquerade?" she crowed.

"Cinderwench at the masquerade!" Maybelle chimed in. She took up a knife and grabbed a handful of my skirts, slashing and cutting it to shreds. Then she unceremoniously dropped the knife at my feet and with her sister followed after her mother, their condescending cackles bowling me over well after their carriage had left the drive.

Once quiet fell, my demeanor fell with it.

I looked around at the tatters of my life, and for the first time wondered how things had gone so far. What had my life come to? How had a home so full of kindness and laughter, warmth and delight become so corrupted with jealousy, pain, and spite? Why was there no one to protect me? And even if Father were here, I doubted anything would have gone differently. Madame was careful to hide her cruelties to me from him and I never had the courage to share them with his already broken heart. In that moment, I despaired of ever knowing love, or at the very least compassion, ever again.

That glimpse of my future was the final nail for me. I turned on my heel and fled to my corner of the garden, collapsing in tears under my pear tree, over my mother's grave.

THE FIRST MISTAKE

*I*f a girl must cry, she should never do so over her mother's grave under a mysteriously rejuvenated pear tree.

She should not talk to anyone, especially matronly figures.

These rules are unbreakable. There are no exceptions.

I learned the hard way.

As the step-witches were surely reveling in palace finery, partaking of mouth-melting delicacies, and swishing about the masquerade on the arms of dukes and lords, I lay in the mud and cried the years away. Tears had stung my eyes more than once in the years since Madame and her progeny were brought to our home, but I had never dared release the floodgates until then.

I was there some time before the squish of footsteps and the tap-tap-tapping of a stick against stone caught my attention. Someone was definitely coming my way, but as I didn't care to see or speak with anyone, I pressed myself further into the ground, the dirt muddy from my tears.

"Ella?" a gentle voice asked. "What happened?"

Marie. The woman from the other side of the wall. I never knew if she was our neighbor or just a crazy old woman living in the wild fields behind our land. She always seemed harmless, and often enough I shared what little I had with her when she came to rest her feet a while at the wall. She was probably my only friend then, though I really didn't know much about her besides her name. I enjoyed speaking with her if only because she was one of few people who still called me by mine.

"It's no matter, Marie," I tried to reassure her.

I sat up and wiped at my eyes, only to worsen them by smudging the mud across my face. Marie looked at me expectantly. She couldn't be so crazy if she could see right through me. Or rather...

"Tell me, Ella," she coaxed.

I didn't want to, but I did, telling her not just about that night, but all the others that had led to it. When I finished, Marie studied me with pursed lips, fearsome looking enough to make me glad her anger was not directed at me.

I fished around in my pockets for a handkerchief of sorts, when my fingers stumbled against the gold coin the prince had tossed my way. For a moment, I lost myself in sliding my fingers along the surface, recalling, as I had at least three times a day for the past two weeks, the man who had given the coin to me. The little gold coin represented a whole other life, a world so different from mine. A world I had been so desperate to see. One in which I could buy pretty things that belonged only to me. Wearing my mother's dress had been the first step into a paradise awaiting me with gates flung wide open. I should have known Madame would never let me go. Now the coin was only a burning reminder of once more broken dreams.

But sitting beside my mother's remains, I remembered that even when I had nothing, I still had kindness and so I hadn't truly lost everything. I pulled the coin out of my pocket and offered it to Marie without a second thought.

Marie took it from me curiously and examined it from all angles, a hint of amusement teasing her lips. "Whatever is this for?"

"It's for you. Someone gave it to me and I want you to have it."

"And what am I to do with it?"

"Treat yourself to something nice, share it with friends, pass it on," I suggested. "As long as it's something good."

Marie's face cleared, and a kindly smile took hold of her features. She took my hand and gave it a quick squeeze. A simple touch from her would usually make me feel better, but tonight the feeling was hollow. Marie must have understood, because she shook her head at me.

"There's only one thing to do about it, then," she decided. "We must send you to the palace."

I stared at her. Just when I thought her sanity was beyond question, she proved otherwise. I appreciated her trying to cheer me up, but "I'm in no mood for pretend," I desisted.

"Pretend? Pretend?" Marie giggled as if the word was the most delightful one in the world. Her laugh reminded me of little bells chiming merrily in the wind. "Dear Ella, you will be going to the masquerade tonight."

"Please, Marie—" I began, but stopped midsentence.

Somehow, without lifting her skirts, without climbing at all, Marie had appeared on the other side of the wall. I shook my head to clear my sight. Surely in my misery, I had overlooked her clambering over.

"Really, Ella," Marie began, throwing back her raggedy hood with a flourish, "I expected you of all people to have more faith in your faery godmother."

My what? I stared at Marie, the walking stick she always held had taken on a more cylindrical form and each time she swirled her hand, bright sparks of light danced behind it. With her hood back, I saw her face clearly for the first time, and of course the first thing I noticed was—

"Your eyes," I breathed, fixating on her purple gaze. "I can't believe—"

"Yes, yes, enough of that dear."

"It's impossible!"

"Is it? Dear, what have those women done to you?"

"But a faery godmother?"

"Grandmère."

"My grandmère?"

"Heavens, no," Marie chuckled, "you're human enough, so we'll do the best we can with what we've got. But you must have something to call me."

"But...my eyes?"

"We haven't much time, so I'll tell you quickly," Marie conceded. "Long ago, my father was running away from an evil little man intent on killing him so he could steal his magic."

"But—"

Marie held up her hand and shook her head. "My father was badly hurt, bleeding, and near unconscious, so he couldn't summon the magic to heal himself. Even so, using it would have attracted unwanted attention. He stumbled into a stable and collapsed in one of the stalls. Startled your mother terribly when she came back with her horse. Two weeks your mother cared for him, kept his secret, and he thanked her for it."

I blinked, expecting more.

"Well, he made her a promise bound by magic," Marie explained. "That his child would care for hers when most in need, the way she had cared for him. That's how she found out you were coming along, and it seems your eyes were marked by that promise."

I stared at her. "I didn't know," I finally managed to say.

"Yes, well, now you do," she said simply. "And tonight, I shall make good on my father's promise."

Marie shrugged out of her patchwork cloak revealing a simple, but finely made purple gown with gold stitching forming an elaborate pattern of swirls and curls across the bodice. Bright sparks trailed after her with each step.

"Where to begin?"

She circled me thoughtfully, taking note of my wretched state, my knifed up gown, my mussed up hair, my sullied face, and trampled soul. She waved her wand in little circles in the air.

"Ah, yes, a way to get to the palace. Follow me," she commanded, as she floated across the field to the modest garden I meticulously tended behind the house.

She flitted between the neat rows of vegetables, passing over carrots, turnips, and tomatoes, until she found what she was looking for. "The pumpkin will do," she chimed, twirling her wand around until it was cocooned in firefly sparks.

With a few more twists of her wand, Marie set the pumpkin spinning in lazy circles, during which it grew larger and larger with each turn. Within seconds, the pumpkin was bigger than either of us and it paused its transformation a moment before it suddenly jolted. A door, windows, a proper seat for the coachman, and rails for the footmen appeared. The pumpkin burped again and then it was raised up on four large, thin wheels. It wasn't difficult to see that a pumpkin had inspired the design of the carriage, but at least the burnt orange hue was closer to bronze to the eyes of the unknowing.

"How wonderful," I breathed, fully enchanted by the prospect of having a faery godmother and all the tricks she must have up her sleeves. Despite everything that was to happen, I don't ever regret having met Grandmère, though I can't say the same for everything she was to do.

Marie waved away my wonder. "Posh, dear, we're only getting started. Now, what else?"

She swiveled about the yard and I scampered after her. Even the magical appearance of a faery godmother and a carriage would have been enough to carry me through the next few years of scrubbing. It wasn't enough for Marie, though. Faeries are never satisfied with a few flicks of the wrist when they can do so much more.

"Ah, the mousetrap, right here please," she commanded, with a point and a tap on the ground before the carriage.

The mousetrap floated over from behind the kitchen. Small rodents were always burrowing their way under the door and getting into the flour. One morning, Calliope had a fit when she came in to find a fat gray mouse caught in the cage, so we moved it outside. There were two black rats trapped inside the little cage that night. A look at them, and I shuddered.

With a tap of her wand, Marie sent the walls of the cage flying, and I had a brief thought that I would need to build another later. Then, before the rats could scurry away, she tapped four times and, much like the pumpkin, the rats grew and grew. Then their faces grew long and their tails more hairy, their skins darkened and glistened and by the time they stopped growing, there were two impressive, dark night stallions ready to be harnessed to my enchanted carriage.

"Every noble appreciates a good horse," Marie nodded to herself. "Now, for the coachman," she clucked.

She clucked and clucked until her calls were echoed, and a fat white goose waddled into the yard.

Marie's eyes lit upon it. "Ah, there."

"We were saving it for a holiday!" I gasped.

"Nonsense, Ella," she scoffed with a shower of sparks from her wand. "There is no greater holiday than today."

The sparks of magic circled the goose and then he stretched and stretched into quite a rotund, but rather jolly coachman.

"Up you go," Marie pointed to his seat. "The horses must be kept in line."

With a cry that sounded too close to a honk, the goose-man jumped up and ran to take his seat on the carriage. My mind had since gone silent, the reality of my life having far outpaced anything it could have contrived. I refused to acknowledge the worry that perhaps this was all a dream from which I would soon awake cold and alone on my mother's muddied grave.

Marie eyed the carriage a moment. "A footman," she concluded.

She cast her gaze around the garden, looking for the next innocent creature that would adorn her magical creation. Her eyes stopped on a lizard quietly darting along the wall of the house, no doubt trying to escape what it must have felt coming.

"Ew," I whispered.

But Marie had already decided. With a flick of her wrist, she detached the lizard from the wall and brought it to us. Still in the air, she tapped twice, and it grew and grew, until I had a handsome, if somewhat olive-skinned, footman in my service.

"Tongue in, chin up," Marie commanded.

The footman scrambled to the carriage, propped the door open and stood at attention beside it, ready to hand me in the moment I gave him leave to do so.

"Granted, I haven't had much time to prepare considering the short notice, but this should do just fine," Marie mused.

"It's—It's magnificent!" I exclaimed circling the carriage, the horses, the coachman, the footman, delightedly examining them from every angle.

"Well then," Marie cleared her throat, "enough dilly-dallying. You've a party to attend."

"But—"

"But what? Speak up, Ella," Marie commanded.

I glanced down at my dress and Marie's eyes followed.

"Yes, of course," she sighed. "You didn't think I'd send you off like that?"

I didn't reply.

Marie studied me, tilting her head from one side to the other. She picked at the rags that had once been my mother's lovely yellow dress. She eyed the misplaced feather in my hair with distrust. She raised my hem and quickly looked away, even before seeing the simple shoes on my feet. She tapped her wand in the palm of her open hand, sending sparks into the air like a shower of stars.

She aimed the wand at me. "This won't hurt a bit," she reassured, as she sent a spray of glittering sparks my way.

I was too terrified to run or hide. I was too terrified to breathe. I hadn't thought about what being transformed by magic would actually feel like and suddenly, I didn't want to.

It was over almost as quickly as it began. The magical sparks dimmed through the mask that suddenly appeared over my eyes. Breathlessly, I reached up to feel the curving feathers which helped shield the true color of my eyes. I looked down, seeing the kingfisher's colors imitated in the silken shine of a beautiful sea-green gown interlaced with ocean blues. A long, layered tail of the same kingfisher feathers cascaded down the back of my dress. Little jewels of emerald green and cobalt blue were stitched across the dress so it shimmered, even in the moonlight. I lifted my hands to find green gloves up to my elbows, so soft I almost couldn't feel I was wearing them. I raised a hand to feel the perfect ringlets that had taken over my hair. Lifting my skirts, I found my battered shoes replaced by lovely green heels decorated with crushed gems like sequins.

"I—it's—what—I feel like a princess!" I finally blurted out.

"Most appropriate for winning the heart of a prince," Marie declared.

"The prince?" I breathed, hardly able to speak, hardly able to process anything that wasn't that one word.

Would he even notice little me in the ocean of beautiful women at the masquerade tonight? Did it matter? I was going to the palace! I was going to a party with my own horse and carriage, wearing a gown made just for me! I could live one hundred years and never outlive the happiness overflowing within me then.

I stared at Marie in wonder. "I..." I whispered.

Marie answered with an inscrutable smile. "Just say thank you, dear," she said kindly.

I pulled Marie into a crushing embrace, not caring that my magical dress may crease. "Thank you, Grandmère, thank you, thank you," I said, sending the last words over her shoulder up to Heaven itself.

Marie hugged me back before gently pushing me away. She tapped me on the head and sent me off to the carriage. "You needn't worry that anyone will recognize you tonight," she reassured me.

I laughed from exhilaration. I hadn't even considered that anyone would ever think the Cinderwench would show up, especially not like this. If my stepmother saw me, she would have a fit, not just because I had come to the palace, but because I was bedecked in finery that far surpassed her own daughters'. There would be no end to her torment of me thereafter.

The footman handed me into the carriage and shut the door behind me. He took up his place at the back, but before we could leave, Marie handed me my repaired invitation with some final words. "Do keep an eye on the time, Ella dear." Her voice was so sweet I almost missed the warning. "For all the magic will be gone and all returned to how it was at three, when night is at its darkest."

It took me a moment to understand what she'd just said. "You're giving me a curfew?"

Marie smiled widely. "Someone must look after you, dear."

Before I could argue, she signaled to the coachman and the carriage took off. I turned to catch her waving proudly as we flew into the night. I didn't once feel the bumpy road beneath the magical carriage, and I'm quite certain we made it to the palace in less time than we should have.

All the way, I wavered between sheer joy and panicked fretting. If my stepfamily wouldn't recognize me, did that mean the prince and the captain wouldn't either? Did I want them to? Surely, neither had spared second thought to a clumsy girl briefly met by an unremarkable well who was only given an invitation as a courtesy. I much preferred they should think they were seeing me for the first time, dressed as I was. I need hardly go into detail about the irony of a masquerade being the start of what was to follow.

Even after all these years of palace life, I still believe that no feeling can quite compare to the exhilaration of when the carriage finally arrived at the royal palace the first time. The entire courtyard was illuminated with tall, slender candles, their gentle flickers bathing the front façade in an angelic glow. Dutifully, my pumpkin carriage pulled up right to the wide row of steps leading up to the palace entrance, a thick red carpet unfurled down the center for the arriving guests.

By that time, the courtyard had mainly settled down, with only a low murmur of footmen rearranging the rows upon rows of carriages so that any could be accessed when called. My olive-skinned footman opened the door then handed me out of the carriage. Once I descended, I stood perfectly still drinking in the reality that I could scarcely believe was unfolding.

"Thank you," I said, and received a silent nod in return.

I would miss nothing; I would take in everything and carefully preserve it forever in my memories. I would taste what I could and dance with anyone who asked. Tonight was my night. Behind the safety of my feathered mask, I could be anyone but Ella the Cinderwench.

I caught faint strains of an orchestra playing a giddy tune. With those notes, I imagined the people inside, the gowns, the masks, the glitter, the gaiety, the lords, the dukes. The prince. I sucked in a deep breath of sweet, fresh air. Everything, even the stars twinkling in the night sky, was better at the palace.

Or so I thought then.

"Don't go too far," I reminded the coachman. "We'll be among the first to leave."

The coachman honked his acquiescence and drove the carriage away. This was it. Relying on years of hated etiquette lessons—for which Madame would surely condemn herself if she knew I was using them then—I squared my shoulders, straightened my back with lifted ribs, raised my chin, and glided forward as best I could.

Invitation clutched tightly in hand, I carefully ascended the palace steps, glancing over my shoulder after every few to look once more upon the glowing courtyard. The quietude was enough to make me feel like I was the only person in the world, as if all this had been done just for me.

I presented my invitation at the top of the stairs, standing in awe as the large palace doors swung open to admit me. A servant appeared to lead me down a long hallway lined on either side with stoic, purple-clad guards, straight to a large pair of doors at the end of the immeasurably long hall.

There, cushioned by the soft murmur of water surrounding the island the palace sat upon, was a menagerie of exquisitely dressed creatures. The men and women in attendance had outdone themselves with sparkling costumes representing heroes of the past, bright flora, and the entirety of the animal kingdom, though some only wore intricately designed masks to cover their faces. There were masks scaled to look like dragons, elaborate headpieces for black stallions, layers of multihued brown feathers like hawks, and magnificent tufts of fur like golden lions. There were suits and gowns designed to reflect the glittering scales of fish, others were covered in bright feathers of birds, and some bloomed as rare and beautiful flowers.

I stood at the top of a wide, stone-paved stairwell, leading down to the massive courtyard in which the masquerade was being held, mouth agape. It was lit up by hundreds of candles that flamed bright enough to rival the light of the full moon and shining stars above. Just before me was a large area cleared for couples dancing to the elegant refrains of a large orchestra. To my right and left little groups of people socialized and sampled the abundance of refreshments. Overwhelmed, I set a hand on the railing and leaned against it for support, careful to keep my sea-swirled gown from crushing against the side.

Against the outer wall of the palace was a generously decorated dais with a tired, but happy looking man upon it who had to be the king. His hair had long since turned gray and he rested his chin upon his hand, content to watch the revelries unfold without being part of them. Slightly behind and to his right stood a man I was to learn was his most trusted advisor and chief castle steward, Sir Percival. Even from a distance, I could see how alert the gentleman was. Now and then, he dipped his head to whisper something to the king, who often responded with a nod or small smile.

Speckled throughout the grounds stood soldiers bedecked in royal purple, gleaming swords sheathed at their hips, their attention perfect, their focus unwavering despite the jumble of people. I looked around for the captain, but couldn't see him from where I stood, then thought if I could find him, it wouldn't be too hard to guess which of the masked men was the prince. Though I was naively certain that I would recognize the melody of his voice, even within the din of the gathered guests.

Keeping a gloved hand on the railing, I slowly descended the stairs, drinking in the entirety of the masquerade with each step that brought me closer to it. Toward the bottom, I learned that most of the food was in a room behind me whose doors had been flung wide open so it seemed they weren't there at all. Tables and tables were laden with cornucopias of fresh fruit, whole roasted geese, puddings, and cakes and confections that surely took a town of chefs to prepare. Wine and champagne flowed in abundance, a guest's raised hand signal enough to bring a waiter offering up a tray of selections to his side.

But I was not to taste any of the fine food or wine that night. Rather, I would become intoxicated by something far more powerful.

Just steps from the bottom of the staircase, my breath still held in my chest, my mind still reminding it to breathe so I really wouldn't miss anything by collapsing from sheer joy, something happened to wrench the night out of my hands. Whatever I had imagined, whatever I could have dreamed, I could scarcely anticipate what actually occurred. I never found out who prompted the new course of my life, but I'm certain if he—or she —knew what would be, he would reverse time and never lift a hand to unsnap the mask from the person he somehow found out was the prince.

At first no one noticed, even I wasn't sure what the commotion on the dance floor was about. But, within seconds of the prince's striped fur mask falling, a dark purple blur darted onto the floor and with raised sword separated him from all the others. The captain alone was not enough to stop the gaggle of women, who had one by one stopped dancing, from overpowering the prince, but everyone could sense the tension beginning to emanate from every soldier lining the courtyard. A brief second of silence fell, a silence thick enough to be tangible. Even the orchestra froze mid-chord. Something was bound to happen, but everyone was waiting for someone else to act first, to do something to signal which way the night would turn.

Ever so calmly, with grace and patience that warmed my stilled heart, the prince bent down and retrieved his mask. His hair was slightly ruffled, but otherwise he was as perfect as I remembered him to be. His cheeks were flushed, his lips tickled by a smile. Handsome and winsome, dressed in dark blue that striped through gray fur like a rare and magnificent tiger.

As the prince stood, he looked up, and somehow, among the maze of costumed people and voluminous skirts, saw me standing on the stairs. His gaze locked on mine. My heart hiccupped then stuck in my throat. I was trapped, overpowered by his gaze and the memory of blue eyes deep enough to drown me.

What was I supposed to do? What should I have done?

No one else realized what was happening, not until the prince rose to his full height, dropped his furry mask on the captain's sword, then walked straight toward me. As he walked, heads turned to follow him. Soon, everyone's eyes were upon me.

The prince raised his hand to signal the orchestra to start up again, but the musicians hesitated, avidly watching the object of the prince's undivided attention with the rest of the room.

Without warning, time stopped. This new world, my old world, every world real and imagined fell into a void. The handsome men and beautiful women melted away. Even the bright light from the candles was no longer needed. There was nothing in existence save for his Royal Highness, Prince Henri Christopher Charles Alexander walking toward Ella the Cinderwench, the petite girl with faery eyes of purple dressed like a creature of the sky.

Then the prince was before me, his hand outstretched, asking for mine.

My hand took his of its own accord, and he held it aloft as I walked down the rest of the stairs. I presented my best curtsy and only stood when I felt a soft finger under my chin, lifting it and me up along with it.

"Care to dance?" he asked, introducing the tune of what would be the lullaby of my life for the next few years.

I'm sure I blushed furiously. "It would be an honor, Your Highness," I demurely replied.

"The honor is mine," the prince said smoothly, his lips parted in a wide grin to show off his dazzling white teeth.

He raised our joined hands out to the side, placed his other with a feather's touch on the edge of my back, just under the arm resting on his shoulder. I was dimly aware that a slower melody had started, dimly aware that as he swept me onto the dance floor other couples slowly took the music back up, as well. But all that receded into insignificance. I was dancing with the prince. I was *dancing*. With *the prince!*

"It is quite unfair that you still wear your mask when mine has been removed," the prince finally said to me, after a few minutes during which I hoped he'd needed to catch his breath as much as I.

"The invitation specified this was to be a masquerade, Your Highness," I said nervously.

"Yes, but now you have the advantage of knowing who I am," he frowned, though his eyes still smiled. "Have I met you before, at court?"

I was glad of being spared the need to lie. "No."

"Will I?" he asked hopefully.

"Maybe," I replied, in my best attempt to be coy.

The prince's brow furrowed in the most adorable way. "That is hardly a fair answer."

"It really was wonderful of His Highness to invite so many

people tonight," I said quickly, gently steering the conversation away from my identity.

The prince's face lit up in a playful grin. "It is rather grand, isn't it? When Sir Percival first suggested a party with all eligible princesses across the realms, I wanted nothing of it. I've met most of them and care not one bit for a single one. 'This is about your future,' he lectured. 'Then why not invite the whole kingdom?' I asked. 'It's their future, too.' So that's what he did. Sort of."

I giggled, and the prince's smile grew.

"Who is Sir Percival?" I asked. "I should thank him."

The prince inclined his head toward the man I'd seen whispering in his father's ear. "That meddling oaf over there."

I glanced but only for a second, unwilling to take my eyes from the prince at all. "Is he always so serious?" I asked.

"Always," the prince confirmed. "He has no sense for fun."

"Perhaps I should ask him to dance with me."

When the prince's grip tightened on my hand, a warm flutter passed through me. "I won't allow it," he said. "Tonight, you must dance with me until you can dance no more."

I didn't bother to hide my pleased expression. "Now it is His Highness who isn't being fair to others," I teased, my confidence inspired by his partiality to me.

"Hang the others," the prince replied. "It's been decided."

"And if I can dance forever?"

"All the better for me."

We danced the hours away, and it was the prince who tired first. I had one night to live out all my hopes and dreams, while a lifetime of this magical reality still stretched before him. It was only when we stopped that I realized it was already after two; that, as we flew around the courtyard, time had too quickly flown with us.

"May I offer you something?" the prince asked, as he led me toward the room overflowing with refreshments.

"I can hardly eat," I began, but seeing the look on his face, amended, "but am sure I can enjoy whatever you bring me."

"A surprise then?" His eyes twinkled merrily.

"A surprise," I agreed.

It was only when he made me sit that I realized how much my feet were hurting. I could feel my pulse in my toes, but after the initial awareness, I forgot all about them. I was breathless with excitement, too hyperaware of everything else to think after my person. I was at the palace. I had danced with the prince. The crown prince. The same prince who was now coming my way with two delicate chocolate swans balanced carefully in his upturned palms.

His eyes met mine for approval, and I gave it to him with the most delighted smile I could muster.

Before he could reach me however, two familiar forms, one blue and one green, fluttered into view. My stepsisters, in the gowns I had sewn for them with hair and makeup that I had done for them, converged upon me. Marie had said that no one would recognize me, but that didn't keep my nerves from suddenly spiking.

"You must forgive the intrusion, my lady," Maybelle began, "but we had to come introduce ourselves."

Were they mocking? Even after what they'd just seen?

"My sister, Calliope," she indicated to her right, "and I am Maybelle."

They certainly weren't. My own stepsisters, who only ever looked at me long enough to make my life miserable, didn't recognize me. I truly could be anyone tonight.

"It's a pleasure to meet you," I said with a nod to each of them.

"We're so pleased to meet you, my lady!" Calliope gushed.

"Your gown is so magnificent," Maybelle cut in, "and those shoes!"

I couldn't believe what was happening, but I was too happy to be anything but kind that night.

"Thank you," I replied sweetly. "I accept your compliments considering how lovely your own costumes are."

Maybelle and Calliope flushed modestly with the praise. For the first time, seeing them through the mask of my new person, I actually wondered if, unlike Madame, they weren't inherently cruel people. Maybelle had a meaner streak than Calliope, but what else could I expect considering their role model in life? I had been lucky to have a kind and patient mother, and while I could have been bitter, I felt that I honored her by trying to be like her. Though little good that had done me with my stepfamily over the years. It was probably why it had been so easy for Madame to manipulate me into being her slave from the start.

The prince's arrival broke the moment.

As my stepsisters stepped aside to allow the prince to present me with the chocolate swans, I caught a glimpse of the time over his shoulder. Noticing that it was fifteen minutes to three, I stood abruptly, causing him to jump back to avoiding knocking over the swans.

"I had such a lovely time, Your Highness, and I do apologize, but I must leave," I said, already whisking past him to the stairs, biting down my disappointment that the magic wouldn't last longer.

"But—" the prince began hopelessly.

"You really are so wonderful," I bumbled on, "and these swans are so dear. But I must go."

I took them from his hands and handed one to each of my wide-eyed stepsisters, not caring at the chocolate smudging the gloves that would surely soon disappear.

"Wait!" the prince cried after me, but it was too late.

I had already lifted my skirts, and on the euphoria of the night alone, flew up the stone staircase and hurried toward the palace doors. Confusion must have halted the prince's step, and his captain's too, because it wasn't until I had reached the front courtyard that I heard them giving chase behind me.

My carriage was already waiting for me, the door held open by my faithful footman as I fled down the red carpet. I leaped into the carriage and the door was quickly shut, signaling the coachman to send the stallions into a mad dash for the palace gates. As we slipped through, the command to close them coming too late, I looked back to see the flustered prince standing in middle of the staircase, his captain and a few soldiers by his side. Although they called for their horses, they must have known from the speed with which I flew away that they wouldn't be able to catch me.

Thank Heaven magic controlled my horses that night, because we scarce made it to the edges of our land before night struck its darkest hour. By the time we reached the final bend before the house came into sight, what had left as my grand entourage returned as a muddied girl in tattered gown carrying an overgrown pumpkin with a goose clucking at her heels as rats scurried into the grass under her feet. But I was too elated to feel sorry for myself. With a few effortless taps of her wand, Marie had given me a lifetime of fulfilled dreams.

Returning home, I immediately changed back into my usual rags, then buried the remains of my mother's dress in the garden alongside her. Then I told her everything, refusing to allow memory to tinge or tweak details that were, and still are, as fresh in my mind as if they were still unfolding. When I was done, I leaned against the pear tree, happy and content that the dreaminess of the night had indeed turned out to be reality. Even staying in Madame's good graces would not have yielded the night I'd had.

I dozed against my tree and only woke when I heard the rumble of carriage wheels approaching our home. I flew back through the house to the front door and stood at the top of the steps, waiting properly for Madame and her daughters to descend from the carriage. Beyond them, the sun was first beginning to rise, color returning to the sky just as the beautiful rainbow of men and women were returning home from their night of revelry.

They were scarcely out of the carriage and carelessly flinging their capes upon me before words tripped and tumbled from their mouths in a muddled attempt to tell me about all that I had supposedly missed.

"What an incredible night!" Calliope gushed.

"What an incredible party!" Maybelle agreed.

"What an incredible prince!" they chimed together, swooning against each other.

I followed them to their rooms and helped them undress to the tune of their accounts of the masquerade.

"Look at this, Ella," Calliope instructed, before I even had a chance to unlace the back of her dress.

In her proffered hand sat a chocolate swan, its form slightly smudged from the heat of her palm, but the one the prince had brought for me nonetheless.

"How lovely!" I dutifully exclaimed.

"I got one, too," Maybelle cut in. "But I ate it."

Calliope gently set hers on her vanity table. "I'm not going to eat mine," she smiled at it dreamily, "not yet."

"Why not?" I blurted out.

"Because it's from the prince!" Calliope explained.

"It's not from the prince," Maybelle corrected. "It's from the prince's mystery lady."

At that point, Madame appeared at the door, distracting her daughters long enough for me to school my features.

"I have made inquiries about this mysterious woman," she announced, "and no one knows a thing about her. She is either a criminal posing as a lady, or a faery."

Maybelle rolled her eyes. "Or she's just a lady."

"She was too kind to be a lady," Calliope dismissed.

"Her posture was admirable," Madame allowed, and I quickly hid my flushing face in the ribbons of Calliope's dress.

"Mama," Calliope called, trying to jerk forward despite my attempt to unlace her, "may I please have feathers for the next party?"

"Me too, Mama," Maybelle cried out, "and sequins for my shoes and swirls of blues and greens for my gown—"

Madame frowned slightly. "We'll speak about it in the morning."

"It is morning, Mama!" both girls exclaimed at once.

"After some sleep," Madame elaborated.

I should have been thrilled that my stepsisters wanted to imitate the fashion of the mystery woman who had so captured the prince's attentions, which of course meant that after all these years my stepsisters were actually seeking to imitate me. Instead, my mind had fixated on...

"There's to be another party?" I blurted out.

"Surely you didn't expect the prince to find the right girl in one night," Madame sniffed. "There's to be a festival in one week, and you're to make new gowns for both girls by then. In addition to your other chores, of course."

"Of course, Madame," I echoed dumbly.

Madame spun from the room, and it was several excited seconds before anyone spoke. Then Calliope, finally stepping out of her dress, gripped my arms and told me excitedly, "It's so the prince can find his mystery lady, I'm sure of it!"

"It's positively thrilling." Maybelle clapped her hands gleefully. "Will he find her, or," she dragged out the word, "will he gain sense and find someone else...like me?"

"Or me!" Calliope rejoined, and that sent them spinning about the room in the arms of wishful thinking.

My mind was too numb to take any of it in.

For hours, I had danced with a prince, and until Calliope spoke, I had thought that enough for a simple servant girl like me. I was horribly mistaken. Having tasted another life, I suddenly realized how hungry I was, how thirsty for something better than the crowded square of attic I called a room and the soot filled corner that was my world.

I hadn't even thought that there would be another chance to go to the palace, hadn't thought much past the feeling of the prince spinning me across the dance floor.

I couldn't be content with what I already had, not when I now wanted so much more. I had to go again.

THE SECOND MISTAKE

Over the next week, my feet didn't once touch the ground. The moment the prince took me in his arms, the floor fell out from under me, sending me to float above the air of my stifled life. I relived the masquerade every night, from the moment I took those last steps on that wide, stone staircase; to the curtsy; the crook of his smile; his arms; the waltzing; down to those chocolate swans and thrilling race against time.

When no one was watching, I danced with the broom, the duster, the fireplace poker, the trays of food, the chicken feed, and around the fattening goose that had developed a sudden need to follow close behind me in the yard. When I walked, it was no longer a suppressed, minified shuffle, but every step was part of a waltz, a grand waltz that had overtaken my life and showed me a world larger and more dazzling than anything I could have conjured.

It was one of the best weeks of my life, when my enchantment was still fresh, when I had only touched the surface, before I fell in too deep.

My days grew longer, and nights inevitably shrank to keep up with the housework and design the new gowns for the upcoming festival. These dresses had to be fashionable and fun, captivating and classy. Madame had a seamstress whom she relied upon to sew the basic pattern, but I was always called upon to be there in deciding the design, and afterward charged with fixing "this horrid excuse of a dress."

I didn't bother asking Madame permission to go to the palace again. My mother had left no more dresses, and if there were any I had missed, I would never consider them presentable enough after the touch of winged sky I had worn. Madame probably thought my silence a sure sign of my submission, but inside my heart, my mind, my imagination was anything but quiet. While designing the dresses for my stepsisters, I thought only of what other dresses Marie could contrive for me. While affixing sequins to their shoes, I thought only of the sparkle and shine of my hair, my fingers, my own shoes when Marie's magic took hold.

And all this without knowing if Marie would be there for me again. Hadn't my greatest hour of need already passed?

For seven days, I waited for her under the pear tree beside my mother's grave, peeking over the low stone wall, and once even standing on it to look beyond, but there was no hint of her anywhere. I wondered where she went when she wasn't turning sobbing young maidens into beautiful princesses for a night. I didn't just want to ask her if she would transform me again, but also to thank her and tell her every juicy detail about what had undoubtedly been the most magnificent night of my life.

The festival finally came, and I had to slow my hands more than once to make sure they worked at their usual pace. Even worse than not knowing about Marie was the thought that my stepfamily would sense my desire to go and humiliate me enough to wrench that desire from me.

"Does this make me look mysterious?" Calliope asked,

adjusting her kingfisher feather-bedecked hat as I helped her dress.

"Very mysterious," I agreed.

She'd wanted to look like the mystery lady and had described it very specifically, though I embellished it with every stitch I had remembered.

Calliope giggled and spun in place so the material of her dress stretched out to its fullest length. She'd wanted an exact copy of the dress, but I'd convinced her to go with something slightly different. Instead of the stiff silks of my gown, I'd persuaded her to try a much lighter material, a thinner silk that better mirrored the easy flow of water. The material was also an array of blues without greens to better suit her complexion. Twirling now, she looked like a splash of ocean spray, her hat a bird diving to fish beneath the surface.

Maybelle pranced into the room with her kingfisher feather hat already in place. Her dress was of the same material as Calliope's, but in greens and yellows, a steady river beneath a sunny forest sky.

"You look very pretty," I told them both sincerely.

Calliope giggled again and, without thinking, gave my hand a small squeeze. Maybelle looked down her nose at me, but without some of her usual harsh disdain.

"Do you think the lady will be there?" I asked, pretending to revel in a mystery I already thought I knew the answer to.

"I hope not," Maybelle sniffed. "For then the prince will spend all his time with her and I will never get my turn."

"I hope she is," Calliope said. "She was so lovely and so very kind to us."

"Girls," Madame commanded from the doorway.

Even though she wasn't talking to me, I automatically pulled my shoulders back and lifted my ribcage with the others. Madame entered the room and slowly circled each of her daughters, straightening and tightening until all was to her approval.

Finally, she nodded. "Come along, then."

As they went to the door, I followed behind to see them off. Madame let her daughters pass then turned to block my way.

"Cinderwench," she indicated behind me with a nod of her head, "the room."

I stifled my sigh until I was sure she was already down the stairs. Why couldn't Marie appear now to tap-tap the house clean for me? I stared at Calliope's room. She could not keep her space clean for a minute. As soon as she saw an empty spot, she was compelled to fill it with something. What was the use in cleaning up if she would only muddle it all the moment she returned?

Still, I had no choice, so I started with the bigger things and worked my way through the room, then dusted it for good measure. I even went to Maybelle's room and straightened the few things that were out of place. Sure that the upstairs was tidy, I stood a moment at the top of the steps and listened to the quiet of the house. Cook and the other servants had the afternoon off —"no one but Cinderwench will be here, and I will not pay for idleness"—so they were surely already long gone. Even Iris must have been occupied with something else because I didn't even hear him.

Then, like lighting, the thought of returning to the palace hit me and I flew down the steps, out the back door, and to my pear tree, praying all the while that Marie would be there.

"Grandmère! Grandmère!" I started to call after I was only halfway across the yard.

Had anyone been around to hear, they would have surely thought me mad. I have never met, nor do I have, any living grandmère to speak of.

My call received no response, which only made me run faster. She had to be there, she had to be!

Reaching the wall, I leaned a moment against my tree and willed air back into my lungs. All seemed quiet and untouched, but then there was a sudden glow and there was Marie, hovering serenely above the stone wall.

"Ella? What's all the excitement about?" she asked.

"There's a festival today!" the words rushed out of my mouth.

"There is?" She tilted her head. "How delightful!"

"Can I go, Grandmère?" I asked. "Will you help me again?"

"What a question!" Marie waved her wand and sent magical fireflies through the air. I looked at her expectantly. "Of course," she finally said.

"Thank you, Grandmère!" I hopped up on the wall and bounced beside her floating frame. "Thank you so much!"

"Does this mean you had a nice time at the masquerade?" Marie asked, as she led me toward the garden.

"I had the best night of my life!" I exclaimed. "And I danced with the prince!"

"Of course you did, dear. You didn't think he'd ignore you in that dress?" Marie said calmly.

"Will I wear something like it today?" I asked, ready for anything that would allow me back into the palace.

"Think bigger, Ella," Marie encouraged, already waving her wand. "Everyone else will be wearing some variation of it. You must have something new."

Having nothing else to say, I clapped my hands in glee. In seconds, the carriage stood ready, the pumpkin tinted with a soft silver glow. Next, the jolly coachman, who even tipped his hat to me as if he remembered our last ride together and the week following when he waddled after me in his true form. Two squirrels were to be my footmen, and the gray mice caught in the trap became horses shaded a lovely dapple gray.

"There'll be people looking out for you this time," Marie

explained of the changes. "We must make sure you get a chance to slip in before anyone can intercept you."

When it was my turn, I closed my eyes and waited impatiently for Marie to decide what I should wear. I only knew she was done when she asked, "Well, how do you like it?"

I opened my eyes to the shine of a silver dress, lightweight and airy, glowing in the sun like a star plucked from the heavens. Diamonds studded the thin, royal purple embroidery on my hem and bodice, small stars winking in the light. Hiding my calloused hands were crisp white gloves that reached until my elbows, and on my feet were the most wonderful silver shoes. Marie had even made them with extra height under the balls of my feet, to appear a little taller than I was.

Tilted to shadow my eyes was a velvet hat decorated with pearls and gray and purple feathers.

"Oh, Grandmère!" I cried, but then all words escaped me. How could I thank her for what she was doing for me? How could I use words for the beauty she was adorning me with?

"No crying now, dear," Marie said with a catch in her voice that made it sound like she was in danger of the same, "just remember, your family won't recognize you and the magic will be gone by sunset."

"Can't I have until three again?" I pleaded.

"Sunset," Marie repeated firmly.

"Then I won't waste any more time," I decided, and lifted my voluminous skirts to be helped into the carriage.

I waved to her until she was out of sight and only then did I turn to watch the way ahead. This time, I paid attention as we rode through Camallea and over the bridge. The path switched back as it climbed the rocky expanse the palace had been built upon, but the magic kept the ride steady. Considering, it was a rather large island, big enough to host a full town if not more, and the view from each angle was more beautiful than the last.

I had to force myself to sit back until the coachman had pulled the carriage to a stop in line with the red carpet sweeping up the stairs. One squirrel-man opened the door for me, the other handed me out. As it was only early afternoon, there were no candles to illuminate the courtyard, and the sun itself painted it in a golden glow. As much as I remembered every detail about the palace, I had forgotten that feeling of first arrival when disbelief and reality converged to steal my breath away. I had come late, again, but I was glad for the lack of guests that could've impeded my arrival.

"Keep the carriage close," I reminded the coachman, who grinned back reassuringly.

Marie may not have given these creatures the power of speech, but at least they had some sense.

Walking up the steps toward the palace entrance, I noticed that one thing had changed since the last time I was there: Then, no one had looked twice as I slipped in late. Now, with each step I felt the eyes of other footmen, coachmen, valets, soldiers, and servants upon me. For the first time in a long time, I was being noticed.

I hurried in, if only to get away from those curious eyes. Following a servant down a new hallway, I tried to stay in the shadows as I walked its carpeted length. Soldiers stood stiffly at attention along the way, but I felt the eyes of each glance then retreat as I passed.

Just before we stepped outside, I stopped to gather myself. What if that spark between the prince and myself wasn't as strong in daylight? What if he wasn't as excited to see me as I was to see him? What if he'd only been enamored with the mystery, but a week in the palace had turned his mind elsewhere? What if he didn't notice me today and I was picked up by a duke or a baron who wanted me only because I had danced with the prince? What if this was all only in my mind?

I didn't allow myself to think on it further. I was here, dressed in finery Father couldn't afford to give me even if he'd wanted to. Marie had gone through the trouble of thinking up this whole charade for me and I would play it out to the end. Whether that ended in humiliation when the truth of who I was became known, or simply returning home to fade into the black soot of my life until even Iris couldn't pick me out of the ashes, I could not guess.

The servant held open a door and bowed to me as I took my cue and stepped outside. Large stretches of green lawns rolled on and on, a perfect place for palace sports. Directly across from where I stood, colorful rows of seats had been built for spectators to enjoy the feats of strength and knighthood to be displayed in the specially constructed arena below. By then, most of the seats were filled with the glistening rainbow of guests already in attendance.

"Miss—Lady—" a deep voice rumbled hesitantly beside me.

I knew even before I finished turning that it was the voice of the captain. Meeting his soft brown gaze, my lips clamped shut, wondering if Marie's promise that I would be unrecognizable counted for people I didn't live with. Would the captain recognize me, the girl from the well? Would he give me away? I knew little about him, but he had a sharp intelligence that couldn't be ignored. A keenness that warned me from assuming such a discovery beyond his abilities.

The captain was studying me closely, perhaps searching for clues of my identity beneath the tilt of my hat, so I figured it best to keep moving.

I gave him a small curtsy. "Good afternoon, Captain," I said evenly, pleasantly, playing the part given to me with a few taps of a wand and a shower of magical sparks.

The captain returned my greeting with a short, crisp bow. "I'm under orders to bring you to the prince the moment you arrive, my lady."

I couldn't hide my flush of pleasure, the worries from before vanishing completely. The prince did want to see me again!

"Please lead the way," I said amicably, taking his proffered arm.

Despite our outward pleasantness toward each other, a sudden silence fell, and I was too anxious to let it last long.

"Are you going to compete today?" I politely inquired.

The captain glanced at me, opened his mouth to say something, then closed it and glanced away. "Yes," he finally said.

"Will the prince?" I asked.

"Yes," he said again, and I'll admit to being excited at the prospect.

We came upon a short flight of steps that led to the large royal box, placed front and center to offer the royal family and their personal guests the best view in the arena. Having never been to an event such as this before, I wondered why they had filled the playing field with so much sand. As soon as the program began, I understood soon enough that it was comfort for the bare feet of strong men and acrobats, a giveaway for the paws of hunted animals, and a sponge for the blood of beaten men.

As the captain led me toward the royal box, a noticeable hush swept across the stands. Unlike my first time at the palace, the music kept on playing, guests continued to talk, but it seemed all with an eye on me. I yearned for the attentions of the prince, not the eyes of hundreds of nobles, men and women who would never notice me without my magical transformation.

"There seems to be a sudden increase in feathers here," I commented, having had a chance to better survey the attendees.

"The kingfishers may migrate early because of it, my lady," the captain replied dryly.

Thinking of the sudden clamor that must have been made over their feathers, my grip unintentionally tightened on the captain's arm. "I did not anticipate this," I whispered.

The captain must have heard the regret in my voice because

his response was much kinder. "Those used to being unseen rarely do," he replied softly.

His response brought me up short. Was he so quick, his vision so clear that he'd already figured out who I was? I didn't think he'd make such a comment if he had thought me a lady or forgotten princess as everyone else seemed to. I was preparing a response to allay his suspicions when we were fortunately interrupted.

"Well done, Captain!" the prince cried merrily, detaching himself from his father's side to intercept us before we could reach him.

Having completed his assignment, the captain turned to me and bowed again. I responded with a curtsy in kind. "Thank you, Captain."

"I hope the lady enjoys the day."

I couldn't hold back my smile. "I wish you luck in the competitions, Captain."

The captain simply nodded his head in thanks.

I turned away from him to catch the prince's bright blue gaze lingering upon me. My heart leapt forward. My stomach flipped. If they were to continue with this behavior, then it would have been better to leave them both at home.

"May I?" the prince asked, and without waiting for a response, took my hand and tucked it into his arm. "I prayed you would come again," he whispered, as he led me toward a quieter corner of the box.

A warmth spread through me, starting from my belly and riding my blood, from the tips of my toes to the roots of the hair on my head. His simple touch, the song of his voice was enough to make my past vanish, to heal and soothe every kick aimed my way, every nasty word meant to poison my spirit. That moment, then, was what I was there for.

"I've had to converse with such droll individuals," he told me.

"I'm sorry to have kept His Highness waiting," I murmured. "Perhaps I should try one or two droll conversations myself, not to be rude."

"Out of the question," the prince replied. "You're here for me and needn't bestow your attentions on anyone else."

I melted, truly melted at those words. How was I to know then that the words were not sweet and romantic but possessive and demanding? What clarity can an overlooked sixteen-year-old hope to have in the face of a prince's devotions?

The prince gently dropped his other hand over mine, acting as gallantly as I remembered him to be. This was my third time meeting him, and his charm had grown threefold. His sandy hair was perfectly combed, a few strands escaping to dip perfectly onto his forehead. Today, he wore pants of royal purple and a white jacket with purple stripes down the side. Two downward rows of gold buttons kept it closed and snug across his certainly strong chest.

"You'll leave me no choice but to hold an event for which hats, masks, and feathers are forbidden," he informed me.

"Perhaps I would not like to come to such an event, Your Highness," I replied.

"Then I wouldn't attend either," he declared.

"But you are the one to have it," I laughed.

The prince's hand tightened on mine and he leaned in closer than was considered proper. "Don't tease," he pleaded, with the right touch of tragedy in his voice to melt my heart all over again.

"I won't," I promised, and the prince rewarded me with a smile I would have walked across the world to see.

"I'm to compete today," he told me.

"I wish His Highness much success," I sincerely replied.

"Oh, I wouldn't worry about that," he said easily, then too quickly for me to stop him, he plucked a purple feather from my hat. He tickled me under my chin with it before fluttering it between us. "I would like this though," he said impishly. "As a token from you."

"The prince is welcome to it," I answered with a shy smile.

The prince kissed the feather then took up my hand to kiss it, too, before tucking it back into his arm.

"As I will not be able to sit with you the entire afternoon," he told me, "I have found someone suitable enough to be your companion in my stead."

I wasn't entirely disappointed, as I knew that when I wasn't sitting next to the prince, I would at least be seeing him. I didn't have much time to ponder what it meant that he was leaving me under someone else's care though, as he promptly led me down the box and settled me into a seat next to one of the most gorgeous women I had ever seen. The small tiara tucked into her hair marked her as a princess, though not of our kingdom, as the prince had no siblings.

Her beauty was so strong it was almost palpable, her features visible even in the canopy's shade. Her lips were red as blood, her skin white as snow, her hair black as ebony. She was dressed in a gown with significantly less layers than the rest of us in attendance, the ruby-red silk almost scandalously shaped to her body. One shoulder was shockingly bare, the rest of the material sweeping past her neck, then tumbling behind her, cinching the dress closed over the other shoulder. Despite the cut, the dress's neckline was high, rather than immodestly low like my stepsisters' and most other eligible women's in attendance.

The irony was that despite the dress, her face was so riveting the rest of her was barely noticed. Her face could have been attached to the neglected bottom half of Madame's etiquette swans and she would still be the most captivating creature in the room. When I met her gaze, a small, seemingly permanent smirk played at her lips as if she knew all this about herself and then some.

"Won't you look after her while I prepare for my turn, Little Lyla?" the prince told more than asked the princess.

"How could I say no, dear Henri Christopher Charles Alexander?" she sneered in response.

"Snow White," he snapped back.

They suddenly stopped, as if remembering I was still there.

"I hate my full name," the prince explained to me apologetically.

"I think it charming, Your Highness," I said.

The prince's face brightened, and Princess Lyla rolled her eyes. "I won't be long," he promised, taking his time letting go of my arm. He shot the princess a sharp, meaningful look before turning toward the steps that led down from the box.

I was both relieved and terrified to be alone with Princess Lyla. Relieved because I knew she couldn't possibly know who I really was, and terrified because she was so certain of herself, so confident, so sure in her place and the power it gave her. I was to learn this wasn't always a good thing. I perched at the very edge of my velvet chair just enough to be sitting, but ready to flee at a moment's notice.

"I never cared much for these festivals," she confided, as we both pretended to turn our attention to the happenings below.

In the arena, servants were raking the sand after the horses had kicked it up during the jousting, smoothing it over for feats of hand-to-hand combat. When they were done, a well-muscled knight, now stripped of his armor and wearing soft leather breeches, was led in to polite applause. After a dramatic enough pause, the prince entered, wearing only pants as well, his admirable torso highlighted by the sun. His skin was taut over his sculpted frame, and from the royal box I was just able to make out a few thin scars, tiny white lines cutting through his sun-kissed skin. I thought then that they were only leftover marks from the wars he'd fought defending our borders, but I would learn soon enough that, like most anyone, he had scars that ran much deeper as well.

The crowd rose to its feet in thunderous appreciation of His Highness, who rewarded all with a dazzling smile. He bowed to his father then looked to where I sat with the beautiful princess, raised the feather he had taken from me to his lips then slipped it into his pocket. From the heat on my face, I'm sure my blush was crimson.

"You like him," Princess Lyla said more than asked.

My blush turned the color of fire. "He-He's my prince," I stammered.

"You're infatuated," she continued. "It's all over your face."

Involuntarily, my hand flew to my cheeks and the princess chuckled.

"It's not a bad thing," she said easily. "Though it'll wear off soon enough. Nothing is really as perfect as it may first seem."

I glanced quickly to her when she said it, but her eyes were turned away from me, watching the prince gain the upper hand over his foe below. She said it so simply, I couldn't decide if she was merely speaking or giving me fair warning. A few weeks before, I would have thought her words over more carefully. Then, I had given myself over to the dream, losing myself in it more and more as it slowly replaced reality.

"We're cousins, you know, of a sort," she said next. "The prince and I," she added, probably in response to my blank stare.

"Of a sort?" I questioned.

"His mother and my stepmother were sisters," she elaborated.

The blood chilled in my veins. I had heard stories about her stepmother, how she had been jealous of her stepdaughter's beauty and sent a huntsman to cut out her heart and liver. I always wondered how true the story could be, but meeting Princess Lyla now, experiencing her beauty for myself, I believed every word of it.

"I have a stepmother," I let slip.

This caught the princess's attention. "Do you?"

I nodded, not trusting my voice on the subject of Madame. At least, she'd never tried to kill me. Not like that anyway.

"Do you like her?"

I emphatically shook my head no. "She hates me," I confessed. "She was never a mother to me."

A short, harsh laugh escaped the princess. "We have something in common," she said. She studied me a bit closer, sizing up tiny little me, deciding something. "He wants me to find out more about you, that's why you're here with me," she revealed.

I tried to lean away from her, but there was really nowhere for me to go.

"You needn't be afraid." Princess Lyla's smile suddenly turned malicious, she grabbed my hand and at the same time, whipped out a mirror from some hidden pocket in her dress. "Mirror, Mirror, from the wall," she began chanting before I could stop her, before I could pull away, "who does Prince Alex think fairest of all?"

The face of the mirror swirled, the silver backing melting in spirals before reforming into my face, my face without any mask. My cinder–streaked skin, my rag-clothed body, my guarded eyes. Princess Lyla frowned at the image.

"Is this you?" she asked pointedly.

I nodded confirmation. That blasted mirror would probably tell her everything anyhow.

"Your father?"

"A merchant."

"Your stepmother?"

"A baroness."

"Does she know you're here?"

"No."

Princess Lyla pursed her lips at the image in the mirror. "Did she do this to you?"

"She calls me Cinderwench," I said, as if that was explanation enough.

Princess Lyla studied me and my image again. "Faery?" was all she finally asked.

"No," I replied, shaking my head for good measure. "Just the dress."

She went back to studying magic me and then the real me. It grew too quiet. I couldn't stand it anymore.

"Please don't tell him, Princess," I begged her. "Please don't tell a soul. The crier said anyone with an invitation could come," I added desperately.

Princess Lyla pursed her lips. "The prince is not fond of magic."

I frowned at her careful choice of words, neither adequate to hide the overly controlled timbre of her voice when she said them.

"Why ever not?" I asked.

"He thinks it ruined his father," she replied shortly. "Mine, too."

That didn't make sense to me. I may not have known about everything that happened in the kingdom, but surely I would have heard if our king had been destroyed by magic.

"I-I did not mean to overstep," I managed to squeeze out.

The princess shrugged. "We're not all magic-obsessed like King Rainn over in Farthington," she said. "Besides, everyone has a line, right? Just make sure he doesn't find out."

"And you-Your Highness won't tell him?" I asked meekly.

She shook her head and I quietly exhaled a sigh of relief. She hadn't told me much, but from the tone of her voice and the look on her face, I could tell that the prince was a little more than "not fond" of magic. A lot more. I would never want to find out.

At the same time, despite the dream I was living, I never really thought that my secret would ever be something I'd have to worry about past that day. Surely, the prince would never find a magically dressed Cinderwench to be the most favorable maiden of all. Right?

The princess studied me a little more. "What's your name?"

"Ella, Your Highness" I replied.

"Ella," the princess repeated.

More silence, then slowly the princess nodded. "I won't tell him," she said, "but I won't lie if he asks."

"Thank you, Princess," I said, and I meant it.

She slipped the mirror back to wherever she'd brought it from, then absently patted my shoulder. "The mirror can only answer one type of question," she informed me offhandedly, as if that knowledge wouldn't have affected the entire conversation until now. "Now we must pretend like we are having a lovely time," she said with a glittering smile, adding in a small laugh for good measure.

I could scarcely process what had just occurred. The princess had just tricked me into revealing intimate details about myself and now she was treating me like her closest friend. I didn't know what to do with myself, but I knew I would have little help from the others in the box. So I turned back to the arena where we watched the prince decidedly beat his foe, then rose to my feet with the rest of the crowd to cheer his heroics. The prince raised his arms triumphantly in the air, and the noise only grew louder. I'll admit to feeling a slight surge of pride seeing him there, strong, graceful, and undefeated.

The prince bowed once more to his father and then turned to leave the arena. In so doing, he pivoted close to his opponent then stepped over him to exit. Had I not been watching him so intently, I would have missed the way the knight winced when the prince walked away from him, only registering later that the prince had stepped on his hand on the way out.

"I really wish he wouldn't do that," Princess Lyla muttered, more to herself than to me. I wasn't even sure that's what she'd said.

The knight was led from the arena as another two entered. They both looked to be knights of the kingdom, but when the second one again received a greater cheer than the first I looked closer. That soft brown hair, those discerning eyes: the captain. I ducked my head before my gaze strayed any more across his exposed torso.

I turned my attention back to the princess beside me, hoping she hadn't noticed, and thought of the trick she'd pulled with the mirror. My initial awe of her burned off in a simmer of annoyance. So emboldened, I dared asked, "Why be here, if you so disdain all this?"

Princess Lyla shook her head, unfazed at my impertinence. "Alex wrote to ask if I'd ever seen or heard of a lady like you, and I was too intrigued not to come. I agreed to find out what I could."

"But you can't tell," I said quickly, hoping her promise to keep my secret still stood.

"So you must tell me something about yourself that I can," she countered directly. "What are some things you like to do?"

"Like to do?" I repeated dumbly.

The thought of doing something, anything simply because I enjoyed it had become foreign to me. I couldn't very well tell her that I liked to live within my fantasy, that it was the only place I was ever really safe and somewhat happy. I dug through the stores of my memory; surely there was something there befitting the behaviors of a lady.

The roar of the crowd tried to pull me from my thoughts, but I refused to look at the arena. Not even to see if the man who'd once helped me gather my boxes by the side of a well was winning. Instead, I forced myself to think of my childhood, to think of a time before Madame had beaten me down.

"Drawing," I finally said. "I've a fair talent for it."

"Do you?" the princess seemed genuinely interested. "Are you very good at it?"

"I haven't had much time for it in a while," I admitted, "only to help my stepsisters with their cosmetics."

"Oh," the princess's lip curled into a disdainful sneer, "there are others."

The crowd cheered again, and this time I did allow myself to look. The knight was on the ground and the captain stood above him. He bowed to the king then briefly raised a fist in triumph to the delight of the crowd. He turned back to his opponent and offered him a hand up. Clinging to his dignity, the man refused, forcing himself to stand without assistance. When he did, the captain offered his hand again, and the knight clasped it in a brief gesture of mutual respect. Both left the arena without a backward glance.

"My sisters treat me as Madame does, but I don't think they are as bad as her," I rushed to explain, turning back to our conversation so my thoughts wouldn't dwell too long on the captain's considerate behavior. "They didn't have a very good example to follow."

The princess sniffed at that. "Are they here, too?"

"Would you like to meet them? They'd be in fits to meet a real princess."

The offer slipped out before I could stop it, but there was something about the princess that loosened my tongue. Maybe because she was the only one who knew the truth about me, and there was real relief in that. Or maybe I just wanted her to see the family that had created the girl in the mirror, so she would understand the need for a mask. Either way, it was a few long seconds, which felt like hours, before she nodded her head.

"The day's already odd," she allowed.

We watched the rest of the events with half an eye. By then, the sun was visibly lower in the sky, and I glanced at it nervously, willing it to slow its path. I was too anxious to watch the performing acrobats or the group of knights chasing a lion back into its cage. Time was short and none of it interested either of us. Even before all was done, the princess motioned for me to stand up and follow her down the steps and out of the box.

We passed by the king's raised seat on our way, and we both stopped to drop him a curtsy. The king beckoned Princess Lyla forward, and she stepped up to kiss her uncle-of-a-sort on his cheek. The king gestured toward me and the princess leaned down to tell him something I couldn't hear. Even if she'd said it loud enough, I doubt I would've heard anything above the pounding of my heart in my ears. I couldn't believe I was standing before the king. I couldn't believe he had motioned toward me, that he noticed me among all these beautiful, eligible women.

Behind him, Sir Percival kept his ever-astute gaze upon me, eyeing me suspiciously until the princess retook my arm and led me away. She reddened his cheeks with a flirtatious wave, but that did not stop his gaze from boring into me as we went to seek out my stepsisters.

"What did the king ask?" I wanted to know.

"He was just inquiring after you," the princess said with a reassuring smile. "I told him you were a new friend of mine."

"Not very specific," I said, wondering if she would dare lie to a king.

I felt the princess shrug. "Until the prince decides he wants to marry you, the king need press no further."

"Marry me!" I exclaimed, stopping in my tracks.

The princess tugged me forward. "It's what these events are about, after all," she calmly reminded me, "for Alex to find a wife."

Suddenly, I couldn't speak. What if the prince decided he wanted to marry me? What if he didn't? Would our time together mean anything if he didn't choose me? And if he did, how would I explain to him who I really was? Could I escape my home and come to the palace without giving anything away? I doubted it. Did I even want to marry the prince? What a question!

Once away from the arena, the princess led the way toward the long tables of food and refreshments set up all along the grassy fields. Guests lingered all about and I kept my eyes alert for my stepsisters, trying to find their familiar dresses in a sea of dresses that swallowed them up in imitation of mine from the masquerade.

Then there they were, right as we came upon the last of the champagne fountains. Maybelle's and Calliope's faces were flushed from drink, or because they both dangled on the arms of young lords who were smiling at them with adoring eyes.

"Good afternoon," I greeted them, painfully aware of the shadows from the sun blending into dusk as the sky bled color above us.

At the sound of my voice, both swiveled to stare wide-eyed at me. Then their gaze shifted to the princess, her tiara, and back to me.

"It's lovely to see you again, Ladies Maybelle and Calliope," I continued.

I said their names more for Princess Lyla's benefit, but the effect on them was well worth it. Calliope flushed, and Maybelle's lips worked like a fish, trying to form words that wouldn't come out.

"She knows our names," she finally managed to sputter in unabashed awe.

"This is the prince's cousin, Princess Lyla," I introduced, and the two dropped into curtsies that would make Madame proud.

"I do hope you're enjoying yourselves," Princess Lyla said to them, amusement playing at the corners of her lips.

Knowing what she was capable of, I wondered if perhaps it wasn't the best of ideas to introduce them to her. She'd quite easily managed to extract everything about me, and I couldn't imagine what she would do to them, knowing how they, and their mother, treated me.

I was saved from further worry by the song of a voice I would slay the fiercest dragon for. "There you are!" the prince, unfortunately now fully dressed, called. He removed my hand from the princess's and took it in his. A significant look passed between them, which I knew had something to do with a talk about me later.

"I've nearly had to chase you across the whole island," he admonished.

"His Highness is surely capable," I replied sweetly. "As today's victory evidenced."

The prince beamed at me. "All for you, my lady," he genially admitted, brandishing the feather from my hat.

Maybelle and Calliope giggled at the sugary words, but I hardly heard them. There was nothing for me in this world so long as those wonderful, clear-blue-sky eyes locked on mine.

"I brought you these," the prince added, presenting me with two small flower confections, perfect white lilies decorated with pink and yellow at their tips.

"Lilies," Princess Lyla said, her voice indicating pleasure at seeing those particular flowers.

"They're lovely," I breathed.

I took them from him, and for reasons still unknown to me, looked up to find one of my squirrel footmen at the doors leading back into the palace. I don't know how he found me, but I did know he only risked it for one reason.

I was dangerously close to overstaying the magic. It was time to go. Now.

"Here," I said, thrusting the two flowers into my gaping stepsisters' hands. I turned to the startled prince and pressed his hand in mine. "Thank you so much for such a wonderful afternoon, Your Highness," I said, already hurrying away. I smiled at Princess Lyla. "It was an honor to meet you, Princess."

"But, but, you can't leave," the prince sputtered. "Not again."

"I'm so sorry, I must go." I lifted my skirts so I could run away faster. I couldn't resist one backward glance. "My charming prince."

"I won't let you! Not this time," he called, lunging for my hand and almost slipping off my glove.

But I was too fast for him. I ran across the grass, burst into the palace, and was already rushing down the hallway, just a few feet from the main doors when I heard his footsteps in close pursuit.

"Captain!" he cried. "My horse, your horse, now!"

More footsteps joined his, but I didn't waste time turning around. To this day, I still don't know how my tiny feet were able to outrun so many grown men, and soldiers at that.

I rushed down the carpeted steps and leaped into the open door of my carriage, not even bothering to be helped in by my footmen. The coachman cracked his whip the moment I was in, and I scrambled to close the door even as the squirrel-men ran to catch up to the fleeing horses. Two dull thumps told me they'd made it, though it scarcely mattered. They would be turned back into squirrels in the next few minutes, and it didn't matter then who saw them.

We had already made it over the bridge and onto the main road of the capitol, when I realized that some of the horses' hooves I was hearing were not from my own carriage. Daring to peek behind me, I saw soldiers chasing after us. They must have had the horses prepared in advance today, because they already seemed too close, even at the pace my magic carriage set. My heart leaped, but not in the way it had earlier. I was, without a doubt, falling head over heels for the prince, but so close to sunset, he was the last person I wanted to see now. Actually, the prince, the captain, the soldiers, even Princess Lyla, were all on equal footing of the people I least wanted to see.

"We're not going to make it," I yelled to the coachman, who may not have heard me but honked his acquiescence anyway.

Why did I take so long? I berated myself. Why couldn't I have just looked at the sky and slipped out before the prince found me again?

Because I hadn't wanted to go home.

Because I had forgotten that my appearance was only magic.

Because I was greedy for every moment I could get with the prince and this other life.

The sun was completely below the horizon now and by dimmed light we raced wildly across the main road, peeling through Camallea at speeds unsafe for a carriage. At some points, soldiers would suddenly appear beside the carriage window, scaring me out of my wits as they tried to cut us off from alleys and side streets. Somehow, the goose skillfully evaded them all.

We were safely out of Camallea and well on the way home when I felt the first jolt from the bottom of the carriage. I thought we'd lost a wheel, but when I didn't see one rolling away behind us, I realized that we'd lost a wheel because the pumpkin was transforming back into its natural state. As we careened around a corner, two squirrels leaped off the back and scurried into the trees lining the way. The carriage became more orange, bumpier, and I knew I had to get out of there before it transformed back with me still inside.

I waited until we were coming across another bend then yelled to the coachman, "Turn straight into the trees!"

He did as he was told. The carriage veered off the main road, I pushed the door open, and soon we were tumbling down an incline, one goose, four mice, a pumpkin, and me. When we came to rest at the bottom, it took me a minute to get my legs under me. I picked up the pumpkin and clucked the goose to my side. When

I was finally able to stand, I ducked right back down again, hearing approaching horsemen, their confused cries, their sudden halt right across from where I was.

I willed the goose to keep his bill shut. But no longer a magical being, he was scarcely under my control. He let out a sharp honk, which turned heads and brought footsteps in our direction. I debated running away, but knew I wouldn't make it very far, and would only increase suspicion. Instead, I grabbed a handful of dirt and quickly smeared it across my face.

The approaching footsteps turned out to be those of the captain and two soldiers. Though I knew he wouldn't recognize me, I was still relieved that the prince was not with them.

The captain fixed his sharp gaze upon me. I lowered my eyes so he couldn't see them. "Miss, what are you doing out here after dark?" he wanted to know.

I fished around for an excuse. "Chasing after the goose," I replied lamely.

"Do you live around here?"

I nodded.

"Did you see a carriage go by not three minutes ago?"

I shook my head no and the goose honked again. The blasted animal was going to be the death of me. The noise seemed to shake off some of the captain's focus.

"Look at me," he said softer, but with as much force.

I hesitated before looking up. I couldn't meet his eyes.

"How old are you?" he asked.

"Sixteen," I replied.

He nodded, but his brow furrowed, as if something had taken ahold of his memory, endeavoring to match two seemingly random bits. I needed to get out of there before anything fell into place.

"I really should get home, sir," I said politely. "Father will worry."

He nodded and let me go without further comment, but I could feel his eyes following me as I climbed back to the main road, ushering the traitorous goose along, lugging the pumpkin under my arm. It was a few moments before I heard him return to the main road, where he was forced to divert his attention from me to take care of his soldiers' reports.

"Nothing," one man said. "Not a clue, not even a track."

I didn't hear the captain's response, as it was then that I passed by the prince's horse. I knew it was his because of the fine white coat, the soft, black leather boot in the stirrup. Sound faded to a buzz, but I refused to look up. Last time we met like this, the prince had mistaken me for a little girl. After two wonderful encounters, I couldn't bear that indignity again.

It took well over thirty minutes to finally reach the path that turned off to my house. By then, all other emotions had quieted, and I was left only with the pleasant warmth of more hours spent among royalty. I was already replaying the afternoon for the third time when I reached my mother's grave. I placed the pumpkin on the low stone wall and sat with my back to it as I told her about all that had happened.

Then I climbed the pear tree high as I dared and looked out toward the palace, searching for the lights I thought would be lit and burning bright. I couldn't see it from my vantage point, but my mind saw it as it should be.

When my stepfamily returned later that night, my stepsisters had understandably worked themselves into a tizzy.

"We met the mystery lady again!" Calliope was the first to tell me.

"She introduced us to a princess!" Maybelle said. "Princess Lyla, the most beautiful woman who ever was."

Calliope nodded in solemn agreement. "She must be somewhat important if she is friends with a princess!"

"And so she ran from the prince again!" Maybelle cried out.

"What is it about him that repels her so?" Calliope asked, and the two fell into fits of laughter.

It only took five years for me to answer that question.

Calliope pulled herself together. "Do you think her disfigured? For she always covers her face?"

"Perhaps her nose is too long, or one eyes droops like so," Maybelle suggested, half-closing one eyelid to demonstrate.

"Perhaps she simply doesn't want to be known," I offered, and both stared at me incredulously. My face flushed under their disbelieving glares, which would be beneficial cover for the words that followed.

"Do you not think the prince would like to know the name of the woman who took his heart?" Calliope asked.

Took his heart? Surely, he wasn't pining after me, not as I was for him. He had a kingdom filled with beautiful women to choose from. I had only him.

"Will he marry her then?" I whispered.

"If he can catch her!" Maybelle exclaimed.

They looked at each other, then burst out laughing hysterically.

"Maybe at the grand ball," Calliope said when she was finally able to catch her breath again.

"The ball?" I asked, not believing this could really be happening.

Calliope nodded. "A *grand* ball. The final event, where the prince must choose his bride, or marry whomever his father chooses for him."

My stomach thudded to my feet at her words. Surely, Marie would concoct something for me so I could go to the palace again. When once I would have been simply happy to be there, I knew now that I could not find happiness again without the prince. If I didn't make it to the grand ball, then he would be forced to marry someone else. It couldn't happen. Marie couldn't allow it. I wouldn't allow it.

And what about the truth of who I was? I wondered that night, as sleep stubbornly stayed away. Would he be able to forgive my use of magic? Could he see me as the enchanting woman who'd caught his attention or only as the young girl from the street? Would Princess Lyla speak up on my behalf? Why should she? Because we'd both been the object of a stepmother's hatred? Was that enough to make her raise me to a princess? A cousin of sorts?

It didn't seem possible. And who knew if she would even still be there by then. She had her own kingdom to get back to, her own prince, her own happily ever after.

Thinking about the princess made me wonder about what she would do in my place. Having heard the stories and then met her in person, I knew she was smart, knew she was someone who got things done. Did I have it in me to do the same?

I doubted it.

THE THIRD MISTAKE

*T*icking down the days until the grand ball proved a much harder task than for the first two events. It would be in one week's time and some days the hours flew by and others they ambled along at their leisure. My emotions rollicked along with them: Sometimes they were a rush of ecstasy, of pure joy and elation at the two incredible chances I'd already been given. Others, the agony chewed away at my stomach, from the uncertainty of whether or not I could go, whether or not Marie would allow the magic to stay around long enough for the prince to ask for my hand.

The night before, I had concluded that I would never be able to accept my life here again if I didn't at least get to try.

I never should have gone to that ball. No matter what I was feeling in the days leading up to that night, no matter the insecurities and uncertainties, the surety I had then of what I felt I *had* to do turned out to be one of the most misguided decisions of my life. So what if the prince married someone else? Once I attended that grand ball, all the events that unfolded from that night were inevitable, from the moment I tried to flee to the moment I came back to the palace for good.

Without Marie to turn to, I discussed these worries high up in my attic with my goldfish night after night. Most responses I received were wide eyed bubbles, but there were times when it moved its fins and that was answer enough. Some nights, the worries sent me to sleep in tears, others, joy cradled me in her arms and hummed me to sleep with a loving caress.

As they had after the masquerade, Maybelle and Calliope were intent on imitating the mystery lady's gown. Although at this point both were agreed that they would rather spend more time with the lords who paid them attention than with the prince who didn't, they still hadn't yet given up hope that the right dress might turn the prince's handsome head. The path to royalty was too great a temptation, too intoxicating a dream to so quickly relinquish. The mystery lady, for her part, had to content herself with being a style setter, a role she was most unaccustomed to, no matter that it would be part of her life at the palace.

I tried as best I could to temper my stepsister's desires for replication. I convinced Maybelle to add deep blue to her silver and purple design, and Calliope to include green in hers. Admittedly, the outcomes of both were most flattering, and I was sure, if they wanted, they could tie up their young lords' hands in marriage before the night was over. They, like most others it turned out, chose to go without anything to hide their faces that third night, as it seemed the contest for the prince's heart was already won. If not, they wanted the prince to see them as they truly were, and both girls were very lovely. However, that did not stop them from wearing pearl and feather headbands in their hair in salute to the mystery lady's hat.

Two days before the ball, Madame led the way into Camallea, intent on finding an extra little something special for her girls. When once I would relish any time away from the house, especially in the vibrant burst of capital life, I dreaded the trip with every step I took. At that point, I didn't even care that they treated me like a pack horse, unceremoniously dumping packages into my already full arms. I just wanted to get out of there, and fast. I kept my head ducked, my eyes lowered the entire time we were there, praying in agony that the sun would set early or that a sudden thunderstorm would close up the shops and send us on our way.

Neither was to happen.

Looking on it now, I was rather foolish to think that anyone would recognize me, that anyone would notice me beneath my soot-stained skin and patchwork head kerchief. I didn't know then what types of questions the prince had asked Princess Lyla, what answers she'd been forced to tell. For all I knew, the prince had sent out word to arrest the Cinderwench, the unworthy servant who impersonated a lady and dared touch the heart of a prince.

The person who worried me most was the captain. At the masquerade, at the festival, he hadn't seemed entirely blinded by my disguise. Considering it further, since that day at the well in the quaint piazza behind the confectioner's, no matter what guise he saw me in, he had never overlooked me. Fortunate for me, neither the captain nor his soldiers were in the streets that day.

Madame finally found what she was looking for in a small glassblower's shop toward the end of the main market. I was dragged inside behind the others where whatever anxiety I had endured until then compounded when I, weighed down as I was with packages, suddenly found myself in a room full of delicate glass pieces, charms, and figurines. One too strong breath, even from little me, would destroy years of the owner's work. Then my life would surely be over.

Madame slowly circled the shop, as if knowing that every prolonged second could be the death of me. She thoroughly examined every piece, biding her time, as a slow trickle of sweat started somewhere around the nape of my neck and eased its way down my spine. I finally prayed she would just stab me and end my misery, a first and final act of mercy for the girl she'd habitually stomped out like stray cinders from a fire.

"It if would please the lady," the servile glassblower tried to steer Madame's attention to a small pouch he'd set on the counter, "perhaps these are worthy of consideration?"

He carefully slid out the small pieces from the pouch to a collective gasp as every breath was stolen away. Dangling from a thin, silver thread were three pieces of glass, at once opaque and translucent as they sucked in the light from the room and swirled it into a kaleidoscope of colors within their sandy depths.

"What is this?" Madame asked, reaching for the glass. Even she wasn't able to keep the wonder from her voice.

For his part, the glassblower didn't react to her awe. Humble and obsequious, he still knew how to play his part in the game. "Castarrean glass, my lady," he explained, his Maridonian accent matching his origins with the method of glassmaking. "I made it myself, right here in my shop."

Madame took the chain from him and examined each piece individually. There was no specific shape or pattern to any of them, but that only added to the allure of the actual glass. The pieces themselves were thick, jagged, and pointed, as if someone had dropped a large jar then picked out the biggest shards from the remains. The ends had been rounded to keep the glass from cutting, but that didn't negate their sharp angles. Beyond all these details was the inexplicable way the glass toyed with the light in the room.

"It's a very tricky method to make this kind of glass," the merchant went on, "not many have the skill or patience to get it right."

Madame gave no sign that she'd heard, but her stillness gave her away.

"Exquisite," she finally declared, and only then did we let out our held breaths. Not too much though, I was still balancing boxes and inordinately afraid I would topple them and the lovely glass on display. "We'll take them."

In a moment of unprecedented concern, Madame refused to entrust me with the carefully wrapped pieces. Instead, she insisted on carrying them herself and I was too relieved to feel slighted.

Once I finished helping my stepsisters get ready the night of the grand ball, they hurried downstairs, and only then did Madame affix the necklaces of Castarrean glass around their necks, with a sharp order of, "Don't touch them!" Then they spun on their heels and flounced out the door.

I stood at the top of the stairs, watching their carriage recede into the night. I knew I should be hurrying to the wall, but something stayed me for a time. Perhaps I sensed this was the night that would irrevocably change my life forever. Perhaps I knew that there was no turning back if Marie would be there to dress me fit enough for the prince's ball and the bearer of his heart. Perhaps, somewhere deep and subconscious, I knew this night was a mark of the end.

When I finally shook myself to act, I flew to the low stone wall near my pear tree.

"Grandmère, Grandmère!" I called for her. "Grandmère, you must come, please!"

At first, all was silent, the echo of my voice dying away in the fields. Fear overtook me. Maybe Marie wouldn't appear? Maybe she sufficiently fulfilled her father's promise, and this was it of my other life, so close to the finish yet unable to see it all the way through.

I refused to let myself cry or fall into despair. If Marie wouldn't come to me, then I would go to her. I was already swinging my second foot over the wall when a familiar voice asked, "Wherever are you going, Ella dear?"

"Grandmère!" I spun around happily, and there she was, floating over the wall as if she'd been there all along. "I wasn't sure you would come," I admitted.

Marie let out a soft chuckle. "And let you miss the biggest night of your life?" she asked. "My dear, whatever rags the magic contrived until now, we shall outdo them tonight!"

"And will you, can you, let it stay?" I asked hopefully, looking up at her through wide eyes, praying she would give in.

Marie shook her head sadly. "I'm sorry, Ella, the magic will only stay until midnight this time."

"Midnight!" I exclaimed. "What if I run out of time?"

"You'll think of something," Marie assured me. "A man who only loves you for your clothes is not a man who loves you very much at all."

I wanted to protest—appearances were always important—but I didn't have patience for clever phrases. Tonight was my last chance with the prince, and yet she insisted it all end by midnight, which gave me even less time than before. Even if I was fool enough to think he would ask for my hand by then, couldn't she at least give us until morning, allow us one untainted sunrise together before the cinders darkened my world forever?

Marie was already enroute to the garden, and I scurried to catch up. If this was to be my last night of magic, then I wouldn't miss a single spark of it.

True to her word, Marie outdid herself that night, the pumpkin became a magnificent golden carriage that glowed and sparkled from within. We could make the journey to the palace in the dark of night by the light of that carriage alone. The goose was once more turned into my faithful coachman, for which I was glad. He may have thrown me to the wolves before, but he was unrivaled as a coachman.

Four fat rats were turned into four powerful stallions, white coats pure as untouched snow, white as Princess Lyla's skin. Two lizards once more became my footmen, and though the squirrels had proven more than adept at their jobs, I was glad to have the lizards back. It reminded me of the beginning, like the whirls of all the parties were coming full circle.

As for myself, Marie didn't transform me right away and I didn't rush her. I knew she wanted tonight to be grandest of all, but tonight, other considerations had to be made. Should I go as myself? Should I be recognized tonight of all nights, if tonight could be the night my future was stamped with a royal seal, the night someone was finally willing and unafraid to love me?

I exhaled in relief when I finally felt the magic take hold. I relaxed into the familiar tingle, and even felt some comfort as it worked. I opened my eyes to find my dress glowing with the same spark that seemed to ignite my pumpkin carriage.

Marie produced a mirror so I could fully appreciate her masterpiece. "Well?"

My gown was all gold, a continuous piece of material that wrapped around me without any visible stitches or seams. Small canary-yellow diamonds were interlaced throughout my dress, affixed with unnoticed real gold thread. If I could sell it, the dress alone would bring in enough money to feed an entire village, and its livestock, for at least three years, if not more. A gold mask, delicate as lace, stretched across my eyes. The now-perfect ringlets of my hair were piled atop my head fronted by a thick gold headband sprouting a five petal gold flower. Even the gold silk gloves covering my hands were luminescent in the moonlight.

"Marie, you have outdone yourself," I said, reverence quieting my voice. "So much gold," I muttered numbly.

A flick of the thumb and the glint of gold tumbling in the air. Marie deftly caught the coin I'd given her before making it disappear again. "I had inspiration."

"So you haven't used it, nor have you shared it with others!" I accused.

"Would you like me to?" Marie asked.

"If you truly have no need for it," I replied, "please share it with someone who does."

"Your mother would smile upon your kindness," Marie said. She tried to wipe away a tear discreetly as she assessed me a final time. "Beautiful, you're absolutely beautiful."

I didn't think about it until later, but till today I will never forget how she spoke only of me and not the dress. I was so young then, so naïve. I thought the hardships I'd known were the worst I'd ever have to bear.

I lifted my gown to peek down at my feet and a small gasp escaped me. "Glass slippers?"

"Castarrean glass," Marie replied with a warm smile.

And really, there was only one type of glass I had ever seen or known of that could take the light around it and fracture it into an endless rainbow of color. The gold, the canary-yellow, it all swirled together in a shine more brilliant than the sun, more varied than the most creative artist's palette. And the glow from my gown would be illuminating into them all night.

I hugged Marie then, so hard and so tight that were she not a faery, I fear I may have hurt her. But I didn't know how else to thank her anymore, how else to put into words the wonder she had given me these three times. I could only hope now, as I did then, that she felt it was worth it.

"Are you sure this is what you want?" Marie asked suddenly, tenderly.

"A prince?" I asked, incredulous she would even ask. "Of course it is!"

"Then off with you," Marie commanded, pulling out of the hug. "You have a ball to get to."

"Goodbye, Grandmère," I called to her, as the footman settled me into my golden orb. "I hope to see you again soon."

"You will, Ella dear," she promised, and was gone even before we rounded the final bend of the house.

In what I anticipated to be my last night at the palace, I refused to allow any thought or emotion to cloud my mind. I dulled all my internal workings and sharpened my senses so I could take in everything, soak in everything, one final time.

By now, I knew the way to the palace very well, not just because I had imagined it so often, and not only because I was forced to walk much of it barefoot. Late one night, I had snuck into my father's study and taken out the maps of the kingdom. Iris, unlike that pigeon-brained goose, had remained silent when I came, emitting only a soft squawk to say he was glad to see me. I tickled the top of his head to let him know I was glad to see him, too, and promised him I would never let Marie bedeck me in macaw feathers.

Finding the map of Camallea, I had traced all possible routes the carriage could take over and over, envisioning it unfold in my mind even as my fingers walked across its renderings in thick black ink on parchment. I even pulled out maps of other realms to trace Princess Lyla's journey to ours. Now, as we rode, I could see the way the route unfolded on the map, could see how the coachman had changed routes on the way there to keep us out of sight of anyone watching for us on the road.

Tonight, the other coachmen and footmen didn't pretend to shy their heads away when my goose-man guided my carriage into the palace yard. Even if they weren't curious about me, my coachman must have been somewhat of a legend in his ability to twice evade the palace guards.

My carriage rolled to a stop before the main entrance, my door perfectly aligned with the red carpet that would lead me up the steps for what I thought then would be the last time. A lizard-man helped me out of the carriage and as before, I stood in the courtyard soaking it all in, knowing how the candlelight, the very moon and stars must be illuminating my headband, my dress, my shoes.

Though I wanted all the time I could hoard with the prince, I didn't hurry. At the top of the stairs, I turned once to look out over the candlelit courtyard below, imagining it as a painting in my mind, imagining how I could turn this fleeting moment into a memento that would last me all my years. Once inside, I again kept a steady pace, even going so far as to smile and incline my head toward the soldiers when I felt their eyes upon me. I didn't know what the rules of etiquette mandated then—Madame had never deigned to cover how to address a servant who was also a protector in any of her lessons—but I cared little for that tonight.

The first time I came to the palace, I was nervous and giddy, unsure of how my night would unfold and who, if anyone, would notice I was there. Tonight, I was serene, knowing full well that everyone would be watching, knowing that *he* would be waiting. A servant ushered me through the doors of the main ballroom, and suddenly, once more, a whole new world burst open below me.

The chandeliers caught my attention first and would continue to do so for my first few years at the palace. Golden candelabras were lit all along the walls but hovering above the dance floor was a line of three, crystal draped chandeliers made of solid gold. At least fifty candles blazed in each, and I wondered how long it took for them to be lit. Surely it took about a dozen or so servants to shine them so brightly they hardly needed candles at all. I gaped in awe at their extravagance.

The center of the marble floor was filled with dancing couples, perfectly synchronized to the eye of anyone watching from above. The men were smartly dressed, every soldier and lord proudly beribboned, their polished leather boots gracefully leading their women about the floor.

And the women...who knew so many pretty women could exist in one room? How could the prince be expected to pick just one jewel in a treasury overflowing with such shining, precious gems? The colors of their dresses were like the first flowers of spring, a rainbow of color springing from the ground after a long winter's night with the promise of youth, beauty, and life. Their hair was twisted fancifully up and studded with gems, their necks wrapped in pearls, their wrists and fingers sparkled with gold and silver. I wished my mother could be there to share in my bedazzlement.

A thirty-piece orchestra held court along one wall of the dance floor, the violins, the harps, the flutes, the trumpets bringing down the music of angels to us mortals on earth. The wall adjacent to them had large glass doors propped open to allow in the cool night air, while also ushering guests out onto moonlit terraces and surely romantic gardens as well.

I stood at one leg of a grand two-pronged marble staircase, which met halfway down at a landing that joined both sides into a sweeping staircase leading right to the tip of the dance floor. Each guest was supposed to be announced before descending, but when asked, I couldn't respond. My eye had caught the prince waiting for me on the middle landing, and the servant must have seen it too because he didn't press. I saw the prince before he saw me, saw his long-strided pacing and anxious glances toward either side of the split stairwell. He wore a dark, royal purple jacket with gold buttons, the gold sash draped over his shoulder angled across his chest. He wore gold gloves on his hands, and even his hair twinkled golden in the chandeliers' light.

The captain stood stiffly to the side, his eyes following the prince. I wondered if I should call to him or if I should find my voice, my name, and my grand entrance.

As it turned out, I didn't have to decide. The moment the prince saw me, he jumped a little, then bounded up the steps. I was sure he was about to take me in his arms and swing me around, but unfortunately decorum got the better of him and he settled for a huge, uncontrollable smile, awakening a mad flurry of butterflies in my stomach.

"Good evening," I curtsied to him. "Prince Charming," I added for good measure.

The prince reached out to raise me up, and for a moment extended both hands so he could cup my face. I wasn't shy enough to not lean into his touch.

"You made it!" He seemed genuinely elated.

"It seems so, Your Highness," I replied, accepting his proffered hand. It felt so natural then to be taking it, so natural for my hand to rest on his arm, for him to be leading me, for me to be at his side. That feeling would not fade for a long while.

"I will not leave your side for one moment tonight," the prince declared. "I cannot have you running off again. My poor heart cannot take it."

My face flushed with pleasure at his words. Nothing on earth could compare to hearing a prince say that to me of all people. Blasted magic, I would have stayed with him forever if it would only allow.

As we passed the captain on the steps, a significant look passed between him and the prince. I should have known then that something was afoot, should have known then how that look signified the end of my charade and all that I'd known in my life. But I was blind then to anyone but the prince, deaf to any sound but the tune of his voice and the rhythm of his heart. The entirety of my senses was overloaded with only him and would remain so for far too long.

"I want you to meet my father," was the next thing he said to me, and that was almost enough to shock the entire world back into sharp focus. Almost.

As it turned out, he introduced me to his father at just the right time. I was barely able to execute my finest curtsy and give him my requested hand when Sir Percival saved me with a gaggle of dignitaries it seemed the king had to meet. The king kissed my hand—*kissed my hand!*—and sent me off with a kind smile. I would have fainted away in the arms of my prince had I not been intent on racing the magic to enjoy every possible minute with him.

The prince whisked me into a dance and for the next few hours, my feet didn't touch the floor. My heart was so full of love and happiness, I was sure it was the only anchor keeping me from floating away from this world.

Before I knew what had happened, the prince had spun me off the dance floor, through a double set of glass doors, and into the cool night. I'm sure we passed some people on our way out, but I only remember the two of us, just him and me in a small blossoming garden under the vast starlit sky.

It seemed only then that we stopped dancing, though I'm sure we had sense enough to walk once we were away from the music. For a moment, neither of us spoke, simply looking at each other, simply being together was enough.

The prince broke the crystalline silence first. "You look beautiful tonight," he said, reaching out to tuck a stray wisp of hair behind my ear. "The first time I saw you, I thought you were the most beautiful lady I'd ever seen."

I smiled happily but wasn't about to correct him then.

"The second time I saw you, you looked even more beautiful," he continued, "and now, how is it possible?"

"Ever the charmer," I murmured.

The prince leaned closer to me and my heart just about exploded in my chest. If it had that night, at least I would have died happy.

"I love it when you say that," he said, his voice a tickle in my ear.

He pulled back and studied me with his shining blue eyes. There would never be a look to match the one he gave me then, that moment when all the love and joy and possibility he felt melded into one moment. That moment, when we were still content to just be, the moment before he found out the truth of who I was, before I found out the truth about him, that was our only bit of ever after.

"I admit I was rather upset when Father and Sir Percival insisted that we have these silly parties," the prince told me without letting go. "I was just weeks away from quieting the borders and all they wanted was to marry me off."

The prince paused and studied my face, drinking in every part he saw.

"The masquerade began as expected," he went on, "as I expected at least, then I looked up and there you were. A kingfisher angel come to rescue me." He reached out as if to touch my cheek, but his hand hesitated. As if doing so would prove there was really nothing to touch, that I was a dream, a fantasy. "How can you be real?" he whispered.

I would have said something, but it was difficult to talk with my heart in my throat. It was difficult enough to breathe.

"I wouldn't be here if I wasn't," I finally managed to squeeze out.

The prince didn't respond right away. A small smile played at his lips, before he abruptly leaned forward and pressed them to mine. The kiss was too quick to feel anything but softness because the prince pulled away just as quickly and granted me a radiant smile.

"You're right," he said, and firmly took my hand in his. "We must tell the king at once."

"Tell him what, Your Highness?" I asked stupidly.

The prince let out an exuberant laugh. "Do you not wish to marry me?" he teased.

So it was true. The mystery lady had captured the prince's heart and he was willing to let her keep it. It was too much for me. My mind shut down. My heart ballooned in my chest. I gripped my prince's hand fiercely, and that was all the answer he needed.

Triumphant, he led me back into the ballroom, making straight for his father, and I would have gone with him had we not passed the clock on the way in. It was seven minutes to midnight. The prince had my hand in his grip. I had to get out before the magic released me and I would embarrass myself, and even worse, him.

I looked around frantically for a solution. I needed a distraction. Or better yet, a blade. Could I take a sword from a soldier and fight my way out without anyone minding?

Heaven sent me my release, for which I have offered thanks every day. My stepsisters, Heaven bless those two wretched souls, appeared suddenly in our path with their young lords in tow, blocking our way forward. Perhaps my kindnesses to them the last two times we'd met there had emboldened them enough to approach us without permission. However, I couldn't be upset with them, not then. Seeing how happy they were with their young, enamored lords made me think for a moment that perhaps, having also grown up under Madame, they too were in need of a little love.

They did have the manners to blush at their own impudence and immediately dropped into perfect curtsies. "Your Highness, my lady," they murmured.

The prince bid them rise, but said little else, visibly ready to end this encounter.

"How delightful to see you two again," I said with more meaning then they could know. The clock continued to tick treacherously forward behind me.

Calliope held out a small bouquet of yellow wildflowers. "For you," she said, blushing fiercely.

Reluctantly, the prince released my hand so I could carefully take the flowers from her. It was really a silly, misguided thing, them offering me a small bundle of flowers as if I was a bridesmaid. It was only later that I understood it for what it was. Their awkward, bumbled attempt was only because they were so unused to genuine kindness they didn't know how to respond, how to thank me for it. It was proof that a little kindness can truly go a long way.

"Thank you," I said, pausing with my nose in the flowers, and that was the signal to end my night.

Without warning, I darted away from the prince and my stepsisters, diving through the crowd and toward the steps as the frantic cry of "Stop her!" tore from the prince's throat after me.

But the room was so full and the music so grand, even a prince couldn't yell over the noise. He could be right behind me, though. Still foolishly clutching the flowers, I grabbed up my skirts and took the steps two at a time. By now, the music was grinding to a halt and I could clearly hear the commotion I was leaving in my wake.

Right outside the hallway, I ran smack into the captain, who was as startled to see me in his arms as I was to be there. He looked down at me and in that moment I'm absolutely sure he saw through the lace to the frightened purple eyes beneath. This time, no confusion clouded his face as he remembered the two other times he'd clearly seen those same unusual eyes. And the type of girl they belonged to.

"Your eyes—" he began, but I didn't let him finish.

Because, in the end, he was the one who'd always seen me, no matter what I wore.

"Please," I whispered, my eyes begging him to let me go. "Please."

Only then did confusion etch across his face. The captain hesitated, and with years of sneaking away and darting Madame's wrath coloring my instincts, I saw that brief pause and I took it. I broke his hold and ran away from him, leaving him with the small bundle of flowers. He turned sharply to follow after me, but fear compelled me forward, pushing me faster than I ever ran before. Perhaps the slippers had a little magic speed in them as well.

I burst through the palace doors and turned sharply to scurry down the front steps, wanting to hug the rail so I could bound down two and three at a time, even in my Castarrean glass slippers. Did it even matter what happened to them if they would anyway be gone by midnight?

At the bottom, my carriage was already waiting for me, the coachman's whip raised above the horses, the footmen ready to toss me in and jump on.

After the second step, I felt my foot catch and to my horror looked down to find the stairs covered in a viscous, black substance. The smell gave it away. Pitch. Was that the look I had seen pass between the prince and his captain? Had he really gone so far to keep me here? I would have been flattered, melted into the very pitch, had I not been so desperate to get away.

I yanked one foot out and leaped toward the carpet, but when the other released to follow it felt too light. I glanced back long enough to see that one of my slippers had stuck in the pitch. There was nothing to do about it. It would be gone within the next three minutes when the clock struck midnight anyway.

As I had used the captain's hesitation to my advantage, the brief pause on the step cost me. The captain, with the prince and a handful of soldiers in tow, burst out of the palace doors, even before I reached the bottom of the stairs. Heaven bless the lizard that leaped up the steps to grab me in his arms and somehow toss me gently into the carriage. The carriage took off like lightning, thundering down the road toward the bridge, a shooting star in a dark night sky. The footman who'd tossed me in stayed behind at the palace steps in an attempt to distract the prince and his soldiers for the last two minutes until midnight, the last two minutes it would take for my carriage to make it across the palace bridge and into the streets of the capital.

Thank Heaven for the hand of foresight that led me to study the maps of the city, because scarcely after we had made it across the bridge the magic fled, and everything fell apart. The carriage sputtered to a bumpy stop, landing hard on the cobblestone streets of the quiet capital city. The rats and remaining lizard fled, the pumpkin smashed into bits, and it was only me and the goose who would never again tip his hat for me but maintained an inexplicable fondness for me all the same.

I didn't have time to wallow in self-pity, and I wanted even less to be sitting in the mud when the others came by. I had to get back home before anyone could find out I was missing, and the walk ahead was a long one. I could already hear the pounding of the horses giving chase to my now ruined carriage. I stood up and felt a strange limp in my foot. Praying nothing was broken, I glanced down to see a swirl of colors in sand, a sparkle of glass showing I still wore my remaining glass slipper. How had the magic missed this? Or was it a lasting gift from Marie? Was its mate still stuck to the palace steps? Was the light being sucked into the glass now turning into the colors of hope?

I didn't have the time to figure it out, especially because having on one shoe meant my others hadn't been returned to me. I tucked it into my apron pocket, then gave the broken pumpkin two or three quick shoves to send as much as I could into the gutter. I chased the goose into a dark alley and hunkered down with it, mentally pleading it stayed quiet until the soldiers had passed.

For once, that blasted goose cooperated, but I still stayed there with it a long time, even as the cold from the cobblestones traveled up through my body, even as the chill from the night entered my bones. I was sure I would be sick after this, and miserable, too, because being sick was never an excuse for not doing my chores.

After a long, long while, well after I heard the clock chime one and then two in the morning, well after I was sure the hoof beats I now heard were the disgruntled men returning from their fruitless chase, I finally allowed myself to stand. The goose had fallen asleep at my feet and though I hated to, I had to kick it awake. It had been good to me, but it was too heavy for me to carry all the way home.

In my mind's eye, I pulled up the maps I had so diligently studied and wove through Camallea's dark streets, pressing close to walls and staying in shadow until we broke through the city and were forced onto the widened path that led home. I was barefoot, but too overwhelmed to feel the pebbles sticking into my heels, too tired to begrudge the dirt coating my feet.

We walked for hours, and I still don't know how the goose kept up. Maybe some magic still lingered in its addled brain. I didn't know what Madame would do to me if she found out the goose had run out under my watch, but I was beyond caring at that point. All I wanted was a long hot bath to wash away the dirt, the grime, the magic, the feel of the prince's arms around me.

For all I knew, I was done. This was it for me. It was all over. My imagination had drained out when faced with the reality of what magic could do. I didn't even have the will to run away anymore.

We had been walking so long, I was almost relieved to see the turn down the familiar path to my house, almost relieved to round that final bend and see it as I once had when I was still a child, a little slice of paradise made just for my family.

I trudged up the long walkway as the first rays of morning light began stretching awake across the sky. I barely had enough time to hide the extra slipper in my attic room and wash my blackened feet before the dreaded sound of hoof beats and carriage wheels announced my stepfamily's return.

I had to work very hard to keep myself together while my stepsisters almost tripped over themselves to recount the night I knew too much about. I had already gone through it all, had already ripped my heart in two running from my prince. I didn't need to hear it all again. I didn't need to hear it from them.

"The mystery lady ran away again—"

"Three times she fled the prince—"

"She left a shoe behind—"

"Castarrean glass. All of it Castarrean glass—"

Even now, it remains in my mind as broken snippets I couldn't quite keep out.

I readied them for bed as swiftly as I could then made sure the house was in order before collapsing onto my narrow mess of straw. A blessed sleep, free from all dreams claimed me and it wasn't until much later, when such peaceful sleep became scarce, that I would appreciate how curative it really was. A final quiet before the raging storms began.

SHATTERED SLIPPER OF GLASS

*T*he next day started late but rambled along like any other. I was too numb to feel anything, even fatigue. My mind and body were subject to unending ripples of shock that mercifully delivered me from contemplating the end, from knowing that the world Marie's magic had opened before me had slammed shut as surely as my pumpkin had been smashed to bits and left to rot in the uncaring gutters of the capital. I didn't even have the heart to worry if the king would force the prince to marry some other girl of his choosing.

After years of keeping me together, my dreams were failing me. My imagination gave up. I grasped at threads of another world fluttering in the wind, just beyond my fingertips.

Three days passed with me functioning at minimal capacity. Three days during which I endured the brainless twittering of my stepsisters, the cynical skepticism of my stepmother, the topic of conversation always returning to the mystery lady, regurgitating every recycled rumor, every theory no matter how inane. And I, the only one who *knew*, had to keep silent.

Those three days were some of the longest of my life. I half expected, half hoped that Princess Lyla would send some word of encouragement, but she only knew my face and not where I lived. I didn't know if she cared to find out either.

The young lords who'd been ensnared by my stepsisters actually sent word requesting to call upon them. Although Madame had not yet forgone her ambitions of at least one of her daughters marrying royalty, both men came from wealthy, established families, and both had titles before their names. Good enough to allow their attentions. I would have rejoiced over their visit, over the hours I was able to spend in mind-numbing tedium preparing the house for their arrival. I was certain they would distract my stepfamily from this vicious cycle of gossip they'd dropped into, give them something else to talk about, someone else to fawn over. As it turned out, their arrival would herald in something far worse.

I should have known it would happen too, because that morning Madame sent word that, in honor of their visit, we were to roast the goose.

The goose hardly made a sound when I had to wring its neck, turning away from it so I wouldn't have to see its still-trusting eyes.

"Well, what did you expect?" I asked when it was done. "This is what you were born to be."

I plucked and gathered its feathers. The culmination of his life would be the warmth it provided as a blanket, or even a pillow. Even then, it was far better off than me. I would never be anything.

The lords arrived on horseback, gaily prancing around the bend on their fine chestnut mares just as the sun tipped over in the sky to signal afternoon. I realize now that I never did learn their names, or which was which. Then, they both seemed the same to me, and as long as someone was there to keep the step-witches out of my hair, I didn't care much either.

It was a cruel irony that led me to serve up my coachman on a platter the moment I heard the words that would change my fate. I was just bearing the tray into the room, wondering how it could still weigh so much after all the hours it took us to walk home, when I caught the excited end of conversation.

"...he really?" Maybelle exclaimed.

"Really what?" I asked, forgetting I wasn't supposed to be seen or heard.

The step-witches were too caught up in the news they'd just received, and one of the lords unwittingly answered my question for me.

"On my honor," he replied, addressing the table, "the prince will be traveling all over the land to try the glass slipper on every eligible maiden. I heard the news myself from Sir Percival's valet's assistant."

Maybelle and Calliope let out giddy shrieks of excitement. I had to wonder why, as not only did we all know the slipper did not belong to either one of them, but they had their own men plying them with attentions. Chance does some funny things to people's heads.

The tray of goose fell from my hands with an indelicate thump on the table. Madame glared at me, her gaze burning through my skin, but there was nothing she could sear me with that would hurt worse than the news I just heard. If the prince was so intent on finding the owner of the slipper, then it was only a matter of time before he came here. And if he came here... then what?

Would I try on the slipper for him? Could I allow myself—rags, soot, and all—to watch a prince bend down and slide a Castarrean glass slipper onto my dirty little foot? And I knew, as others didn't, that there was little chance he would find anyone else to fit that slipper. No eligible maiden was made tiny as I. I was sure of it.

So where did that leave me? Was I worthy enough to step forward, accept a prince's heart, and one day sit beside him to rule over his land? Dressed for the ball with the feeling that magic gave me, I would have said yes, but not anymore. And I doubted Marie would be here to rescue me yet again. She couldn't see the future, but she'd made it pretty clear the night of the grand ball that it would be the last time magic would dress me. Weren't the pair of slippers it had left behind proof that it was over?

I was only Cinderwench. I didn't get more than I already had.

One of the young lords took up the knife to carve the goose, allowing me to back away from the dining room and general revelry as quickly as I could. I had to wait a few more agonizing hours until the meal was over, dessert was served, the lords sent on their way, and the family to bed. I don't know how I made it through then, but somehow, my years under Madame's cruelty taught me to dull my senses enough that I was able to scrape by. As soon as the last bedroom door shut, I fled across the yard to my mother's grave and fell into bitter sobs upon it.

Marie didn't show, and I didn't even have the blasted goose to wander after me anymore.

For the first time since my mother passed, I felt completely and utterly alone. But not the type of loneliness that stems from being stranded on an island in the middle of a tumbling sea that no one cares to sail past. Rather, I had fallen head over heels into a dark and slippery well, yelling for help from passersby. I was able to see daylight, I was able to see potential escape, but they did not look down, and they could not hear me call. Worse than being alone without anyone is being alone among others. Little did I know then, but in the ensuing years, that awful solitude would revisit me more times than I ever care to count.

Somehow, the night passed, and the morning sun rose without a care for those in the world. It may have been my imagination, but it was almost brighter, sunnier, illuminating our garden in such a way as to bring out life and colors I hadn't noticed before.

Blasted sun. Even it couldn't hide its glee of a new day behind a cloud long enough to commiserate with me.

Once the first bit of news about the prince and his plans for the slipper reached us, it seemed that updates would not stop coming. The prince chose to start at the furthest reaches of the kingdom, thinking that was how the woman hid her identity for so long, and then work in to the capital. The royal entourage had chosen large cities where they would set up in the main square and allow all eligible maidens in the area to try on the shoe. Noblemen and other wealthy individuals living in the surrounding countryside were not made to suffer such indignities. For them, the prince joined the entourage and showed up at the house himself.

Each week, we received word on failure in new cities. Each day, the prince came that much closer to us.

I would be remiss not to say that the entire prospect excited me a bit. To think I had made such an impression on the prince that he was willing to go door-to-door, willing to wait for hours while women tried on the shoe I left behind was, quite simply, flattering. It was more than that as well. No one, ever, had gone to such great lengths for me, and even though the prince didn't know who I was, I was too humbled and gratified to bother with the difference. At the same time, worry gnawed at my stomach until I wondered how there was anything left of it.

"I would do anything to make the shoe fit," Calliope announced one day.

"Would you even cut off your toe?" Maybelle wanted to know.

"Certainly!" she replied.

"Would you even cut off your heel?" Maybelle pressed.

"Absolutely!" Calliope affirmed.

Maybelle arched her eyebrows. "So you would cut off your toe and cut off your heel, mutilate your foot for the rest of your life, just so you could marry a prince?"

"Yes," Calliope insisted. "And don't pretend you wouldn't do the same. A queen has servants to carry her anyway."

Foolish girls. The ring that came with the shoe was not worth losing a toe over.

As the prince and his entourage circled closer to the capital, Madame kept us busy scrubbing down every nook, cranny, and corner of the house, because this time the prince really was coming here. The cleaning did me good, as each night I collapsed into bed too tired to consider the endless possibilities of what could be. Not knowing when the prince would arrive also proved to help somewhat, because I could always push off his arrival until tomorrow which was so much easier to think of than today.

According to the route he'd taken, which I later traced for myself on a map, the prince had to ride through Camallea to get to our little corner of land. Because of that, his progress slowed as his entourage decided it best to just get it over with there once they were already passing through. Therefore, as things turned out, our house was one of the last ones the prince visited.

Actually, it was the last one.

The prince arrived late morning, as good a time as any to ruin my life. I was in the study cleaning out Iris's cage when Madame came rushing in with a feverish look in her eyes.

"He's coming," the words tumbled out.

I stared at her a moment, honestly unsure of what she wanted from me then.

"Go upstairs and change your dress," she told me impatiently. "Try to find something clean."

Iris squawked.

"And take that beast with you!"

I dashed out, bringing Iris along.

My heart was beating too loud when I reached my attic room, so I never heard the footsteps that followed me up. In fact, I wasn't aware of another presence until I was slipping on my less tattered dress, tucking the other shoe into my pocket, and hearing the key in the lock.

"No!" I ran toward the door and banged fruitlessly on its hard wooden surface. "No, no, no!" I sobbed. "Why?"

"Because you are too good," came the unexpected response, cool and uncaring. "Because you are too kind. Because even covered in soot, you outshine all those around you and I can't abide by your little foot fitting that slipper."

The acidity of her hatred was strong enough to melt the lock between us. However, even then, it was almost a relief to finally hear her say those words. It was the first time I entirely understood I was not to blame for my troubles, but she and her hatred were. It would take a long time to digest, but it was finally a start, a release of sorts.

Would she have known then, could she have seen the years to follow, she never would have locked me in my attic room. Instead, she would have bathed me herself, dressed me in her finest gown, dripped me in jewels and the three Castarrean glass necklaces, and lent me her title of Baroness on a silver platter. She would have presented me to the prince at the top of the stairs and tried the shoe on my foot herself.

But she didn't know what was to be and, of course, neither did I.

So my heart shattered like glass when she locked me inside with a screaming macaw diving over and over for the door as if it was a woodpecker whose beak could chop straight through. Between my crying and Iris's berserk screams, I'm surprised no one heard us sooner. I also understood then how cold Madame's heart must be.

My cries died down well before the prince and his entourage rounded the final bend toward our house. I didn't want to stop, but I was too tired, weak, and thirsty to go on. Marie could've sprung me free in an instant, but whatever magic had once allowed her to come to me wasn't allowing it now. As always, I was on my own.

Funny as it may seem, and even though I didn't know then if I would ever be let out or left to waste away in my small piece of room, the first thing I did after I stood up was wash my face and fix my hair. Putting myself together seemed to give my mind permission to pull itself together as well.

Then I spun about the room and considered my options.

Madame hadn't even seen fit to give me a whole attic to myself. Instead, the front part of the room was cluttered with forgotten household items, baby toys, little girl's clothing, broken mementos, none of which proved sufficient to break me out. I turned every crate inside out, scratched at every nail until my fingers bled, but to no avail. Iris had calmed down somewhat as I desperately turned over the room, but as soon as I sat down in defeat, the macaw flew up and started screeching again.

The blasted bird was driving me mad and I wouldn't last another minute without killing it.

Seeing no other recourse, I piled crates up and pushed open the tiny round window that let a miser's amount of light into the room. Calling Iris to me, I held out my hand as a perch, then thrust it out the window as fast as I could, slamming the pane shut before it could get in.

The quiet lasted but a minute before Iris squawked and flung himself against the window over and over again. What was wrong with the goose-brained bird? I had just set it free, and it wanted to come back in?

As it turned out, that was to be the most fortuitous and most injurious decision either of us could make.

I have yet to gather courage enough to ask the captain if he ever regrets what came next. If he regrets his bat-like hearing that caught onto the jamming shut of a windowpane just moments before a blur of red and blue feathers started screeching like a banshee, something only he heard and noticed in the din of the leaving entourage. Does he regret staying the prince's hand when his foot was already in the stirrup? Does he regret the simple question that irrevocably changed our lives forever?

"Baroness, is someone else in the house?"

I couldn't hear it then, but I can hear the question now, hear the way the words must have rumbled out of his throat, menacing and magnificent, like water rushing over the edge as it plunges to its fall.

Of course, the little glass slipper hadn't fit either of her daughters, and having seen the size for herself, the baroness knew that I was the only one in the house with a prayer at winning the heart of royalty.

She tried her most innocent look on a man trained to see the guilt lurking in the hearts of the innocent. "Whatever do you mean, Captain?"

The captain only looked up but didn't answer. The look on Madame's face, that initial annoyance she didn't yet have time to hide, was all the answer he needed.

"Your Highness," he told the prince, "we may not be quite finished here."

"Sort it out, Captain," the prince commanded with a wave of his hand.

He was desperate to find his lady, but he was tired, too. I couldn't blame him. Having spent more than two minutes in the house with Madame and her girls, he was must have been willing to swear to a life of celibacy just to get away. And they were only two girls of many, many others.

The captain strode back into the house. He didn't pause as he made straight for the steps and climbed them to my prison. He rapped lightly on the door, the unexpected sound near startled me to death.

"Madame?" I called tentatively.

I had no idea what had happened outside, could not even guess, because at this point my mind was fixed on that obnoxious bird. Subconsciously, I knew that Madame would never have knocked, she considered this house and every being and item in it as her personal property, so she needed no one's permission. I highly doubted that either Maybelle or Calliope had come looking for me, but I couldn't fathom who could be on the other side of that door. Father, as usual, wasn't home. Maybe Cook had finally taken pity on me after all these years?

Unsure of what was about to come through the doors, I grabbed the faery sword and brandished it before me, ready to do what I must, ready even to face the hangman's noose for murder if it meant leaving that place.

I heard the doorknob rattle and a roll of thunder demand the key. Apparently, it didn't come fast enough because first I was commanded to "Stand back" and then the door was kicked in by a finely polished leather boot. The rest of the captain joined his foot in the room and his eyes widened at the sight of me. A wave of sadness passed over his features, but he blinked, and it was gone. I knew I saw it there, even if I didn't understand why.

"I don't think you'll need that, miss," he said kindly, reaching his hand out for the sword.

I hesitated, knowing he wouldn't hurt me, but not wanting to give up the only thing that may have been my last hope of getting out. I was so fed up by then. The charade, the magic, the shoe, my nerves, I was frayed to the root and Madame locking me up was all it took to snap it. I was holding on by a thread, which it now seemed the captain was scrambling for to tow me back to safety.

Begrudgingly, I handed over the blade, and I couldn't hide my smirk as I saw him quickly admire the sword before he found the sheath and slid it safely into his belt.

He turned back to me. "Aren't you going to let the bird in?" he asked softly.

I flushed and turned quickly to the window, clambering up the row of crates to let Iris back in. He calmed as soon as I took him in my arms. Turning to climb down, I was startled by a black-gloved hand in my face.

It was the captain's. With one hand keeping the crates steady, he offered me the other. I took it in a loose grip and clambered down as quickly as I could.

"Are you all right, Miss—?"

"Ella," I said quickly.

The captain tried the name out. "Ella."

A moment of silence.

"Captain!"

A voice from beyond the steps broke the silence, a voice whose musical refrain I would recognize anywhere.

I blushed and tried to duck my head into Iris's little body, hoping to hide my reddening cheeks in his far redder feathers. The captain glanced at me, and I didn't understand then the mix of emotions swirling in his eyes. Like a fine mist, it was gone as soon as I noticed it.

The captain looked at me seriously. "Are you ready, Miss Ella?"

I took a deep breath and nodded yes. No more needed to be said. He—only he—already knew. Too much it would seem.

The top of the stairway was too narrow for both of us, so the captain went down before me to prepare the prince. And by that it just meant that he handed me down the last few steps and told him, "I found her, Your Highness."

The prince didn't react at all when he initially saw me. I knew then that he didn't recognize the girl from the well, couldn't place me without my magical dresses and jewels as the one he'd singled out each time at the palace. How could it be that the lady who shone like silver and glittered like gold was one and the same with the tiny, sooty girl before him?

"She is nothing but a Cinderwench!" Madame protested

snidely, her voice coming to me through the haze that overcame me the moment I locked onto the prince's beautiful cerulean eyes.

He must have heard her clearly though, because a cloud passed over the skies of his eyes before he managed to push it away. My heart ached seeing him again, and I knew then that I never could have been happy again in my life if I hadn't. He was as handsome as I remembered him, his cheeks slightly flushed, his sandy hair adorably mussed, as perfect as he could ever be.

He was here. For me.

I dropped a perfect curtsy. "Hello, Prince Charming," I said softly.

A grim smile of recognition tugged at the tight lines of his lips.

"So this is you, and this is where you live," he replied just as quietly, though I couldn't decipher the tone of his voice.

"This is my father's house," I said in a rush, somehow feeling the urge to explain away my current state, to assure him that looking like a Cinderwench didn't mean I always was one.

"And the dresses?" he asked.

My mind flashed to the moment when Princess Lyla warned me that the prince didn't like magic, but the truth was the only thing to say.

"My faery godmother," I admitted.

"Magic?"

"The dresses were," I emphasized.

I was too young to know that I didn't have to explain such things; no, that I shouldn't have had to explain such things. The invitation had been open to everyone, after all.

"Sire?"

From somewhere behind, Sir Percival's voice cut into whatever was going on between us. My heart had almost stopped beating at the sight of the prince, but I couldn't decipher what was going on in his heart. Though he was in my house, wasn't he? Hadn't he traversed the kingdom to find me?

Sir Percival's voice, or perhaps something in it, jolted the prince back to being His Highness, restoring his poise and graciousness. Then he no longer hesitated to take my hand from the captain, to lead me to the front door where he ushered the valet to bring the shoe up for me to try on. The prince, the captain, and I all knew it was unnecessary at that point, but so much significance had gone into trying on the shoe that it had to be done. Considering the looks on Madame, Maybelle, and Calliope's faces, though, it was evident they were finally realizing this wasn't my first time meeting the prince.

The moment the valet bore the little glass slipper aloft in the late morning sunshine, I knew that it was mine. There was no mistaking the pure work of Castarrean glass, the way the slipper grabbed the light of the sun and fractured it into endless prisms and rainbows that radiated around the pillow and even spilled over onto the valet himself.

To my surprise, Sir Percival appeared right behind the valet, following behind him with a thick rolled up parchment, possibly his list of all eligible maidens who didn't fit the shoe. We waited for them to reach us at the top of the step, and I didn't comprehend the extent of my stepmother's pride and jealousy until the moment she pretended to fall forward and tripped the valet carrying the little glass slipper.

The valet tried valiantly to stay upright, but he lost his footing and even the captain wasn't quick enough to catch the slipper before it smashed upon the steps.

Total silence descended upon all present. Myself, my stepsisters, the valet, Sir Percival, and the rest of the entourage were quieted by the impudence of what Madame had done. The prince wavered between wondering if it even mattered anymore and wanting to punish Madame for her insolence.

The captain was the only one with any sense left among us.

"Surely," he began slowly, looking at me as he spoke, "surely, this slipper was only one of a pair?"

That jolted me back to reality. The answer was simple. A happy smile stretched across my face and I pulled from my pocket the slipper I'd stuck there earlier.

I will forever rue that moment. I should have feigned ignorance, should have pretended the mate was missing and then left the final decision to the entourage to decide. But once I pulled that slipper out, once that unmistakable Castarrean glass sucked and fractured the light, once the prince delicately slid it onto my foot, he had no choice but to marry me. Too much ceremony had been made for it to be otherwise.

Time has given me perspective now and I can look back and see all that really unfolded then through the clear magnifying glass of hindsight, no longer tinted with a faerytale haze. For in truth, as soon as Madame smashed my little glass slipper, the prince had the out he was looking for the moment he found out that his beautiful mystery lady was nothing more than a Cinderwench bedecked by magic. It didn't matter who my father was, who my stepmother was, it only mattered that I was a lowly servant girl with a faery godmother.

No one remembers, because in the rush of things no one noticed, how Sir Percival put a hand on the prince's shoulder as I was steered to a seat in the house. No one remembers how he leaned over to whisper a few words in the prince's ear, how the prince nodded in resignation, then took a breath to steel himself before he knelt down to slide the shoe on my foot.

No one remembers that the prince was willing to leave me among the fragments of shattered glass.

What everyone does remember, and loves to tell over, is how I had the other slipper hidden in my apron pocket. How perfectly the little slipper fit my little foot and how, after, the prince gathered me in his arms and carried me away from my wretched home.

Well, he didn't quite carry me.

After we confirmed the slipper fit, the prince pulled me into his arms and I heard him take a deep breath I mistook for relief. Then, smiling widely, he efficiently gathered me up and carried me down to his horse, brusquely brushing past an indignant Madame and shocked Maybelle and Calliope.

He bounded down the stairs as best he could, eager as I was to get away from the house that had so long held me prisoner. He lifted me onto his magnificent white stallion and swung up onto the saddle behind me. He flicked the reins and off we rode, never once looking back.

I never said goodbye to my father. I don't even know what he knew or didn't. The man who had once loved me, who'd taught me how to wield a sword and taught me how to laugh had been buried eight years ago with my mother. The man he left behind was no father to me.

We made straight for the palace, the prince riding tall and regal, confident in who he was, his place and power in the world. And I? I nestled into his warmth and rode with eyes clouded with faerytale love, straight into the arms of my treacherous happily ever after.

ONLY FAERIES LIVE IN FAERY TALES

*T*he next few months were a flurry of preparations during which I hardly saw the prince at all. The wedding was set for the beginning of fall when the days were just beginning to cool, and much work was needed to get everything ready, especially to get a Cinderwench ready.

Once the prince brought me to the palace, I was home, and I never returned to the place where I had grown up. Fortunately, as the soon-to-be princess, I didn't have to. I had a bevy of servants eager to please their new mistress with just a ring from a little gold bell that was never too far from my side. At first, I was uncomfortable with all the attention, didn't understand why I needed so many people to serve me, but live with it long enough and it's easy to get used to such things.

My personal maid was Javotte and she was mistress of all my servants and ladies-in-waiting. She was a straightforward middle-aged woman, strong, capable, and very dedicated to her duties. She was always deferential, always respectful. She would save me from court humiliation more than once in the coming years, usually with a sniff at my dress, my hairstyle, or my shoes and a simple, "Are you absolutely sure, Your Highness?"

I knew she was just a maid, but it wouldn't be long before I would consider her a friend, too. One of the few I ever had.

My quarters, handpicked for me by the prince—or so I was told—were lovely, too large for a tiny girl like me, so for the first few months I feared getting lost inside them. As it was, I was having a hard time navigating the endless corridors of the palace.

My sitting room had wide, large windows framed by thick, purple, gold-tasseled drapes that looked out over a side garden I would come to adopt as my own, not least because my prince ensconced my famed slipper in a glass case in the center so I could always see it from my room. For the first two years, and especially the first three months until my wedding, I would glance out to see all manner of people stopping by that case. Some stayed longer than others, some dared to touch the glass, others only let their hands pass over, but all came for the same reason, in hopes that some of the magic would rub off into their own lives. No matter the person, no matter the circumstance, there's always need for a little magic.

In better weather, all the windows were propped open, turning the bedroom into an atrium of sorts as sunlight and fresh sea air poured in. A grand four-post canopy bed took up about half the room, and the first morning Javotte came to wake me, she missed me buried in its warmth and thought I was already out of bed. It would be almost unnecessary to add that from the carpets to the tapestries, from the coverlets to the fine tables and chairs, I was unused to being around, let alone possessing, such finery. It would take a while for me to get used to using the delicate and expensive items without a lingering fear that I would ruin it all with my touch.

I hadn't seen the prince in over a week when he finally came to call upon me in my quarters one day, unannounced, it must be said, elegant and upbeat as always. His eyes were the sky, his smile the sun, his whole face the Heavens that looked upon our frail world.

I was standing before a trio of mirrors that had been propped up in another one of the too-large rooms when the prince poked his head in before the valet could announce him. I was enduring the fitting of a lovely purple dress for one of the endless days of official banquets and parties that would follow our wedding day. This wasn't just the wedding of a crown prince, this was the wedding of a king's only child, his only son, the continuation of his dynasty and all that meant for the future of Laurendale.

The purple of the dress brought out my eyes so strongly that they took on a navy blue hue. As such, Javotte and I were deciding if I should wear blue, gold, or purple earrings with it. The platform I was standing on as my royal seamstress pinned my hem at least gave me some height, so I was eye-level with the prince when he came to take my hands in his. The prince tenderly kissed each one then held them wide so he could admire the progress.

"Lovely, absolutely lovely," he sang, and I beamed adoringly at him. "You look much more like you should."

That should have been my first clue into the true nature of the man I thought I was madly in love with. Actually, I was rather mad to think myself in love with him, but it took hindsight to clarify that. Instead, my whole being soared from his praise rather than plummet from how little he really knew about me.

"Thank you, Your Highness," I murmured.

The prince brought my fingertips to his lips and pretended to think even as he focused on bringing them to his lips one by one.

"My love, what can I do to make you happy?"

"I don't know that anything can make me happier than I am now," I replied, unable to think clearly in my delusion.

The prince pretended to pout. "Even marrying me?"

"Only marrying you," I reassured him.

The smile on the prince's face showed how much he liked my answer and I smiled, too, happy and content in the knowledge that I had the power to bring that much joy to his face. I was ecstatic then. I gag at the memory now.

"Yet," the prince pressed, still holding onto my hands, as if I would be silly enough to run away from him now. "Yet, there must be something."

There really wasn't anything more I could have wanted. Even thoughts of my mother weren't able to penetrate my present fog of happiness. Scrambling for something, I realized that there were only two things I still missed.

"My goldfish and my pear tree," I finally said.

The captain had already brought my sword along to the palace and didn't waste time bringing it to my chambers with a carefully guarded smirk and, "Be careful who you wield that against here. Not everyone would approve."

From the look on the prince's face at my requests, though, it seemed I had asked for acceptable things.

And that was how my goldfish, which Calliope apparently kept alive to duck my royal wrath, was given a pond of its own near my pear tree in the garden beneath my window. In time, between them and the shoe, it would come to be known as "The Queen's Garden."

I met the king, too, of course. It was odd to look at this aged man who was my sovereign and also see a man who would be my new father. In the beginning, I was very quiet around him, not quite sure what to say, how to act, where to put my hands.

I also tried not to think of what Princess Lyla had said about the prince's belief that magic had ruined his father. Outwardly, the king didn't appear to be anything less than the monarch he was supposed to be. It made me wonder at how deep the prince's dislike for magic really was. Surely, he didn't fear that whatever he thought had befallen his father would overtake him. Surely, he knew that I had left all magical tricks behind when he carried me off to the palace.

For his part, the king readily embraced the idea of having a daughter, glad for there to again be "a lovely young woman like yourself to brighten things up again."

I did my best, though I really couldn't do much, because the servants generally had everything in hand or there were official court rules about the rest of it.

His Majesty also told me very pointedly that he was "looking forward to hearing the pitter-patter of little feet about the palace," and "couldn't wait for the first morning his grandson woke him too early to play at being soldiers."

I appropriately responded by turning red and praying the conversation would be over soon.

When I later told the prince about it, he chuckled. "He'll see his grandchildren, from this world or the next, he'll see them." Then he spun me into him and leaned close, "For now, however, let's enjoy just you and me."

With such talk, it was a wonder I never saw the future coming. Then, everything was a dream, every word a mirror of my imagination. I never once stopped to think that perhaps it was all a little too perfect to be real.

All throughout summer, they prepared me for my new position with an endless parade of tutors meant to teach me about my new obligations and the way to behave around the respected guests from other kingdoms. The wedding ceremony would be followed by almost a week of parties, banquets, picnics, hunts, and games, which Javotte informed me were not just for celebration, but also to keep the hundreds of arriving guests busy and out of trouble. She also told me that the day of the wedding was to be a public holiday during which shops and businesses would be closed and people all over would gather in their towns for a day full of festivities.

I was overwhelmed by what she was describing. This was still in the beginning, when I had yet to fully appreciate how an action of a prince could shake an entire kingdom. I was baffled at how high I had risen, how my good fortune became the people's good fortune, too.

Because of the endless festivities, because of the visiting allies and dignitaries, because I was to be the wife of the crown prince, I had to have a wardrobe befitting my station. The purple dress was only one of myriads that had to be sewn in time to make me presentable. Unlike other more appropriate choices for a prince's bride, I hadn't anything in my closet to give me a head start when I came. A team of seamstresses worked around the clock to have everything ready, making sure I had at least one new dress a day for the first three weeks. As if the rush of the wedding wasn't enough, I went to bed exhausted every night just from the fittings and stylings.

The night before my wedding, my chambers were oddly quiet. All stray bits and scraps of material had been cleaned up and twenty-two new gowns were pressed and put away. Not even an odd bead or pearl remained from the flurry that had overtaken these rooms until now. My wedding gown was hung up in my bedchamber where I could stare at it all night if I wanted to, which is what I was doing in the silence, wondering about what the prince was up to.

The knock at my door nearly startled me out of my wits, and I pressed my hand against my chest to keep my heart from flying out.

"Enter," I called, when I'd regained my voice.

A head full of wonderfully wavy black hair popped up behind

the door. The color seemed even darker against the white, white skin of the face—

"Princess Lyla!" I cried, jumping up and rushing toward her. I would have been afraid to hug her, but I was too happy then to see a familiar face.

Princess Lyla laughed, glad at the reaction she'd elicited. "It's not Princess Lyla anymore," she said, "for we are to be cousins of a sort. We are just Lyla and Ella."

A princess had just given me leave to call her by her first name! Was there no end to the wonders of my life?

"What brings you here?" I stammered to correct myself. "What brings you here tonight?"

"Us," Lyla corrected, opening the door wide enough for two beautiful women to enter behind her.

The first had long, lovely blond hair that sparkled like gold in the candlelight. Her white skin was luminescent as an angel's and she had beautifully shaped coral lips. Scampering in behind her was an adorable little spaniel, who slid along the polished wood floor each time he tried to change directions.

"Oh dear, I hope you don't mind," she spluttered.

"Not at all—" I began, but she was already rushing past me to chase after him. It was odd to notice then, but she had an uncommon grace about her, even when running after a slippery puppy.

"Mopsey. Mopsey!"

Lyla laughed and shook her head at the puppy. "She'll be running after him the whole night. Good thing the twins are asleep."

My eyes bulged after the angelic woman, captivatingly beautiful, though not in the same way as Lyla. She didn't have one child, but two?

Catching the look on my face, Lyla answered aloud for me. As it turned out, Lyla would be one of my best sources of information on royalty in the palace. Why she ever took a shine to me is still beyond my comprehension, but I'm forever grateful that she did.

"Queen Alaina is a bit older than she looks. The first to be 'awoken' by true love's kiss," Lyla explained with a smirk that hinted at a joke within the wording. "She has a little boy and a little girl and they're both as adorable and mischievous as that puppy. We persuaded her to let the nursemaids put them to sleep so she could sneak here with us."

"I'm very grateful, Your Majesty," I said after the queen, who was working on tugging a fur lined slipper out of the spaniel's mouth.

I wasn't even sure it was my slipper with so many new things to keep track of, and only confirmed it when I noticed that everyone else still had both shoes on.

"This is Princess Kiara of Delphe."

Lyla gestured to the second woman, a true beauty not just because of her perfect ringlets of brown hair or the incredibly delicate features of her face, but also because there was something about her that radiated outward, making her all the more beautiful. I would call it graciousness, patience, or even temperament, all of which I would find out to be true, but the strongest feeling from her was a sense of absolute acceptance of whomever was before her. Her unique beauty was a reflection of the beauty she so easily saw in others, even fearsome beasts.

"She also had two horrific sisters," Lyla whispered to me.

Princess Kiara reached out with both hands to clasp one of mine in hers. "We are so happy for you, Ella," she said with a warm smile I believed to be genuine.

I had to blink back tears, so overwhelmed was I that they had come to visit, that they so readily accepted me into their august circle. All had journeyed from their kingdoms to be here, and instead of taking the night off, they had chosen to see me. Ella. Cinderwench. Of all people. I felt so out of place in that room.

Neither a beauty nor a princess, I had no gifts from faeries, only tinted eyes and tiny feet. What could I add to this little royal group?

"Now," Lyla began, and it was then I noticed the bottle of wine in her hand, "as you'll be too excited to sleep tonight, we'll while away some of the hours with you."

"*Some* of the hours?" I repeated.

The other three laughed at my innocence.

"We won't be here all night," Kiara elaborated, "just long enough to calm your nerves. You'll have time enough for beauty sleep—"

"Which really works," Alaina interjected with a wink.

"—though you scarcely need it," Kiara finished.

It was becoming clearer how she could be the one from the four of us to have married a man once considered a beast. Little did I know...

"Come now," Lyla called, beckoning us to my sitting area and popping the cork on the bottle to pour us each some wine. She handed out the glasses, then motioned us to raise them with hers. "To Alex and Ella," she proclaimed. "To a true happily ever after," she added with an undisguised—I thought then unwarranted— tinge of sadness to her voice.

"To Alex and Ella," the others chimed.

Scarcely had the wine touched our lips then Lyla jumped forward. For whatever reason, she'd set herself on taking me under her wing, and it seemed she wouldn't let me go tonight without making me feel accepted. More than she already had.

"Kiara plays the harp divinely," she said, "and Alaina sings like a nightingale." She glanced around the room as if I kept either of them at hand.

"I don't play any instrument," I told her quickly, before she had a chance to take my rooms apart in her intense search of one.

Lyla stuck out her lower lip, pouting and thinking. "Then we'll have to bring some here!" she proclaimed.

"Surely, Lyla, it's not that important," Queen Alaina tried to temper her.

Lyla glanced at Kiara, who shrugged back in return. "How far is the music room from here?" she asked her.

That was good enough for Lyla. "Come along then," she commanded all of us.

Only Lyla, in a room of royalty where one woman even outranked her, would dare take charge like that. I would realize it was part of her air. Like a streak of lightning across a darkened sky, in the same way she dared anyone to be more beautiful than she, she dared the whole world to try and bottle her electricity. It was both frightening and exhilarating to be around.

After a small tussle involving me figuring out what I could or could not wear for our short walk to the music room and locating slippers unmangled by a dog which took longer as the others admired my new gowns and offered some tips on dressing, Lyla bustled us out of my quarters. Apparently, the palace had three music rooms, and I'd only known of one.

We had just made it out of my chambers and past the cadre of guards—which included some of the queen's, some of the princess', and some of mine—when a deep voice stopped us in our tracks.

"What mischief brews here, Lady Ella?" The question seemed to reverberate in the very floor beneath us.

We turned around to face the captain of the prince's guard, the rest of our guards a few paces behind him. They'd turned to follow us when we thought to sneak out, but only the captain was daring enough to ask the question.

Lyla rolled her eyes at him, a habit no doubt developed from her relatively frequent encounters with him and his prince. "We're having a ladies' night, Captain," she said sweetly.

The captain looked toward me, which I supposed was right, given as I was the one he was now sworn to protect. "Now?"

I answered before Lyla could. "We're just going to play a little music, that's all. I'll be back before curfew," I couldn't help adding in. Lyla snickered beside me.

The captain didn't change his expression. "Very well. Please let the guards know if there's anything you need."

"Thank you, Captain," I said kindly. "Good night."

"Good night, Lady Ella," he replied. He dipped his head to the others. "Your Majesty, Your Highness, Princess."

"I freely admit that it isn't easy getting used to people actually caring about my whereabouts," I confessed to the others as we continued on.

"It's always nice to have someone care if you're there or not," Kiara reassured me.

"You were blessed in so many ways," Alaina added, then she let out a harsh laugh. "My mother-in-law was an ogress."

Lyla shared her laughter, no doubt thinking of her own stepmother who wanted to eat her heart. Walking with them down the hall, I had an eerie moment when it felt that I was really above us, floating along while the four of us chatted and giggled below. Aside from myself, the smallest, the youngest, the most naïve of the bunch, I saw three beautiful portraits of royalty. Three dynamic, courageous women, who had all survived something, who had all accepted, defeated, overcome to gain their happily ever after.

What I didn't know then was that none of us ever truly had it at all.

AS LONG AS WE BOTH SHALL LIVE

*T*here hasn't been, and I suppose won't ever be, much to compare to the day of my wedding. Even now, after all that's happened, the magic of that day hasn't faded. So much of it has to do with the aura, the excitement, the general atmosphere of a royal wedding. On that day, kings and queens, princes and princesses, dukes, duchesses, and dignitaries from all over the realms gathered solely to celebrate together in peace and happiness. So long as no one said something out of line when drunk, there would be no wars between us, for at least another week.

I could spend days describing the ceremony, the celebration, the gowns, the clothing, the jewelry, the food, the people, everything. But try as I might these years later, I have found no words to encapsulate the way I felt that day, when for the first time the sun shone brightly upon my future. Though I had already lived in the palace three months, though I had been catered to my every whim, though a tree had been uprooted and a pond dug in my name, the moment my dress was fastened behind me, the moment I slid on a new pair of Castarrean glass slippers, I became another person. Rather, I stepped into another world and left behind everything and anything I had ever known. My life would never be what it was.

It would be far worse.

But I didn't know that yet. All I knew was that whatever glory Marie's magic had woven for me was little compared to the dress four seamstresses spent three months creating for my wedding day.

Made out of silk billowy as a cloud, so soft I thought my hand would fall through it, and though I was wrapped in yards and yards of it, I didn't feel its weight at all. The entire bodice was covered with tiny crushed crystals which spilled down my waist before tapering off like fine mist over the skirt of my dress. The crystals were so small they were hardly visible, but they caught the light and shone like dozens of tiny rainbows. Were I to stand in a dark, mirrored room, one candle could illuminate my dress and thusly the whole room in a kaleidoscope of color.

Along the bottom half of my layered skirts, attached with real silver thread, was a garden of delicate white plumerias clustered along the front of the dress then scattered behind onto the long, long white train of my gown as if I was dropping them as I walked. Fresh dahlias had been cut and wrapped in a thick white bow for my bridal bouquet. A comb was stuck into the frail lace of my diamond studded veil until the prince would lift it and my world would be full again.

"Kings and queens, princes and princesses, noble people of the realms," the ceremony began, "His Royal Majesty, King William Robert Alexander, the fair and just, welcomes you to Laurendale in celebration of the wedding of his son, His Royal Highness, Prince Henri Christopher Charles Alexander, to the Lady Ella."

I haven't much to say about the rest of the ceremony itself

because I don't remember it. I was too dazed with disbelief, ecstasy, and exhilaration to register anything before the moment the prince slid the gold ring onto my finger and the guests threw rice as we retreated down the aisle. As for the guests, I didn't know most of them, but I knew all were important.

I recognized Lyla, of course, and assumed the handsome man standing beside her with hair streaked gray like a wolf's was her Prince Daimyon. I caught sight of Queen Alaina beside her king, each struggling to contain a squirming toddler, and I suspect from the way the queen kept sliding her foot, a loveable spaniel as well. Princess Kiara stood next to a mountain of a man who, though handsome, looked as though darkness clung to his shadow. Only Kiara, dwarfed as she was by his enormous frame, could still so distinctly shine beside him. And, though it may have only been my imagination, I'm quite certain I saw Marie hovering briefly somewhere past the crowd.

Aside from the prince, and perhaps my new friends, there really was no one else that I cared for to be at the wedding. I don't even know if my father came. The only thing that would have made a perfect day complete was if my mother had been there to see it.

After the ceremony was over, my new husband took my hand and led me down the aisle to the cheers and good wishes of all gathered. We had just crossed the threshold of the chapel, ready to lead everyone to the first of several days of festivities and feasting, when three swirls of color materialized at our feet. We pulled short abruptly and looking down was the only time that day when my joy was not absolute.

On the ground, groveling at our feet, were Madame, Maybelle, and Calliope. I did not know then how they got there. Had anyone asked, I would have refused them entry to the palace island. The captain had already cleared the path for us, Sir Percival was the only other member of the royal entourage who could have recognized them and sent them on their way. He had also exited with the captain and the only one who had left the chapel before us. From what I would learn about him, I suspect that little scene at the entrance was Sir Percival's doing.

My prince kept his poise intact, but not without an annoyed click of his tongue and a quick flick of daggers from his eyes. He didn't want to see them either. He had no patience, no desire to be reminded of the house or circumstances I had come from.

While her daughters couldn't control their scared doe-eyes from darting back and forth between me and the prince, Madame focused her stricken gaze upon me.

"Please—" she began.

"Rise," the prince growled at her.

Hesitantly, she stood, her legs unsteady, her head bowed. After the initial courage that brought her to our feet, it took her some time to find her voice again.

"Please, Cinder... Please, Ella," she pleaded, "please forgive us for what we've done to you."

Perhaps, if we were alone somewhere in my chambers, perhaps if I had nothing else to do but pick a new color paint for my room, I would have stood over her cowering frame and demanded she recount for me in detail every one of her sins against me. I would have liked to know if she even knew what she'd done, if she'd known the extent of the damage her words and actions had on an innocent, motherless girl. I had given her a chance to be mother to me. I had offered her my love and my kindness. But she wanted none of it. She'd thrown it all back at me, the only things I had to give, into the gutter where she thought I also belonged.

And now she had the audacity to confront me on my wedding day and ask for forgiveness. She truly couldn't leave any good untainted.

However, it was my wedding day. I had just become royalty,

bestowed with favor beyond the cumulative treasures of my imagination. Hundreds of people were gathered to celebrate and thousands more would hear of all that occurred. Could I not forgive her in the face of it all?

Only my husband knew how my hand tightened in protest around his arm.

Yet it was something more that led me to say the three simple words, "I forgive you," loud enough that anyone who cared to could hear.

As soon as the words left my mouth, I felt that my mother had come down to bless my new life after all. It wasn't until then that I understood that there are some parts of me that would never change, because even with nothing—even with everything—I always had kindness. Madame had nothing, even when it seemed she had everything.

I didn't stay around for thanks I didn't want and wasn't anyway sure were coming. I didn't need anything from them anymore. I sincerely hoped that no one expected me to ever invite them to the palace. Lentil soup would be on the menu if they ever were. I walked away and left them behind with everything else from my past.

The rest of the week flew by in a blur, but the one thing that needs mentioning, the one thing I remember clearest of all, was that first night the prince came to my chambers. The rest of the palace hadn't yet gone to sleep, and their merrymaking would continue into the wee hours of the morning. As for us, we were exhausted, and simply wanted to be alone.

His gentle knock announced his arrival and the flutter it set off in my stomach was enough to produce one butterfly for each flower on my wedding gown. Earlier, Javotte had prepared me for the prince's arrival, and though I was excited I was nervous, too.

"Prince Char...Alexander," I greeted him as I opened the door.

"Princess Ella," he replied with a kiss.

The prince didn't seem to be sharing my nerves. He sauntered into the room with a jug of wine, though I'm sure now he'd had enough before he came. He smiled as if he'd conquered a neighboring kingdom. Lyla's most likely. He set down the jug and scooped me into his arms, spinning me around and around, me giggling and clinging to his neck, until he was too dizzy to stand. Even when he stopped, he didn't set me down right away. He held me closer as if he too were savoring every precious first moment of the rest of our lives together.

"A prettier bride, I never did see," he sang, as he prepared two glasses and filled them from the jug.

"Certainly more than the groom," I teased.

The prince spun to glare at me before he realized I was joking.

I stepped closer to him. "And why would I want them looking at you, anyway?" I wanted to know.

The prince gave me a look that weakened my knees and sent my mind tumbling. Up until the end of what was between us, he was always able to do that, always able to turn me to mush with just a look from his precious, perfect face. He reached out a hand and gently pulled me to him, holding me close even as he tried to finish pouring the wine.

"You know, it's well past midnight," I whispered, suddenly unable to use my voice any more than to scratch those few words out.

The prince bent over to kiss my forehead. "I'm just being cautious." And he held me even tighter to him.

He placed a cup in my hand and I peered into its plummy contents. The liquid was warm, and the sweet scent of mulled cinnamon-and-spiced wine drifted up to me. I really wasn't in the mood for wine, or drinking, or anything of the sort, but I also didn't want to tell my husband 'no' right after we'd been married.

I looked at him. "What is this?"

My prince smiled down. "Wine," he answered. "From the year you were born," he elaborated.

I wasn't about to refuse the drink then.

I took a careful sip and sputtered. Beneath the spices, and cinnamon, and other delicious flavors was something acrid and bitter. I hadn't much chance to taste wine before, but this one wasn't about to convince me things should be otherwise. The one Lyla had brought the previous night had been much more palatable.

I glanced up at my prince who seemed to be enjoying his cup. I took another sip and coughed, and he looked down at me with an ill-hidden smirk. "We'll have to teach you to get used to some of these finer wines, my love."

I didn't like the way he said that, or what his comment had implied, that I had grown up differently, that my palette, my taste wasn't refined enough for palace finery. At the same time, I didn't want to disappoint him further, so I upended the contents in my mouth and swallowed as quickly as I could. I offered him the finished cup and he took it with a large smile. At least the wine helped calm some of my nerves.

A quiet pause.

Then my prince swept me up in his arms and carried me off to bed.

My first two years at the palace were a constant blur of newness, but there are some memories that starkly stand out to me. Memories of the prince rocking me to sleep with lullabies of what he wanted his kingdom to be. Memories of my little fingers skittering across his broad, muscled chest, tracing each scar imprinted in his torso like a path penciled onto a map.

"What is this from?" I'd ask, tracing a long, river-like scar that wound from one shoulder to the bottom of his neck.

"Dragon talon," he'd reply.

I traced dull pink scars shaped like short dashes above his belly.

"Ogre mace."

I winced, and the prince chuckled at my reaction. I traced another scar above his heart.

"This one?"

"That," he said, giving me his full attention, "is from when you took my heart."

I had never known such adoration could be real, let alone that I could be the lucky recipient of it. Of course, it would turn out that it wasn't.

Not only was I adjusting to being someone's wife, but I had to learn how to be the wife of royalty along with all the protocol for the next in line for the crown. Madame's etiquette lessons were only able to carry me so far, so there was an abundant more I needed to learn in my new position.

I had to learn of a history and places I'd never heard nor cared to know of before. I had to memorize family trees and diplomatic behaviors, those spoken and those not. I had to find new levels of patience and new outlets for kindness. I had to learn how to be alone despite being surrounded by so many people and how to safely maneuver between all those people. I had to learn phrases in new languages, formal court speak, and the political tongue. I took lessons in art and music and games from all over the realms. It was, quite frankly, usually boring. I was rather adept at remembering anything that could be found on a map, though.

There were some bright spots among it all. There were days when I felt that I had been staring at a book so long, my eyes would never detach from it. Then my prince would come sweeping into the room announcing his intent to rescue me, which he did by ushering me out of the room toward a romantic picnic, horseback ride, or quiet walk in the gardens. During those first two years, the prince was as perfect as could be: attentive, patient, and all around charming.

By then, I'd grown comfortable enough in my role as princess and didn't only call him 'Charming' anymore. Whoever was allowed to use his real name called him Alex, but I called him Alexander, rolling the syllables off my tongue like a slowly melting caramel.

For his part, my husband rarely called me Ella. Rather, it was always some version of 'love,' 'my love,' 'my heart,' 'darling.' It was as if calling me by my simple, single name was a painful reminder of my lower class origins. I do think he tried to mean all those pretty little endearments, though as it turned out, he was only using them to convince himself.

But there were some interesting things I learned from those first few years at the palace, too.

For one, the royal family has too many names. Most aren't used and when I saw my name painted beside my husband's on the large family tree that took up nearly the whole of a two-story wall in the library, I felt as little and insignificant as my size had always made me believe.

For two, there are way too many rooms in the royal palace. Most aren't used, unless there's a big occasion, like a crown prince's wedding.

For three, Queen Alaina has insomnia and doesn't sleep more than three or four hours a night. She doesn't know I know, but I caught sight of her many a night in the garden beneath my window. Through asking the right people the right questions, I was able to confirm my suspicions.

For four, though now a human, the frog king will bend down to the floor and leap like a frog when he thinks no one is looking.

I'd never believe it had I not seen it with my own eyes when he was a guest at our wedding.

The point is that I learned that while we were all supposed to be safe and content in our magical ever afters, most of us would never be able to fully escape how we got there. None of us, not even the prince, could ever be rid of the residue left by our pasts.

SUGARPLUM DAYS

*T*hose years, my life was a swirl of happiness. On each wedding anniversary, we held a masked ball, which always stopped long enough for all to listen as the clock chimed midnight, then we'd remove our masks and toast each other into the early morning.

It was only after the start of our third year that I noticed some changes, that I began to suspect that not all masks had been removed. Much of it happened so slowly, so gradually that it was difficult to recognize how our lives were shifting even as they did. I am ashamed to think of how slow I was to regain a sense of reality; how reticent I was to let go of the dream. I had been called a nothing my whole life and I was finally beginning to feel like a something, like a some*one*. So I believed what I wanted for as long as I could.

Until then, once the initial excitement of becoming a princess and living in the palace settled, I was able to see that living like a princess wasn't always as grand as I'd once dreamed. There was the drudgery of lessons, the need to spend hours on my dresses and the way I looked, the constant surveillance of every word and every look that passed my lips and face. I was shy around the other women of the court, attempts at conversation made me feel clumsy, and their attentions made me feel like an object on display, so I struggled to make friends in those early years. I would like to say that I could be myself whenever I was alone with the prince, but that wasn't entirely true. I always felt, and still do now, that I had a standard to live up to, an unspoken expectation that had to be met, for those in the court and for those outside of it.

I had mistakenly thought that all the good that was in my life was from the prince, so I did everything I could to make him happy, like drinking that acrid wine I never acquired a taste for each time he came to spend the night with me. Oddly, he never seemed concerned that I didn't conceive an heir. Maybe he thought we had plenty of years ahead of us. I certainly did. I lost myself in those first few years, lost the girl my mother had dreamed I would one day be. I only found her again when I was forced to, when it was too late to undo what else had been done to her.

I can recognize all these things for what they are now, but my life then was too busy for much thought. There was always something to do and someone to see, so it wasn't long before I longed for the days when I had a quiet corner of my own. Even as a princess, I couldn't lock myself in my room whenever I needed to, and not just because the guards or Javotte were always there. If I did, people would talk, and talk was not always a good thing for the royal family. That everyone was always watching me was a hard and unwelcome fact I only begrudgingly came to accept. Before then, I had always been too small to notice.

There was also the time I decided I had been away too long and finally determined to resume the visits I had once gone on with Mother. Madame couldn't hold me back now, and I had every resource at my disposal. I was still thinking too small in their regard, but I knew then that a true mark of kindness would be to give when I actually had everything.

I was leaving my chambers, wearing the simplest dress I owned, which wasn't very simple at all, when my husband appeared.

"Where are you off to, love?" he asked.

"I—" I hesitated. But then, why should I be ashamed? Surely, he would approve. "Mother used to take me with on her visits to some of the less fortunate families in our area," I explained.

The prince simply looked at me.

"I haven't been in a long while," I continued haltingly, unnerved by his lack of response.

The prince finally smiled and gently pulled loose the ribbons of my bonnet. "Darling," he said slowly, "if you have any concerns, then you need only let me know. Otherwise, we can't have you visiting those areas anymore. The commotion it would cause would be untenable, and besides," he added with a glance at my middle, "your health is too precious to the kingdom."

"But—" I tried to protest. Neither Mother nor myself had ever fallen ill from our visits.

The prince silenced me with a finger to my lips. "They will be taken care of," he assured me.

I trusted what he said to be true, but reluctantly... I didn't like that this simple action had been taken out of my hands, that I still didn't have the freedom I had so often yearned for, that this one connection to Mother was being denied me. Realizing I wouldn't gain any ground with further protests, I pushed the matter to the back of my mind, not to be forgotten, but to simmer. I would come up with something, I would come up with some way to help them personally. In the meantime, there had to be somewhere in this maze of a palace where prying eyes couldn't reach me.

Eventually, I came to find sanctuary in the shaded limbs of my pear tree. It was private enough for me to be comfortable, public enough not to worry the guards, and safely enough in the palace so my precious health wasn't endangered. The first time I scurried away, I was too scared to try and climb up, but staring at it long enough day after day I convinced myself that I didn't have to climb so high to hide. I was pretty small, after all.

The third time I escaped into the tree was to avoid a dance lesson I had neither the time nor patience to attend. And why did I need to learn all those other dances anyway? By now, my prince and I had waltzed more than two nights away and I would never tire of it. He was so tall, so strong, and yet we fit perfectly together. I didn't even need to know how to dance because I was content to simply follow wherever my prince led. As the skilled dancer, he need only take my hand and my feet would automatically follow his.

Besides, the instructor was also trying to blend the lessons with comportment, always urging me to stand taller, to lift my whole frame higher. I don't know what stubborn tick in his brain was refusing to accept that I could grow no more than I already had.

"You must be seen to be admired," were one of the things he was wont to say. "A princess stands above all others."

No, she doesn't, I wanted to bite back in irritation.

"A prince is a gem, and a princess its sparkle," was another nonsensical motto.

I'm more than just a description! I wanted to yell at him.

Was this why it was so hard to find my footing at the palace? Because whoever grew up in this life was taught to always stay at arms-length? Yet the prince seemed to always have his own court of followers buzzing around him. Perhaps it was only me. Perhaps it was the halo of magic around me that kept others at an awe-filled distance.

And I couldn't well expect to become real friends with any of the servants either. I saw the prince's expression anytime there was a reference to my past life. I knew it wouldn't stand. Even Javotte, who was always there, kept a remove of propriety between us.

I have more than I ever had, I reminded myself. *I have the prince, that is enough.*

I told myself that for far too long.

I didn't want to bother with the circle of those thoughts that day, which is why, on my way to the lesson, I made a sharp turn off course and didn't stop walking until I'd gone straight to my garden. I said a quick hello to my goldfish before looking both ways to make sure no one saw me hike up my skirts and clamber up the tree. Years of scrubbing at already clean surfaces for Madame made me strong enough to tuck myself away without much hassle.

It was wonderfully quiet in the sheltered boughs of the tree. The branches were overgrown with lush greenery, though there wouldn't be pears for another month or so. I thought about ways I could at least send my pears to the homes I used to visit, even if I couldn't bring them there myself. Sitting in the tree for the first time since I left my old life behind, I was transported back to the days when Mother was still alive, when every buzz of a bee was a tiny trumpet call and every flower a faery home.

I was thus lost in innocent reflection when I was found out.

I didn't react to the first shakings of the tree limbs. Actually, I went still, hoping that whatever man or animal had decided to call would soon go away. But the shaking became more determined, which was made obvious by the sudden appearance of a black leather glove and the top of a thick brown head of hair. I watched impassively as the captain pulled himself into the tree, settled himself onto a nearby branch and tucked his feet up so his long legs wouldn't be seen. He sat easily on his branch with the same confidence and assuredness he displayed when riding a horse, giving orders, or just walking.

I didn't want to be the first one to break the silence, but I wanted to stay in control of our strange encounter.

"How did you find me?" I asked.

"It is my duty, Your Highness," he replied seriously.

"Don't you have better things to do?" I pressed, not sure if I was annoyed or flattered that he had in fact bothered to look long enough to find me. I suppose it was a bit of both.

The captain chuckled and grinned impudently. "Absolutely not, Princess."

It's odd to think back on that first conversation in the tree, the first of a handful or so. There was so much I didn't know about the captain, so much I didn't yet understand—still, because he had been the first to recognize me, I felt almost comfortable with him. Perhaps 'safe' would be the better word. But not just physically safe, safe to be myself as well. Maybe because he'd been the one to break down my prison door, at my lowest, most desperate point, I thought then I had nothing left to lose before him.

I was horribly wrong. But that was later.

"Have you known the prince long, Captain?"

The captain considered me and the question. "My father was a duke and a dear friend of the king's," he began. "We used to visit each other often, particularly because my father had three sons and the king approved of us as worthy playmates for his son."

"You are the same age then?" I clarified.

"About," the captain replied. "One night, all four of us were bundled into the prince's antechamber, camping out as it were, and my oldest brother told us a particularly unsavory story about ghosts and witches and such things. Throughout the telling, we pretended we weren't scared, but that wasn't the case at all. That night, I reassured the prince I'd protect him, and he slept while I kept watch."

"How noble," I commented with mock gravitas.

"It was," the captain agreed. A man of few wasted words, his tongue, I would learn, loosened easily whenever he had a story he thought needed to be told. "Our fathers found us like that the next morning. I'd fallen asleep sitting up, still holding the butter knife I intended to use to protect His Highness from the terrors of ghosts and witches. As the youngest son, I didn't have much awaiting me by way of land or title at home. It seemed best to train for the prince's guard, so I went with him to the Academy. Considering, it was the right decision."

"So you know the prince rather well then," I confirmed.

I thought about it for a bit, how the captain had tried to stay up to protect his friend, how even as a child, he'd found someone he thought more important than himself to watch over. I hadn't had that in a long time, not since my mother passed at least.

"That will all change now," the captain said, and it took me a moment to understand he was responding to the thoughts I had unintentionally spoken out loud. "You'll have a different kind of life now, Princess. You've become important to...a very many people."

The tone of his voice kept me from meeting his eyes, so I rushed to speak instead. "I don't miss my old life, but there are some things I'm sorry I had to say goodbye to."

"Are there old friends you'd like to see again, Your Highness?" the captain inquired with sincerity.

I shook my head. "I never had any friends," I whispered into the wind breezing through the leaves.

"If it pleases Her Highness, I will be a friend," the captain offered. Blast him and his blasted hawk-like senses. He wasn't supposed to hear that.

"Please don't feel obligated," I hurried to say.

The captain looked at me seriously through his brown eyes, at once soft and rich as melted copper, hard and unyielding as a tree. His expression spoke for him.

"Will you do me a favor then, as a friend?" I asked quickly, veering away from how serious our pleasant conversation had become.

"Anything, Your Highness," the captain replied.

"I would like to go into the capital," I said, "but not as a princess. Just Ella."

The captain took a deep breath, and I knew that wasn't what he was expecting my request to be. I also knew that I'd backed him against a wall, pouncing on his generous offer of friendship, on his willingness to help me feel at home.

"Please, just think about it," I hurried to add. "I understand what I'm asking—but I just—I don't—I just need to be somewhere where no one knows who I am for a while. Please."

The captain nodded, and I wasn't sure if that was to indicate he would think about it or take me into the capital. I didn't push him, though. I trusted he'd tell me when he would. And neither of us was going anywhere else in the meantime.

He cleared his throat. "It would be beneficial to confirm you can protect yourself somewhat, Princess," he said slowly.

"I have my sword," I told him firmly. "I'm ready any time."

The captain nodded. "Tomorrow, late morning?"

"Tomorrow," I asserted.

A short pause.

"Perhaps, Your Highness, it is time to return to your schedule?" he suggested.

I sighed and rolled my eyes. "If I must."

The captain slid down the tree first, then offered his hand to help me climb down.

"Oh, let's just be finished with this," I said, and swung myself down from the tree right into his waiting arms.

The captain set me down and stood me up quickly, but not quick enough that I didn't feel a fleeting sense of security in his arms. If anyone could get me in and out of the capital unnoticed, it was him. I just needed him to say yes.

The next day, I dressed in the simplest, lightest dress I had, which was rather difficult to find and did require Javotte's ingenuity and some last second alterations from both of us. I met the captain in the training room, my sword held loosely by my side. Only Javotte came with me.

The room was blessedly quiet. No doubt, the captain had seen to it that anyone who would think to be here had training elsewhere. At the other end of the palace, perhaps.

The captain clicked his heels and executed a stiff bow. "Whenever Her Highness is ready."

"Captain, I already told you," I said with a smile, "any time, anywhere."

A smirk played at the corners of the captain's lips. "Is that so?" His hand shot forward from behind his back, the silver of his sword flashing like lighting toward me.

I wasn't unprepared, but I wasn't lightning quick either. I flung my sheath away and raised my blade just in time to parry his blow. That didn't stop him, he just kept coming at me again and again. For a long while, I took up defense, pushing myself just to keep his blade from getting too close. I knew he wouldn't hurt me, but he also didn't seem the type to go easy just to let someone, even a princess, win.

We took a quick break, during which I tried to ignore my burning arms and gasping lungs. I wasn't out of shape, I took daily walks through the palace gardens and my tiny frame was too small to allow me to overeat much. Still, it had been a while.

"Whenever Her Highness sees fit to resume," the captain said with a lazy smile. He was leaning against the far wall of the room, hardly sweating from the first round.

"Any time, anywhere," I repeated, and it became the mantra that kept me going through the next two rounds. During the second round, I decided I had enough of always defending myself and struck first as often as I could.

"I'll have you know, honorable Captain," I cautioned between blows, "that I have defeated many an ogre and many a dragon with this blade. Though I am out of practice as it all happened when I was much younger."

The captain's eyes shone from the challenge of cornering my tiny frame, which bobbed, wove, and darted in and out of his reach. He couldn't keep a merry chuckle from escaping at my words. "We must warn His Highness that his princess may take his place in the ballads as the kingdom's protector."

"But my prince can easily defeat his enemy with his charm and wit," I countered. "I must still use my sword."

After the third round, I decided I'd proven enough, and felt I'd done relatively well. Enough that, when I announced, "It's been a pleasure, Captain," the captain bowed low and countered, "It was an honor, Princess." When he straightened, there was a brief light left over from the sparkle in his eyes.

I didn't see the captain for a few days after that, but the next time I saw him, he looked like he needed a good shave. It wasn't out of the ordinary for the captain to have changed something in his appearance. As head of the crown prince's guard, he did have to deal with people and situations that no one talked of and knew even less about. However, when I turned a questioningly gaze upon him and pointed to my chin, he returned the look with a sly wink.

I understood immediately.

"It quite suits you, Captain," I informed him two days later, when the shadow on his chin had grown to a tidy brown beard.

He never did fully shave it off after that.

A week after my request, the captain appeared in my room with a sack containing an old pair of boots, an unremarkable dress, and a short dagger.

"I trust you know how to use this, Your Highness?" the captain said more than asked.

I measured the weight of the dagger in my hand. "I'll manage."

"Then we'll set out tomorrow, after lunch," the captain said. "Javotte will assist you."

"You told Javotte?"

The captain shrugged unapologetically. "We need her help, Princess."

I sighed recognizing his logic. Still, I didn't like that someone else knew where I was going. The captain bowed and spun to leave the room.

"One more thing, Captain," I called after him.

The captain raised his brow, unsure of what I would come up with next. "Yes, Princess?"

"I would like a map of the city," I said.

The captain's brow dropped into a studious furrow. "As you wish, Your Highness."

Good at his word, the captain sent over the map later that evening, rolled up and tied with a ribbon so it looked like a regular missive. I studied the map late into the night, tracing and retracing the streets and alleys of the city, memorizing piazzas and parks, seeking to match memory to sketches on paper. I even searched out the piazza where I'd first met the prince, but it wasn't on the map. The memory of that place was to remain untouched for now.

The next morning, I was so giddy with nerves and excitement, I had to focus to maintain proper composure. I didn't want anyone talking about my altered mood, however slight, because with so many eyes always watching, it was bound to be noticed. Considering my last attempt to leave without an entourage, I knew the prince would try to stop me if he caught on. Or he'd decide to join me, not in disguise, but as the prince, and I would be made to ride in a carriage beside him as we waved merrily to our faithful, rose-slinging citizens. I loved roses, but that was the opposite of what I was yearning for today.

After lunch, word was passed around that I would be retiring to my chambers for an afternoon rest. I slipped into my bedroom and changed into the stiff, old dress the captain had brought. I tied an oversized head kerchief over my auburn hair and, with some difficulty, forced myself into the uncomfortable boots I would have once considered myself lucky to own.

Especially compared to my clothes now, the dress was itchy and all around hideous. I stared at myself in the mirror, trying to find the Ella that used to look like the girl looking back at me. I must have buried her rather deep, because I could find no trace of her in my reflection. Without the hours in the sun taking care of the livestock, gardening, and beating rugs, my skin had lightened. My hair had lost some of its red streaks, but it had also become thicker, fuller, healthier. After months of ointments and lotions, the skin on my hands and bottom of my feet had smoothed, the way a hot drink helped even Madame relax a few moments.

I felt like someone else in those clothes. At first, I was a Cinderwench pretending to be a princess. Now, I was a princess pretending to be a Cinderwench, and one charade didn't feel so different from the other.

Javotte led me out of the side door of my chambers, unused but by my prince at night, from which we turned away from the main hallway, toward a skinny one that opened into the maze of servants' corridors running unseen throughout the palace. She deposited me near a quiet part of the palace wall, purposely well hidden from prying eyes by overgrown ivy.

The captain was waiting for me there, stalwart and stoic as always, even in his patched vest and slightly-ragged trousers, as if we often met each other dressed as we were in peasant disguise.

"Almost like the first time we met," I told him, as he took me from Javotte's care.

"I remember," the captain replied quietly, two words I hated to admit the prince simply could not say.

The captain took my hand and led me through a few more twists and turns until we came across a small stone door, well hidden in the greater wall around it. The captain rapped a code and the door swung open. He pulled me after him, down a steep incline, and into the busy traffic of the palace bridge before I could decipher where we'd been or who'd let us through the secret door he and his network probably used at their convenience. It was the kind of door a princess didn't ask questions about because there were things even she shouldn't know.

Neither of us spoke until we were almost fully across the bridge. At the end, stretching in either direction, was a wide promenade that ran the length of the water surrounding the palace. Sprinkled along the way were benches and parks, much like the one I had been in when I first found out about the masquerade that changed my life. Crossing over the promenade toward the bridge was the main road that eventually forked to either turn toward the city or continue past it.

"You must forgive me, Princess," the captain spoke first, as we turned right to walk along the promenade, two regular citizens out for an afternoon stroll, "but I must have a name to call you by in the city."

"Call me by the name I was given," I replied easily.

The captain hesitated to speak it. "Ella," he finally said, and the deep baritone of his voice made those few letters sound like slow rolling thunder across an open plain.

"And what must I call you?" I asked in return.

"Cap," he said immediately.

I frowned. "That's rather obvious, isn't it? Don't you have a name of your own?"

"I did once, before," the captain replied. "But its lack of use has left me out of practice answering to it."

"Very well, then," I accepted his explanation.

We walked along at a leisurely pace, not rushing to any

appointment or lesson or banquet or party or meeting. The sun angled down on us, warming us even as a cool breeze skipped across the waters. It felt so good to be out of the palace, to be no one for a while.

Then something caught my eye.

Along the walk of the promenade, the side overlooking the water that surrounded the royal island, was a small monument I was sure hadn't been on any map. Some people were milling about it, and I would have passed by had I not seen the too familiar fractured rainbow of color caused by Castarrean glass swallowing the rays of the sun.

I pulled up short and the captain stopped beside me. "Don't you want to go on?" he urged.

"Not yet," I replied, already weaving my way toward the glass.

My breath caught as I came upon it, and tears stung my eyes. Seeing this small dedication before me, this small symbol of hope and something more, left me faint and I floundered to stay upright. The captain gave me his hand for balance and placed his other one gently on my back to keep me steady. He would have to ask forgiveness for being so forward in the palace, but here there were no such rules.

Before me stood a stone pillar, simply carved, simply made, but enduring nonetheless. Sculpted above was a dainty slipper, studded with bits of Castarrean glass, and if I hadn't already understood it's meaning, the inscription at the toe of the shoe made it very clear.

With magic's grace, she came to the ball
With beauty and charm and heart above all
But when midnight struck she made to depart
Taking with a royal heart
That third night
Outwitted in flight

Abandoned her shoe
In final adieu
Her found her a servant, and carried her away
Happily ever after, till their final day
Surrounded by love and joy forever
We wish you dance on, our CinderElla

I blinked away tears as my fingers traced over the words engraved into the statue. I could never be no one again. "CinderElla," I mouthed. Then, more loudly, "Did you know about this, Cap? Did the prince?"

The captain mutely nodded his head.

"CinderElla," I repeated out loud, trying the name on for size. "Why did no one tell me?"

The captain actually looked ashamed, though I wasn't directly accusing him. "Perhaps the prince thought you would not like it," he suggested.

"Would not like it?" I questioned in wonder.

The captain looked at me. "Do you like it?" he asked softly.

I nodded. How could I not? For the people, for my people, it combined the best parts of who I was. A girl with the simple commoner's name my mother had given me raised to royalty from the cinders of hardship. CinderElla. I repeated it over and over in my mind. It was a name of hope.

The captain cleared his throat. "We haven't much time. Wouldn't you like to see something else, Your Hi—Ella?"

"CinderElla," I echoed again.

I studied the statue thinking of all the places I could see. A wide smile tugged across my face. I wanted to do everything, see everything, smell everything, taste everything! But I had to start somewhere.

"There is a place I'd like to visit first," I finally said, and with that we were off.

⁓

I stood beside the captain in the glassblower's shop, enjoying his admiration as the craftsman showed off his few trinkets of Castarrean glass.

"Aye, I made the glass for that shoe," the craftsman confirmed, a little more confident when safely outside the glare of a baroness. "And two others like it. One for a goose and one for a pumpkin. They'll be all over the kingdom soon enough."

I blinked, unable to comprehend the first statue and now hearing there were more. Why?

"For the people," the man replied, and only then did I realize I'd voiced the question. "Maybe they never saw the princess and maybe they did, but they see her in their mind often. When life gets too weighty, her story is there, a reminder that things get better, that there's tomorrow."

This was not at all what I was expecting when I persuaded the captain to sneak me into the city. I was supposed to be free from all people and responsibilities for a while, not run head first into more. Perhaps, sensing my mood was to become too serious if I stayed there much longer, the captain thanked the man and gently tugged at my arm to get me out of the shop. "There are other things to see."

I followed numbly. We stepped into the bustling marketplace, and it didn't take long for the sights to take over the reins of my thoughts. For a while, we simply strolled along, passing stalls that sold everything from the exotic to the mundane. The captain kept close to me, his large frame shield enough to protect my small one, his hand reaching out now and then to reassure himself that I was still beside him.

After an hour, the aromas got the better of me and we stopped to buy fresh bread from a baker's shop. Stepping out, nibbling at my small roll, I noticed something curious in the alley across the way, something I'd noticed in quite a few of the alleys we'd already passed. I didn't remember having ever seen them before on my few trips into the city with Madame and her girls, but I was also accustomed to looking down then.

"What are those?" I asked the captain, pointing to the small, huddled shapes in the alley.

"Poor," he said without emotion. "Hoping for the luck of some dropped coins."

I stopped mid-chew, then slowly lowered my roll. Without even realizing it, my feet had already taken a few steps forward, but the captain's hand urgently grabbed me back. "Where are you going?" he asked.

I looked back at him. "To share my bread," I replied, as if the answer was obvious.

Looking back now, I realize it wasn't, not to him. Perhaps because I knew what it was to be hungry, perhaps because of Marie, it was the only choice for me. I never thought that despite all I'd been through there were still some with less than me. Even the people Mother and I used to visit still had a roof over their heads, if little else. It seemed Heaven had sent me a way to directly help the less fortunate after all.

The captain blinked at me, once, twice. "If you give away your roll, and I buy you another, will you give it away as well?"

I nodded.

The captain drew a thoughtful breath. "Very well, then," he agreed.

And he spun me back into the shop, where he spent the last of the coins he had with him on a basket full of rolls and the basket, too. We left the shop and crossed the alley, where he hovered over me like an eagle as I shared bread to a grateful chorus of praise.

After that alley, we walked some more until we found another one filled with the wretched shapes. We shared with them and continued on, finding a third alley, where we gave out the last of the bread.

"Please take," I offered a roll to an age-stooped figure at the end of the alley. "Eat and be in good health."

"It brings me extraordinary joy to know you haven't lost your kindness," the figure replied.

"Pardon, ma'am—" I began to say, unsure I had heard right when the figure straightened, tossing back her hood to reveal, "Grandmère!"

I threw my arms around her, clinging to her in the fear that she was a fantasy, a fleeting remnant of my past bound to be carried away on the winds of change. The captain rushed forward when he saw me hugging a strange, elderly lady, unsure of what exactly was going on.

"It's all right, Cap," I reassured him, wiping at tears I only realized then were falling, "this is Marie, my faery godmother."

The captain gave Marie a small bow, and she smiled back knowingly. I never could figure out what was going on in that head of hers.

"I've missed you so much, Grandmère," I half-admonished her. "Why have you never come to visit?"

Marie smiled sadly. "The palace isn't for me," she replied.

"Oh posh," I echoed her objection from the long ago night that started this all. "It would be so marvelous if you would come."

Marie took my hands to answer, but suddenly her face clouded in concern. "Ella, dear, have you been ill?" she asked, and the captain who was only half listening as he watched the alley, suddenly regained his singular eagle like focus for me.

"I just needed some time away," I said airily, wondering how on earth she knew about those spots when the floor seemed to spin beneath my feet, when sudden bouts of nausea doubled me over crossing from one room to the next. I hadn't told anyone about them, because those instances were always brief and far between, so I always forgot later. But they had happened, and somehow Marie was sensing them.

"Ella," Marie began, but I didn't want her to say anymore. Especially not with the captain right there.

"Really, Grandmère, you mustn't worry," I said quickly. "My life is so much better than I could have ever dreamed."

Marie studied me intently, and soon I was feeling the warmth from her hands flowing throughout my body. I hadn't had an incident in a while, but suddenly all of me felt better, and I knew that I had been carrying something ill inside me.

"Thank you," I whispered, for her ears only.

Marie smiled, then something in her expression became vague and far away. "I must go now, Ella," she began.

"Please don't," I begged. "Please stay with me."

Marie stroked my cheek. "I'll see you again, dear," she promised. "And if you ever truly need me, call for me under your pear tree."

That branch *had* been enchanted!

Marie pulled me into a quick hug before she secured her hood and trundled down the alley toward the marketplace. At the last moment, before she turned, she flicked her wrist, and I'm sure I saw the glint of a gold coin turning end over end in the air. Then she was gone, and she took some of my good cheer with her.

"Shall we turn back?" the captain asked kindly.

I nodded. "But not through the marketplace," I said.

"As you wish," he replied, and we turned down the nearest street in the general direction of the palace.

It was only a few streets before our route began pairing itself with the maps I had studied the night before. I quickly gained my bearings and confirmed I knew where we were when I correctly predicted the street we were coming upon. It was about that same time that the captain leaned into me and whispered, "Don't speak, only nod. Do you have your dagger ready?"

I nodded, looking into his eyes to ask why.

"Two men are following us," he explained. "Perhaps because they saw how ready we were to share." His lips quirked upward, but I knew he didn't say it unkindly. Besides, two men wouldn't be much of a match for him. Still, avoidance would be best.

We were coming upon a piazza, and recognizing it from the map, I took the captain's hand and urged him toward it.

"What—?"

"There's a piazza up ahead with turns for five different streets," I explained quickly. "If we're fast enough, we can lose them there."

The captain quickened his stride and I had to run to keep up with him. Entering the piazza, there were indeed five different ways before us, and we made a sharp right turn into the one closest, but also slightly behind us. I intended to follow the street to the end, but the captain pulled me back and into him as he immediately pressed himself into a doorway. I just barely reached his chest, which about left me with my ear pressed to it.

We held our breath as we waited silently for the telltale signs of following footsteps. They came soon enough, setting my pulse to pounding, though through the captain's filthy shirt, I could hear his heart beat steady and true. That calmed me somewhat. We waited a while longer for the footsteps to recede, and I only knew it was safe to move on when I felt the captain's body shift.

I glanced up to catch him looking down at me, and maybe it was a moment of madness, but in that instant, I saw the world in his brown, earthy eyes, illuminated like the sudden spark of a shooting star as it blinks over the earth.

I stepped back from him out of the doorway, telling myself I was shaking from the receding fear.

"Well, that was something," I understated. "At least I'm still adept at eluding people, so I haven't lost all my old skills."

"Being friends with you, Princess, really wears the heart," the captain replied with a grin.

There was so much more to what he was saying than his actual words. As with most other things, I didn't know it then, and can only speculate now.

I answered him with an annoyed click of the tongue before turning away toward the piazza. Following the map in my mind, I chose the third path, knowing it was only a few more turns to the main road leading toward the bridge.

We were almost out of the last street when I suddenly turned on the captain. "Marie wasn't keen on visiting at the palace," I commented. "Why do you think that is?"

The captain didn't respond at first but the way he pressed his lips together told me he knew the answer.

"Why?" I pressed.

The captain sighed. "You know the prince's mother was the sister of Princess Lyla's stepmother?"

"Yes," I confirmed.

"There are many who thought," the captain continued, "though it hasn't been proven, that our late queen used magic to win and keep the king's heart."

"Did she?" I barely whispered.

The captain gave me an indecipherable look. "It's hasn't been proven," he repeated, "but she did have the king's heart and ear completely. The king never refused his wife anything, even when he didn't agree with her...even when it meant going back on his word. The prince despised his weakness and swore that no one and no magic would ever control him. Marie must know that he wouldn't welcome her sincerely."

I thought about that. I supposed it made sense, why the prince would be so reticent about magic. But—

"I didn't use magic to win the prince's heart," I told him.

Again, that same inscrutable look. "I know," the captain said.

"Does he?" I dared ask. "Be honest."

The captain tried to fight my command, but he couldn't in the end. "He really tries," he finally admitted.

A moody silence fell between us as we came upon the promenade.

"These questions of yours—" the captain began with a shake of his head.

"I want to know," I insisted, then thought for a moment. "If you want to know anything," I stumbled for the right words to offer, "we are friends, after all, you can ask me whatever you wish."

"Can I?" the captain asked with a grin that almost made me take back what I'd said. "All right, then, Ella," he began, and his grin grew wider, "I wonder if I count to ten and let you run first, would you still beat me to the bridge?"

"Captain!" I exclaimed.

"One, two—"

I didn't wait to hear the rest. I grabbed my skirts and took off running as fast as my little legs could carry me. I knew he had only suggested the race to distract me, but I didn't care. I wanted so much for the dream to be real that I was eager to push away any thought or feeling that might threaten it. I didn't care that every moment I chose the illusion chipped away at my very self.

It was only a few long strides that put the captain in the lead, and I tried to keep up even though I knew I couldn't. We must have looked like fools, choking on laughter as we raced toward the bridge.

It was a good trick to make sure the outing ended with a smile.

"Captain, I think it would be wise to stay in practice with my sword," I said, after we caught our breath. "Wouldn't you agree?"

"Is that an order or a request?" he teased.

"A request," I replied. "Please."

The captain tipped his head. "Any time, anywhere, Your Highness."

"And I hope," I pressed, "that if at times I trust you with some gold coins, you'll know how to use them."

The captain nodded silently.

"Thank you, Captain," I said. I reached out and gave his hand a small squeeze. "Thank you for today."

The captain simply bowed his head again.

We slipped back in the same way we'd entered, and when the captain returned me to Javotte, she almost flung herself at me.

"I was so worried, Your Highness," she said, barely keeping back her tears.

"I was in competent hands," I said with a nod that both thanked and dismissed the captain.

Javotte ushered me quickly into my rooms, where she stripped me down and burned the clothing I had worn.

"Did you know they call me CinderElla?" I asked as she hurried about, dumping buckets of hot water into my bath.

She paused only a moment to answer me. "I do, Your Highness."

"Do you like it?" I asked.

"I do," she replied, without hesitation.

She deposited me into the bath and insisted I stay there for at least half an hour to draw all the grime and dirt from the street out of my skin. That was well and good by me. So much had happened that day, though my mind and heart were well more exhausted than my body. Javotte came by to wash me twice, so I was almost glowing when she was done. Her recipe for freshness must have worked, because the prince followed me back to my chambers after dinner that night.

He poured me a glass of that blasted wine, which I tried to choke down slowly. I would've stopped drinking it by now, but he seemed pleased each time I finished the cup, and I wanted nothing more than to please him. I also wasn't sure if he was mocking my lower class tastes, which made me more determined to drink the horrible stuff, or if he really was trying to refine my palette. Either way, I had learned to drink so it went straight down my throat, touching as little of my tongue as possible.

We sat close together as we drank, the prince tangling his fingers in my hair. It drove Javotte mad, and she'd mutter to herself as she teased those infernal knots out, but I never rebuked her for it. Frankly, I didn't understand why the prince snarled my hair either, but it made him happy, so why stop him? I suspect now he probably didn't even realize the trouble he caused.

"Alexander, dear?" I broke into his reverie.

"Yes, my love?"

"I was wondering, what do we do for the less fortunate in our city?"

The fingers stopped twisting. My prince gave me an expression that was better suited to something more ridiculous, say if I'd announced my intentions to dance with the court jesters.

"Still on that, darling?" he asked with a chuckle. "Why ever do you wonder about them so much?"

I shrugged. "I was one of them," I dared remind him.

The prince stiffened. "Yes, well, not anymore."

"Alexander," I soothed, "it's only the question came to me and I didn't have an answer."

The prince smiled and stood up, taking my cup from me, then taking my hand to pull me up toward him. I doubt he was really listening to me at that point.

"Really, love," his breath warmed my skin, "you need no longer worry about such things."

"Isn't it my obligation as a princess to worry about my people?" I questioned.

"Your obligation," he enunciated, letting his fingers wander in the most distracting of ways, "is to voice your concerns to those who can take care of these things for you."

"I want to know that they're taken care of," I insisted, not yet responding to his advances.

The prince paused, realizing I was entirely serious. "What do you suggest? That we give them whatever they need? There'd be no end to the line of people wanting a handout. The money would run out before the people and what help would that be?"

He was right. Still, "There has to be something."

"I already told you I'd take care of it," he promised, probably just to end the conversation so he could regain my attentions. He lightly traced the outline of my jaw with his finger, his blue eyes intent on my every feature. My stomach wobbled, a shiver ran down my back. "I'm the luckiest prince that ever was," he whispered.

I was still worried about the poor, gray shapes I'd seen huddled in the capital that day. I really was. And inwardly I insisted that I'd figure out a real solution. But when my prince held me in his arms and said those few little words, I couldn't stop myself. I gave in completely.

A few days later, the captain was announced in my quarters, which he entered rather rapidly. His face seemed a little paler than usual, and I knew something was wrong when he gave an abrupt bow and began straightening even before I'd finished allowing him to.

"Captain," I greeted him. "What worries you?"

The captain stood up, back straight, posture perfect. His eyes darted over the others in the room, before landing on my face to search mine.

"Come sit with me over here," I said, leading him to a table in the corner of the room where we were less likely to be overheard.

The captain, as his job would expect, stayed overly cautious.

"Your Highness, I don't mean to disturb," he said, "but I have some information you may have use for."

"What about?" I inclined my head, openly curious.

"The matter spoken with the prince some nights ago," the captain's voice lowered, "it seems he relayed certain concerns to Sir Percival."

Contrary to what the captain thought, I was delighted at this news. Why come in looking like the sky had fallen?

"Why the concern, Captain? I think it wonderful."

The captain pursed his lips to keep whatever he was about to say in. He started to speak, looked around the room, then thought better of it.

"Perhaps Her Highness should speak to Sir Percival directly," he suggested.

His whole behavior was too odd to dismiss his worry. "I shall go to him immediately," I announced.

The captain nodded and excused himself from the room.

I followed close on his heels, as I really did intend to speak with Sir Percival straightaway. I came to his office and, scarcely had his valet announced me, then I swept into the room. There were some perks to being a princess that I enjoyed, after all.

The office was neat, spacious and, with all the windows open, fresh and airy. The walls were lined with overflowing bookshelves and the outline of the desk was made known by stacks of papers in varying heights. Sir Percival was barely out of his chair when I entered, his look more amused than confused at my unexpected appearance.

"Your Highness, welcome," he bowed obediently. "Will you sit?"

"Thank you," I replied, declining his offer. "I'll only be a minute."

"What brings you here, Princess?"

"It was recommended I come speak with you about the matter

of the poor people in our capitol," I said. "My husband spoke with you about it?"

A dark cloud passed quickly over Sir Percival's face, but he did his best to hide it. "Yes, he did, Your Highness," he murmured.

"And?" I pressed.

Sir Percival smiled apologetically. "Really, Your Highness," he tried to deflect, "there is no cause for further worry over this."

"I shall decide what I will or will not worry about," I insisted. "Now, Sir Percival, it is my solemn duty to care for my people, and I will have my answer now, please," I said in the most authoritative voice I could muster. Being so small, I had learned since coming to the palace that, without size, sometimes tone was everything.

Sir Percival looked away as if to decide, then faced me squarely. "His Highness suggested that we simply remove them from Camallea, because of the 'undue stress' they cause his wife," he said flatly. "He worries it may 'adversely affect' her wellbeing."

I scrunched my brow, forcing down a rising sense of indignation. "I'm sure I don't understand what you mean."

"His Highness," Sir Percival repeated slowly, "would like for us to arrange transport to remove all poor from the city."

"And where will they go?" I asked.

Sir Percival shrugged.

I frowned. "This doesn't sound like an efficient solution."

"It's what I was commanded to do, Your Highness," Sir Percival apologized, not seeming very thrilled with the idea himself.

"Then I must command you to wait," I said, "or slow the process as much as possible. Surely, the prince will change his mind if we offer a more reasonable solution."

"I'm not—" Sir Percival began, but I cut him off.

"There must be something," I said, turning to leave. "If you can't, then I'll think of something."

"I'm sure you will, Your Highness," Sir Percival replied, but his tone suggested otherwise.

That night, I rolled out my maps and called for Javotte.

"Where exactly are you from?" I asked her.

Javotte, obedient but confused, pointed to a little hamlet about two hours ride from the capital.

"And you return for a visit once a month?" I queried.

"Yes, Your Highness," she replied, her expression showing she had no idea what I was driving at.

"And how do you get there?" I pressed further.

Javotte oriented herself on the map, then dragged her finger along her preferred route.

"How much more time would this or this way add to your journey?" I wanted to know, tracing out two more routes with each hand.

Javotte shrugged. "More than an hour, most likely."

"And if there was a request for you to alternate your routes," I said, "and perhaps 'lose' some clothes, or food, or coins in poorer homes along the way, how much more time would that add?"

Javotte considered me carefully. I don't know how much she knew about my foray into the capital with the captain, but by then, we had surely spent enough together for her to guess at what I was really asking.

"And who shall I say sent me?" she asked.

I shrugged. "No one. Anyone. It doesn't matter."

"Well," she said slowly.

"I can arrange a horse," I quickly interjected.

"Then I'm sure that wouldn't add very much time at all."

I smiled at her. "Then I shall request it of you."

Javotte dipped her head. "Thank you, Your Highness."

She went to turn down the blankets to ready my bed for sleep, but I stayed focused on the maps. Maybe Sir Percival and I would concoct a real solution, maybe not, but in the meantime, I had the captain, I had Javotte, I had the handful of coins I would be skimming from my monthly allowance. It was certainly *something*.

The map shows how all this land looks from Heaven, Mother's voice echoed through my thoughts.

I was only a princess stuck in a palace, but as I was married to the crown prince. I had to try and make a difference for someone. My fingers traced routes all along the maps.

Down here, everything is much farther apart.

There were less fortunate souls all over the kingdom. Perhaps there were others like my Mother who took their daughters and cared for them, or perhaps these families had never seen any of the many faces of kindness. The prince was right about one thing, I couldn't just keep giving and giving or their lives would be stuck in a cycle of taking without ever improving.

I was sure it would take more than one answer to help all these people, but at least we were getting started. A new feeling gently began to surge through me.

Standing over those maps, thinking of my mother and her eternal legacy to me, well, in that moment I didn't feel so very small at all.

FRAGMENTS OF GLASS

*I*n light of the little things I had started doing, I was beginning to feel more at home, to find my footing in the palace as our third anniversary approached. I remember most the feeling of security, the feeling of warmth, the feeling of bliss, a constant hope as if every day was the first day of summer and only long hours of sunshine lay ahead.

Though there were some things, some things I look back on and recognize as warnings, signals that I ignored because I had wanted so much to believe in my faery tale. They were small things, little incidents that sprang up without pattern, little hints to remind me that no man is as black-and-white as he's painted to be.

One such occurrence happened that fall. I was traveling with the prince to visit a duke whom he considered a close friend from his time at the Academy. The visit was to be over the weekend, so the prince and the duke could hunt, gamble, and do all other manner of leisurely activities befitting those of noble blood. As such, we were traveling with a small chest of gold coins, though intended for gambling, the sum was exact, and every coin accounted for.

By then, I had been all over Laurendale and could finally match almost every major point on the map with images from memory, but a trip like this one still excited me. My life had only ever been as large as my father's estate and the world in my mind, but around the kingdom I saw lives and places far more interesting, far more complex than anything I had ever conjured.

We were traveling along a quieter section of the kingdom's main highway. My hand was propping up my chin so I could gaze out the window, luxuriating in the deep reds, oranges, and yellows of the changing leaves, the still giddily blooming wildflowers, the buzz and hum of insects reveling in their surroundings. The carriage suddenly slowed. It stopped. Then came the slow rocking of the carriage turning around.

The prince and I glanced at each other quizzically but said nothing as the horses soon picked up their regular pace. Not twenty minutes later, the carriage halted again. Alexander and I exchanged another questioning look. We heard voices, the whinny of a horse, grunts, shouting, then nothing. The captain and a select cadre of guards were traveling on horseback ahead of us, so we trusted we were safe. Still, this was curious.

The prince hopped out of the carriage to investigate. "I need to stretch my legs anyway," he explained.

I waited patiently for him to return, and soon he did, popping up beside my window to tell me that a farmer and his family were ahead of us. Their cart was in a muddy rut and though it wasn't blocking the road, it wasn't out of the way either.

"We've only come this way because a bridge washed away on the path we were supposed to be on," the prince added, slightly irritated. He muttered something about it being gone over a year and roads made unfit after rain.

"Can we not navigate around the cart?" I asked.

The prince furrowed his brow. "Be back soon," he promised.

A few minutes later, I smelled smoke. The prince hadn't yet returned, but some clomping brought the feet of an enviable white stallion into view. Seconds later, the captain slid down and faced me from the other side of the window.

"All right, Princess?" he asked amiably.

"All right, Captain," I confirmed. "But it smells like something's burning."

The captain nodded. "The farmer's cart," he explained simply.

I scrunched my brow. "What? How?" I wanted to know.

The captain kept his face neutral. "His Highness said the wind shifted and blew sparks from their cooking fire onto the wheat they were carrying. Unfortunately, the closest river is back the way we came."

I looked at the captain. He looked at me.

"What cooking fire?" I demanded.

The captain didn't blink. "The prince said," he replied adamantly.

I stared. The prince hadn't said anything to me about a cooking fire. I would have smelled if there was one. Surely, that wasn't what had happened. But if not, then what? The captain wasn't likely to tell me, I was sure of it. Almost. Then again, he'd only told me what the prince had said to him. Unbidden, the image of the prince stepping on the hand of his opponent as he left the arena the day I met Lyla came to mind. I shook the image loose. I don't know what he'd been thinking then, or now, but things were different since the festival. I was here now.

Without considering further, I raised my hands and removed the earrings I was wearing. A simple pair that I really adored, they were shaped like soft golden teardrops, three on each one, each tear attached to a thin gold chain that lowered it just below the teardrop above it. I handed them to the captain.

"Your Highness?" he questioned.

"Please give them to the farmer and his wife," I said without feeling the need to explain myself further. He'd helped me distribute the bread in the capitol. Now and again, he lost coins for me all over the kingdom. Surely, he of all people understood.

"May I ask, Your Highness, what a simple farmer and his wife are supposed to do with these?" the captain asked, but not unkindly. "Were he to try and sell them he'd certainly be imprisoned for theft."

Color rose to my cheeks, but I refused to let it spread. I'd make a mistake. I would fix it. I bent toward the prince's side of the carriage and removed two gold coins from the small chest under his seat.

"Please give these to the farmer and his wife," I instructed as I placed the gold coins beside the earrings.

The captain raised his eyebrows at me. He knew, as well as I, that the prince would notice if any coins went missing.

"As you travel ahead, bring the earrings to a nearby village and sell them to a jeweler with explicit instructions that they be melted down."

"These may be worth more than any one man can offer out here."

"Take whatever you're offered for them, even less than their worth," I ordered. "Bring me back two gold coins, if there is more, buy food and clothing for those who don't have enough."

I didn't need to add that this had to stay between us. The captain was a smart man. He knew the prince well. He knew what had happened with the cart.

The captain closed his hand around the coins and earrings, his grip tight. He studied me a moment, his look suggesting he wanted to say something but wasn't sure how or what. He finally settled for, "It's unwise to undervalue personal property."

"Even more so the property of others," I retorted evenly.

The captain bowed his head, but not fast enough for me to miss the approving grin he struggled to keep from his lips.

"One more thing," I stayed him, suddenly remembering the prince's mutterings from moments ago.

"Yes, Princess?"

"If the bridge was swept away over a year ago," I asked, "why hasn't it been rebuilt? Why aren't the roads draining properly?"

The captain regarded me seriously. "It takes a long time to recover from four straight years of war," he replied. "There may be a lack of men or resources or both."

That made sense. "Thank you," I told him.

He rode away as the prince came back, sliding into the carriage and jerking the door shut with a loud thump so the coachman would know it was time to move on.

"Hope you didn't fret too much without me, love," he said with a rakish smile.

"Barely," I grinned back.

The carriage jolted, then began to sway beneath us as the horses resumed their trot down the road. After a few quiet minutes, I looked up to notice the prince studying me with an odd expression on his face.

"What is it, Alexander?" I asked.

He started to speak, shook his head, stopped, then decided to go for it anyway. "It's a silly thing really, but I was almost certain you were wearing earrings today. Those lovely gold teardrops I gave you for our anniversary."

My hands flew instinctively to my ears, and I rubbed the empty holes, even though I knew nothing was there.

"It seems I forgot with all that was going on," I said sweetly. "Perhaps, I had only spoken of wearing them. I must ask Javotte if she remembered to pack them."

The prince nodded slowly, as if to accept my answer only because there wasn't any other that fit.

I felt bad about lying to him, stretching the truth was more like it, but I didn't think he'd like to hear what I'd done with the earrings. I'd have new ones made before he could ask again. Besides, it was for something good, I excused myself.

And why not? I was already excusing the prince to myself. Why couldn't I do so for me?

~

That particular trip wound down with a surprisingly pleasant detour on our way back home. The prince and I were sharing a companionable quiet in the carriage, when suddenly the prince's head shot up in response to something he noticed outside. Immediately, he began pounding on the roof of the carriage, signaling the driver to stop. I peered out the window, anxiously searching for the cause of the prince's odd behavior.

Seconds later, the captain's horse was pulling into view beside the carriage window. The captain leaned over and addressed the prince.

"Something the matter, Your Highness?"

"Captain," the prince replied with a wide smile, "I must say there's something enchantingly familiar about this forest."

The captain didn't respond right away, perhaps taking the time to examine the forest for himself.

"It is rather familiar, Your Highness," he conceded carefully.

"And would it not be unforgivably discourteous if we were to pass through your brother's lands and not bother to inquire after his health?" the prince demanded, his smile growing ever larger.

"It would indeed, Your Highness," the captain agreed reluctantly.

"Indeed. Now, ride on ahead and notify them of our imminent arrival," the prince commanded, "with our apologies that it is so...imminent."

"As you wish, Your Highness."

The captain kicked his horse into a gallop, shooting away so quickly its hooves hardly touched ground long enough to spray up dust behind it. The prince leaned back in his seat with a self-satisfied smirk.

"I hope you don't mind the diversion, my heart," he said to me.

"Not in the least," I replied honestly. I was rather intrigued to see the home where the captain had grown up.

"You'll like them," the prince reassured me. "They are quite a lovely family."

"Wherein the captain is part of the rule and not the exception?" I inquired.

The prince grinned. "Indeed," he agreed.

The carriage resumed its travels, turning off the main highway to follow a clear but shaded path, which probably marked the beginnings of the captain's familial estate. The prince, in an obviously nostalgic mood, began talking about the boys he had grown up with.

Although all the brothers had spent years at the Academy, only the captain was still part of the king's active service. His eldest brother, Alaryx, had taken over the family's estate after their father's passing, and it seemed he was quite happy to stay there and raise his growing family.

The second brother, Daedryk, had been an exemplary military strategist during his years in the Academy, which had led to some very important roles in many of the defining battles that secured our borders. The prince said it was well known that any battle Daedryk had a hand in planning had a much higher chance of victory, as well as a much lower casualty rate. The result was a chest full of ribbons the prince claimed could "accessorize a small bridal party."

Our carriage rolled up to the front steps of a wide, sprawling brick structure, very similar to a fortress, except it was only a façade for the prettier and more welcoming home behind it. There was no drawbridge, but there were two heavy wooden doors that could easily barricade the household inside. The captain was already off his horse and waiting for us when we came. At the top of the steps stood two large men, both with thick brown hair and chocolatey brown eyes. All three brothers wore versions of the same features.

The carriage door was scarcely opened before the prince was already out and bounding up the steps to the captain's brothers. Without permission, Alaryx scooped him into a large hug and squeezed him hard enough to lift him off the ground.

"Release me, you big ogre," the prince commanded good-naturedly, pounding his back for good measure.

"Our home is always ready to welcome you, Prince Alex," Daedryk greeted him with more restraint.

"He looks well," Alaryx commented to Daedryk. "Doesn't our prince look well?"

"He looks very well, indeed," Daedryk confirmed.

About then, I came upon the group, having been helped out of the carriage by a footman and offered an arm up the steps by the captain.

"Gentleman," the prince announced, "my wife, the Princess Ella."

The brothers dropped into chivalric bows.

"Surely the reason His Highness looks so well," Daedryk loudly whispered to Alaryx.

"Enough of that," the prince waved at them dismissively.

"To the terrace then? For some refreshments," Daedryk gamely offered.

"Absolutely," the prince replied, and they sauntered off together toward the back of the house.

I watched them go, pleased at the mutual warmth between the prince and this family. I had never known of such happy relationships and being allowed a glimpse into one now was just one more example of how much my life had changed for the better, and how much I wanted a family like this of my own.

The duke turned to his youngest brother and tugged at his short beard.

"Disguising yourself as a bear for your next assignment, Captain?" he teased.

The captain tried to bat his brother's arm away. "It's not a disguise if you insist on announcing it," he retorted.

Alaryx laughed, then turned to me with a wink. "Quite a troublemaker this one," he told me, "had us all doubting the honesty of his future."

He ruffled his brother's hair affectionately, and the captain pulled away quickly, though not without some unwanted traces of a blush coloring his cheeks. He turned on his heel and went in search of his prince.

Alaryx grinned after him and offered me his arm. "Kaitryn's present condition prevents her from getting about as much as she would like, but she's eager to meet you, Princess," he said.

"I'd like to meet her, too," I replied sincerely.

As it turned out, the duke's wife was seven months pregnant, her face shining contentedly despite the assumed discomfort of her swollen belly. Three more children were about the terrace, the oldest looking to be about six whereas the youngest must have just learned how to use his feet because he tottered about drunkenly and lost his balance often.

The duke and his wife weren't shy about the abounding pride they had for their children, and I watched them curiously, wondering if this was the way parents really were supposed to be, would have been, had my perfect life not ended with my mother's death. I knew my mother had loved me, knew my father had once been proud of me, but it had been so long since a parent had shown me approval, the feeling was quite foreign to me by then.

The terrace was a paved outdoor area directly behind the house that was wide enough and long enough to hold a fairly large outdoor party. It ended with an open flight of steps that descended onto crisp green lawns stretching out as far as the eye could see. The glint of the sun shimmering on something in the distance suggested there was some sort of pond or lake at the edge of the property, and to the right of that was dense forest, which was certainly the host of many a hunt.

The men kept themselves busy; apparently there were some new horses Alaryx wanted to show the prince, and I sat with the duchess enjoying the refreshments and the fresh air. While sitting there, the second to youngest child, a darling little girl with curling brown hair and large doe eyes made herself comfortable beside me.

"What are you holding in your hand?" I asked gently, nodding toward her clenched fist.

The girl slowly opened her fingers to reveal a bright yellow wildflower. "I'm saving it to keep in my room," she told me.

"Well," I said, "that's a lovely idea, but you have to be careful not to crush it like that." I carefully took the flower from her and began to straighten its petals.

"Why not?" the little girl wanted to know.

She couldn't have been older than four, if even. My heart puddled from her wide, innocent eyes.

"Well," I said, and all at once I was taken back to another estate in what felt like another life. There was a little girl there, too, one who loved to explore every flower and the wide promise of magic each petal offered. "Well," I said again, "because tiny pixies live in these flowers, and if you crush them up then they can't stay there anymore."

The girl's eyes grew even wider. "Really?" she asked.

"Really," I confirmed, slipping with surprising ease back into the sunshine days of my most imaginative years. I held the flower up to my ear. "If you listen closely, you can hear them singing." I hummed along to an unheard melody. "You try."

The little girl delicately took the flower back, then, with some hesitation, held it up to her ear and screwed her eyes shut as she listened intently.

"Do you hear it?" I whispered.

She shook her head no.

I frowned. "Perhaps they already left this flower," I said. "Should we find another?"

The young girl nodded eagerly. I stood up and brushed off my skirts, "You'll have to show me where they grow," I told her seriously. "Only children know which flowers are pixie homes."

The little girl jumped up and slipped her small hand into mine. I thought then to look back at her mother. "I hope you don't mind?"

Kaitryn smiled back widely. "Not in the least, Your Highness."

So I went with the little girl, each step bringing me closer to innocent days painted with broad strokes of naiveté. By the time we had uprooted at least a half dozen more flowers, the little girl was finally convinced she could hear the pixie music, too. She hummed along with me as we walked back to the terrace, her little hand tucked into mine, her other carefully holding the prized flower aloft.

The men were waiting for us, their amused expressions at our return revealing that they had been let in on what we were after. The little girl ran to show her father her find, and in one motion Alaryx lifted her up and pressed his ear to the flower. He tried to hum along with her, though she couldn't quite keep the tune I'd taught her.

"It's time we were returning, my love," the prince said to me. He turned to the captain's family. "We thank you for your hospitality."

"It was our pleasure," our hosts chimed as one.

The duke, still holding his little girl, and Daedryk walked us back to our carriage. The prince, it seemed, would not be riding with me, as he was now the proud owner of a new chestnut-colored mare. He stroked its mane lovingly while he waited for the rest of us to get settled. The captain was already back on his horse and calling out orders for the rest of the journey home.

The little girl whispered something in her father's ear, and he turned to me with a soft smile on his face. "She wants to give you something," Alaryx said.

"Of course," I replied sweetly, not in the least suspecting what it could be.

He set her down and I bent to receive whatever she intended to give me. I was taken quite by surprise when she placed a quick, shy peck on my unsuspecting cheek. I still smile when I think of that moment, a single, pure gesture to wrap up a lovely, unexpected afternoon.

The duke once more held his daughter and offered his free hand to help me into the carriage. I settled in and he closed the door behind me. I leaned out the window so I could tell the little girl, "Thank you. It was so nice to meet you."

"If it's not too forward of me, Princess," Alaryx suddenly said, "I feel I must thank you."

I looked at him in surprise. "Whatever for?"

The duke fidgeted. "I'm not quite certain how to say this, Your Highness, but while my brother has always been an honest and loyal soldier, there's been something missing in his service." Here the duke stopped and rubbed his fingers together, as if that motion was enough to fabricate the words he was seeking. "He's proud to serve the prince, but he lost a part of himself in those wars. Only recently does it seem he's finding himself again, as it were."

"I'm not sure I understand your meaning," I said frankly.

Alaryx took a deep breath, his eyes wandered over to his

brother, watching him, studying him a moment, before turning back to me. "Simply put, in a good way, he wasn't like this before you came to the palace."

I still didn't understand what the duke was trying to get at, though I have my assumptions now.

"The captain is a very good friend to me," I replied.

The duke nodded slowly. "Yes, a friend."

We didn't have time to discuss his odd comments any further, because the carriage started forward and we were on our way.

"Safe journey, Your Highness," Alaryx called after me, leaving me to wonder after our strange parting the rest of the way home.

Later that night, after we had safely returned and been settled back into the palace, I sat with the prince over hot cups of tea and made sure to tell him what a wonderful time I'd had at the duke's house.

"It was a lovely visit," the prince affirmed.

"Their estate is just charming," I went on, "and the children, what a delight!"

"Hm? Yes, very delightful," the prince agreed.

I had contemplated different ways of bringing up the topic of children to the prince many times before that night, and I figured then was as good a time as any for us to discuss our future family. I was happy for the time we had alone, but my visit today stirred my desire to have a child of my own. Besides, wasn't the need for an heir part of why the prince had been pressured into getting married so soon after returning from war?

"And that little girl," I gushed, "was just so darling."

"Very darling," the prince echoed. "It's always nice to visit with old friends."

He stretched and leaned back in his chair, settling comfortably against the cushions with a contented smile.

"Did I ever tell you about my first day at the Academy?" he asked.

"No," I said hesitantly, trying to hide my disappointment at his move to change the topic of conversation.

"Well," the prince began, "Alaryx and Daedryk were already there, but it would be the first time the four of us would be together again in some time..."

I listened with half an ear to the rest of the story, which I would have been happier to hear almost any other day.

I should have known then, should have sensed from his actions the truth about the prince's thoughts on expanding our family. Now, after all that's been, I can say plainly that the fault was with me. Not because of who I was, but because of who I refused to see. There was something not right about the man who couldn't even be bothered to have a civil conversation with his wife about having a family. Something suspicious about a prince —and future king—who wasn't anxious for an heir.

THE FIRST CLUE

*C*hanges dark as thunderclouds slowly drifted in as that year went on, changes that would shake up life at court, rocking the foundation like an earthquake that cracks the land to shake off unwanted bits. Even a faerytale princess was not to remain untouched.

The first thing to happen, the first change that set off all the others, occurred shortly after we returned from our trip. The health of His Royal Majesty, King William Robert Alexander, decided it had enough of his body and wanted out. Over the next nine months, the color, the life, the will slowly oozed from the king's body, eventually leaving it bedridden in his chambers.

And I was there every day to watch it happen. After three years living in the palace and never exchanging more than basic pleasantries with the king, I was now by his side every day.

When news first came that the king had collapsed stepping down from his throne, my husband and I rushed to his bedside and stayed there most of the day. The king was still fully conscious then, and even though he seemed to understand that his time was up, the rest of us were still shaking the hourglass, searching desperately for a few more grains of sand.

After a week, it became apparent that though the king would have some days that were better, he would not actually get better again.

"I'm worried about Father," the prince confided to me one winter night as we sat before the fire.

"The king has the best physicians," I reassured him. "Whatever can be done, will be done."

The prince sighed. "I don't even know that he wants it anymore. He was never the same after Mother died, and I suspect he'll be glad to see her again."

"You shouldn't talk like that," I hushed him, though I knew exactly what he meant. I stood to massage his shoulders, kneading out the knots that had grown thicker since the king took ill.

There was no point denying that it wouldn't be very long before the prince became king. I never thought of what that would mean for me, how that would trap me even further in the responsibilities and life I was still growing accustomed to. Then, my thoughts were still only consumed with him.

"It's difficult to see him like this," the prince continued, yielding to my touch, relaxing into it. "Is it horrible of me to say that I don't want to see his decline? It is pretty horrible, isn't it? Someone must be with him, though."

I knew the prince had little respect for his father, though he must have loved him to be so bothered by whatever faults he saw in him. I thought this must be the reason why he was concerned about him now. After all, no man should die alone.

"I'll visit with him, every day," the words slipped out without any thought. It was so automatic for me to say what he expected, what he wanted, what would make him happy. I leaned forward and kissed the top of his head. "And you're not horrible."

The prince tilted his face upward and smiled into my eyes.

Heavens, he was beautiful. After three years of marriage, he could still melt me with a look. "I'm not that horrible," he conceded, grinning.

"Not that horrible at all."

"Maybe even a little nice?"

"Maybe. A little." I stopped massaging his shoulders so I could walk around and face him. "Rather, you're positively charming."

The prince's smile grew to match my own. He pulled me toward him, and we were done talking for a while.

The next day, true to my word, I was announced to the king, who actually made an effort to move from bed to chair for me. I sat with him a while, listening patiently as he rambled on about the kingdom. In the beginning, I listened because he spoke, but as I visited with him every day for months, I began to see the man under the crown, who really wasn't anything like what I was led to believe.

Outside of the respect I showed the king because of his position, I'd never really felt comfortable around him. 'Father-in-law' seemed the term for someone warmer, someone more regular and mundane. As it turned out, the king was a regular man, quick witted, intelligent, and proud of his son, wife, and kingdom. Soon, I began to listen because I wanted to hear what he had to say about the prince growing up, about the history of the kingdom, about the future he wouldn't see. When he spoke of such things, he didn't seem at all like a man utterly controlled by his wife.

But what did I know of such things? It wasn't until much later that I would realize how much I had willingly given my whole self over to my husband, and the prince hadn't used any magic aside from that automatically spun into the fabric of every faery tale.

When the weather warmed up, the king was wheeled to the

gardens, and I sat faithfully beside him. Passing courtiers would be invited to join us. Some did for a while, others only stopped long enough to curtsy and bow. What all did see was my devotion to the king, what all knew was that I wove no spell over him outside of that engendered by constant companionship.

"Why must you eye Lady Rhodellia so suspiciously?" the king once whispered over to me.

I started. I hadn't realized the king was adept at reading my expression. I hadn't realized I'd allowed myself any expression when the lady in question had greeted us two minutes before.

I shifted uncomfortably in my seat. "She likes to talk," I finally explained.

The king waved away my resentment. "People always talk."

"And if it's untrue?"

"That's when they talk the most. But we royals," he grinned conspiratorially, "are above all talk."

Now my expression showed my doubt. "Is it those lovely eyes, Ella?" the king asked. "Do they accuse you of casting spells on my son as my wife cast spells upon me? Or perhaps they worry about the future of the royal line?"

I stared, unable to answer. I never figured the king for a fool, but I certainly never thought him so keen either.

The king chuckled. "While they talk, you act," he advised. "Sometimes they'll admit the truth, sometimes they won't, but at the end of the day, they cannot do the things you can."

I remember that moment so clearly, and for good reason, too.

"Your visits get His Majesty out of bed each morning," one of his nurses once told me as I was leaving. "The king so looks forward to them. He may be hanging on a little bit more just for you."

I reported this to the prince, who warmly pressed my hand between his in gratitude. "Then you must keep at it, darling." He kissed my palm then placed it on his chest. "It eases the heart to know Father's surrounded with such love before he passes."

So, of course, I kept at it. The curious thing about it all was that it became harder and harder to reconcile the man I was beginning to know with the person the captain, and even Princess Lyla, had once described to me. That one day in the capital, the captain had told me about a man too weak to keep his wife from governing him, yet the man I was visiting seemed anything but. He had sound philosophies for running his kingdom, though having been his subject all my years, I can't say that I always saw all of them in action. Still, I had lived a sheltered, if cruel, life and it could be that I had missed much during that time. Either way, it didn't seem like this man could be anything but good. Unless his wife truly hadn't allowed him to be.

By the time the king could no longer leave his rooms, my visits had already become a regular part of my daily schedule. Which could be how Sir Percival knew where to intercept me one day as I was leaving the king's chambers.

"The king is resting," I told him, as the door clicked softly shut behind me.

"I was hoping to speak with you, Princess," he replied.

I shot him a quizzical look.

"May we walk?" Sir Percival suggested, gesturing away from the king's chambers, down a quieter hallway.

I led the way.

"At a time like this," Sir Percival delicately began, keeping pace but remaining a respectful step behind, "one worries about the overall effects such a situation could have on the general wellbeing of the kingdom."

"One would," I echoed uncertainly. I knew he was talking about the king's declining health, but I didn't know why he was speaking with me about it or why he needed so many words to say it.

"And yet," Sir Percival continued, "the expected feelings of uneasiness aren't as prevalent as one might suspect considering the circumstances."

"They aren't?" I repeated dumbly.

"They aren't," he confirmed. "There is sadness, there is loss, but there is also a hint of anticipation, an undercurrent of comfort. A strong undercurrent. Enough to affect a river's course."

I didn't even bother to parrot his words back to him. I looked at him expectantly, ready for the point of this odd little conversation.

Sir Percival held out a small slip of paper to me, and I took it hesitantly.

"This was attached to a new plow in a poor farmer's yard," he explained, "and he is only one of several others to have found something similar attached to a much needed gift."

He gave me a significant look, then bowed and dismissed himself with a "Thank you, Princess," before I even had a chance to glance down.

Alone, I examined the paper.

The one side was blank.

I flipped it over.

Neatly formed, clear block letters, so even the barest educated of men could sound it out.

TO TOMORROW.

A sketch of a little crown made up the signature.

A particular moment in a glassblower's shop in Camallea leapt to mind.

The captain. It had to be.

Was he having these included with every coin—and piece of equipment, it now seemed— that he was losing for me around the kingdom? He'd since recruited two other soldiers noted for their discretion to expand my little cadre of helpers, and it seemed they had been efficient in their work. Through them, how far had I reached across Laurendale? Were the few coins I was sending out really making a difference?

People always talk.

Good, I ducked my head to hide my smile, let them talk about this.

$$\sim$$

Over the months of the king's decline, I saw less of Alexander as he began taking over the duties that the king was no longer able to attend to. About a week before his mind cut off from the world and two weeks before he left it forever, the king took my hand in his and studied me for a long, almost uncomfortable, while.

"My son is luckier than he will ever know," he finally said. "You're a different kind of woman than my wife was. I loved her dearly, but love can blind any of us." He smiled sadly and patted my hand. Something strongly resembling regret flitted across his face. "You'll make a fine queen. And my son will be a worthy king because of it."

I nodded to show my agreement, because I didn't have anything else to say in the face of such a sincere, yet odd statement. The few times he'd spoken about his wife, it seemed to be with respect, yet now his tone was saying it was a good thing, no, a very good thing, that I wasn't anything like her.

Perhaps the rumors were true? Perhaps she really had been the voice of the kingdom, wresting power with magic and wielding it to her gain? The prince admitted that his father had changed since his mother died, but if this was the man he really was, then perhaps he really had been blinded, willing to give in to his wife despite the good of the kingdom.

Perhaps he'd also seen the poor of his city and ignored them. Perhaps the queen had created them.

The king patted my hand again. "And so kind," he said, surely continuing a private thought out loud because it certainly didn't fit the conversation. "Almost too kind."

I didn't know then what he spoke of, but with the years I've figured it out. The king may have been blind to the kind of woman his wife was, but his eyes were wide open in regard to his son and me. He knew, much better than I, what kind of man the prince was. He knew what kind of poison ran in his veins.

Although we knew it was coming, the king's death had a sobering effect on all of us at the palace. Death usually has a way of making people take a step back from life, its finality a push to make us stop and wonder about our own ends. Black ribbons adorned the hats and arms of men and the dresses of women. Black banners were raised from the ramparts, and Javotte admitted that a sadness had seeped into the surrounding areas as well.

However, mourning could not go on forever and the kingdom would not run itself, so it was only one month after the king's death that the palace awakened again under plans for the future. Beginning with my husband's coronation.

Our coronation.

Despite being married to a crown prince, I had never thought much about becoming a queen. Our lives had been good, my marriage happy, why would I ever think beyond that?

With the coronation would come a slew of parties, a celebration for the kingdom and for all the visiting royalty and dignitaries that were sure to arrive for the event. With so much to prepare, I scarcely had time to think about much else. Like the weight of a crown on my head. The new chain that would bind me to the kingdom and lead me to a decision I could never have foreseen.

I noticed soon enough though that Javotte was distracted, as if the heavy cloud that once engulfed the rest of the palace was still hanging solely over her head.

At first, I thought it the strain of preparing for the coronation. Apparently, now that I was to be queen, I was to be moved into the queen's chambers, rooms that had been empty since the death of the prince's mother. The first time I'd stepped into my quarters, I had thought them monstrous in size, but I'd since grown used to them. Now, I was sorry to say goodbye to the rooms that were home for me. The view from the new ones would also be different. Higher up and slightly over to the right, the view made my garden seem that much smaller, not only because of the height, but also because I could now catch a fair glimpse of the extensive palace grounds that lay beyond it. My garden was but a small corner of it all.

With so many servants assigned to help me move in very little time, my chambers, and Javotte's temperament it seemed, were upside down. I only realized anything was wrong after we'd settled in upstairs, because Javotte, much like a lady's maid should be, rarely, if ever, lost her temper in private, let alone in public.

We were in my new chamber, watching as a parade of servants carefully carried in what felt like an endless line of dresses from my wardrobe. Dresses for banquets, dresses for picnics, dresses for hunts, dresses for official ceremonies, dresses for traveling, dresses for balls, until the individual designs blurred indistinctly into singular lines of a rainbow.

"How many are there?" I finally asked Javotte.

Javotte tilted her head, considering. "If you were to wear one each day, you would probably not repeat before three months were up, Your Highness."

"That seems a very large amount of dresses," I commented.

"There are princesses with more, Your Highness," Javotte pointed out.

I shook my head. "And now I must have even more made."

"If you wish it, Princess," Javotte replied, but something bitter in her tone caught my attention.

"Is something the matter, Javotte?" I narrowed my gaze at her.

Javotte stared ahead at the colorful prism of dresses arranged about the room to resemble the full range of a color wheel. She would be up late with the others sorting and putting all these away.

"Nothing is the matter, Your Highness," she answered evenly. "It appears the move is going smoothly."

I wasn't about to be sidetracked. "Is something the matter with *you*?" I persisted.

Javotte glanced at me quickly, then glanced away, but it had been long enough for me to see the worry, the sadness, the frustration in her eyes.

"Tell me," I commanded.

"May we speak somewhere private, Your Highness?" she asked.

"Of course," I replied, ushering her into my new bedchamber and shutting the door behind us. I turned toward her and saw the guarded, carefully maintained neutrality fall from her face.

"Javotte, what is it?" I cried, unsure of what could be troubling her so much.

"May I speak freely, Your Highness?" she requested.

"Yes, please, go on."

"My mother is very ill," she said, swallowing hard to keep her voice steady, "and there is no one to care for her."

I looked at her in surprise. "Surely there is a doctor who can help?"

She shook her head. "We did have a doctor once, but our village is small so he moved to a larger one where he could earn more pay for his work. I have a younger sister, who we once thought could take his place, but he left before she was old enough to receive any training. All she can do now is make my mother comfortable before the end."

"This is absurd! I'll personally send a physician over to her at once!"

"And which physician can be bothered to tend to an old peasant woman?"

"One who doesn't want to be punished for disobeying my orders."

"That's very kind, Your Highness, but once my mother is tended to, what then? What about the rest of my village? Will you send a physician out each time someone falls ill, even just a little?"

I paused to consider her words. She was right. Helping her mother would not solve the greater issue that they didn't have anyone trained in medicine. A farmer too sick to work lost income every day he wasn't in his fields. A craftsman restricted to his bed couldn't very well open up his shop. The coins I had distributed across the kingdom had helped somewhat, but they weren't enough. Of course they weren't. There had to be a greater solution to all this, and I intended to find it. Until then, Javotte's mother was still sick, and she needn't lose her if she could still be helped. I had an immediate solution for that.

I went to my night table and removed a few coins from my purse. "Ask the captain to help you find a doctor in the city willing to help your mother. Pay him extra if you must, and if you need more, I will give it gladly."

Javotte's eyes widened. "I cannot accept this. You already give so much."

"Must I order you to do everything?" I questioned impatiently. "Use this to help your mother, and then we'll find a solution to your village's problem."

Javotte hesitated further. I glared at her. She reached out her hands.

"Thank you," she cried, flinging her arms around me. Immediately, she remembered herself and pulled back, curtsying low and looking up at me though eyes brimming with gratitude. "Thank you, Your Highness."

I waved my hand at her. "Don't risk your mother's life any further. Go now to find the captain."

Javotte curtsied again and scurried out the door. I returned to the other room where the parade of dresses was finally winding down. Without Javotte to direct them on how everything must be put away, the servants moved on to transporting other things, leaving me with some quiet to contemplate the bundles of material about the room.

Three months with no end to my dresses. And I was expected to make even more for all the days celebrating the coronation? My dress for the actual coronation was already complete. It was a lovely royal purple creation with a long, sheer cape that doubled as my train, which could be removed after the ceremony if I so wished. Even now, it stood apart from the others, the purple garnets on it outshining all other stones in the light, haphazardly dotting the dress like bright, glistening shimmers of stardust before they fade into the night sky.

Looking at those dresses, an idea began weaving through my mind, an idea that grew bolder with each wink of those stones. It wouldn't seem like much to most people, but it was a brave step for me, an effort at change. It wasn't the solution I sought either, but with this, I was certainly on the right path.

About a week before the coronation, Javotte came into my rooms to announce the prince. I hadn't yet dressed, deeming it unnecessary since the whole morning would be commanded by an abundance of fittings. I had my magnificent royal purple gown set for the coronation, so now I had only to figure out all the other ones.

Putting my idea into play, Javotte had already gathered some of my least liked dresses and started taking them apart. Making small piles of jewels when necessary, carefully removing silver and gold threads, unwinding ribbons, and folding away any larger pieces of material that could either be reused or given away. With those piles out in addition to my array of dresses, my rooms truly resembled a dressmaker's shop.

So it was that morning that I breezed out of my room and into my husband's arms still in my nightclothes.

Looking past his shoulder, I only noticed then that he hadn't come alone. The captain was right behind him, blushing and averting his gaze at the sight of my indecent state. The prince didn't think twice of it. He'd probably forgotten about the captain, who was now retreating into a corner to give us some privacy. I tried to keep my little frame blocked by the prince for the rest of his visit.

"What brings you here so early, Alexander?" I asked him. "Though it does make for a wonderful start to my day."

The prince gave me a short smile. "The royal treasurer sent me a message about the expenses for your gowns," he said.

I raised my eyebrows. This is what this was all about? "Am I spending too much?" I asked with an innocent smile.

The prince furrowed his brow, his voice and face expressed equal concern. "You're not spending enough. Tell me, do you not plan on making new gowns for the celebrations?"

"Is that what brought you here so early?" I laughed, unsure at the cause for urgency. "I've had so many dresses made in the last three years, some I've barely worn at all."

The prince bent down and placed a hand on each of my arms just below the shoulders, so we'd be eye-level and I could see just how serious this was. "My love," he said slowly, explaining something to a little girl who really couldn't be expected to know better, "those dresses were appropriate for a princess, but they aren't fit for a queen. Besides," he added with a glance at the wardrobe decorating my room, "they are too regular, and you are anything but. I myself have had an entirely new wardrobe made."

"But you just had three new suits made six weeks ago!" I exclaimed.

The prince shook his head. "They aren't good enough anymore."

"Very well," I nodded, forcing composure, to keep from saying anything about how silly that sounded, as if clothing would be responsible for making us better monarchs. "I will send Javotte to personally request the funds for me. My wardrobe will be dazzling," I assured him, though I really had no intention of using any of them for myself. I had enough for now. I would dress like a queen, but it was time to do something about all this largesse. Those monies could do some good elsewhere.

The prince kissed my forehead and released me, sweeping out of the room with the captain at his heel. After she was certain he was gone, Javotte looked at me, as if to ask what to do about the dresses we'd already chosen to fix up for the celebrations.

I pivoted on my toes, taking in the room. "I already have a new coronation dress," I thought out loud, "the rest, it seems unnecessary."

I didn't mean to defy the prince, not after he'd been so good to me, not so close to one of the biggest moments of our lives, but the king's death, even the note from Sir Percival, had done something to me. It hadn't changed everything, but it had propped my eyes open enough to truly grasp the opulence in which we lived. When I first came to the palace, I was awed by it, always feeling the need to touch and taste everything around me. I had grown used to it, but death had jerked me hard enough to take a step back and reconsider. I'd lived with only two dresses for most of my life, and now it seemed an unwritten rule stated that I couldn't wear one more than twice. Why did I need so many?

Who was paying for it all? And why couldn't I write my own rules?

They were unnecessary considering what others in Laurendale were going through, in a country just four years removed from war, so I didn't feel guilty about the truth I had stretched. My dresses had been dazzling the first time I wore them, and they would be dazzling again.

Thusly, we simply altered the dresses I already had, funneled the extra money to pay for Javotte's sister to apprentice to a doctor, and hoped that with all that was going on, the prince wouldn't notice.

There is nothing quite able to compare to a royal coronation.

Over the years, I have been to a few others. I was there when Princess Kiara and Prince Azahr ascended to their throne and again just a few months ago, when Prince Daimyon and Princess Lyla received the crowns of their kingdom. Before then, our coronation was the first I had ever attended, and despite all, it's still a well-protected memory.

The day started early to allow extra time and care in dressing for the occasion. By late morning, my husband came to get me from my room, dashing and handsome as ever in his royal purple suit with gold buttons, sword, gloves, and cape.

"You look lovely, my heart," my prince sang to me, eyes shining with excitement as he caught my hand just as I came out of a full spin that showed off the reach of my skirts.

"You look rather charming yourself," I replied.

Alexander raised a finger to affectionately tap my nose. "I will always be your Prince Charming."

I'll admit, my knees turned to jelly.

We glided down the hall arm in arm, heads high, hearts

bursting with pride at the awesome honor we were about to receive. We walked to the great throne room and waited at the entrance for our cue to step forward. The captain stood there with a thick scroll outlining the laws of Laurendale that the prince was to hold during the ceremony. In one hand a sword, in one hand a scroll, a balance of wisdom and might, patience and strength, virtue and courage. The prince walked the aisle toward the thrones, with me following close behind him, blind to the crowd I knew was present, unable to see anyone through the haze of this incredible moment in my life. Once there, we knelt before the steps to our thrones and swore fealty to the kingdom and her people.

Only then were we led to the seats of the kingdom, the prince settled atop his ornate, centered one, and me in the smaller one slightly behind and to his right. The large gold crown studded with rare gems was placed upon the new king's head, and he sat taller beneath its weight. After, the crown would be locked in a secure vault in the treasury and removed only for very rare and very special occasions. Smaller, lighter gold crowns were made for the prince to wear from today onward.

"... I present to you His Royal Majesty, King Henri Christopher Charles Alexander, Ruler of Laurendale and Protector of the Realm ..."

I don't remember much of the actual ceremony, but I remember that part.

Despite having been warned, I wasn't prepared for the weight of the crown on my head. When it was placed there, I struggled a moment to keep my head up and my decidedly not swan-like neck from buckling. I managed, somehow, and was grateful even then that I would soon be able to switch that crown in for a lighter one. As a princess, I had worn a tiara to mark my status, but only a crown would do for a queen. Unlike the king, I had more variety in being allowed to wear either gold or silver. I had spent some time with Javotte and the royal jeweler designing delicate circlets of each that would quietly and modestly announce my station.

"...and his wife, Her Royal Majesty, Queen Ella..."

My name was so short compared to his, compared to all the other royals that came before me. It was out and over before it had even begun to echo.

The crowd only materialized for me after those words were said. Prince Daimyon and Princess Lyla, whose smile reached from one end of the room to the other; Queen Alaina with her king and twins; and Princess Kiara with the hulking man who was once a beast. Within the throne room itself, only ally royalty and high ranking nobility were permitted entry. The upper galleries of the throne room, usually able to fit over one hundred people had been blocked off by the captain for our security, insisting a live king was of greater use to the kingdom. Still, I looked, hoping for the familiar glow of an older woman, hoping that Marie had put aside her reservations and come to celebrate this day with me after all.

The celebration after the ceremony was open to all levels of diplomats and nobility. To accommodate the expected crowd, the event was held on the back lawns of the palace where there was enough room for every level of landed gentry, and then some.

It was only then, perched on a raised dais where we sat for hours accepting well wishes from our friends and allies, that I remembered that Madame and her daughters were nobility enough to be there. I doubt Madame ever came close to liking me, but that didn't mean she would miss such an important event.

Restless from sitting for so long, I excused myself from the dais, hoping to hide away in my garden, where I could sit under, rather than in, my pear tree. I really only needed a few minutes of quiet to collect myself, a few minutes for the enormity of the day to sink in. Never once, in all my years of travel and dreaming in my corner, did I ever think that I would actually be a queen. Especially not at the tender age of twenty.

As was to be expected, I was waylaid enroute by the very people I didn't want to see. Maybelle and Calliope suddenly appeared, curtsying low, their faces flushed and giddy from the celebrations. They each wore a wedding band on their fingers, so it seemed they had settled for their young lords after all.

I stared at them dipped before me before I realized that, as queen, they were waiting for me to give them permission to rise. There were so many new things I'd now have to get used to. Pulling deep from the well of kindness my mother had begun to dig in me, I put on a patient smile before bidding them to rise.

"We wanted to wish Her Majesty congratulations on this auspicious day." The words tumbled out from Calliope.

"And Her Majesty looks so wonderful, too," Maybelle added. "The color of your gown illuminates your eyes in the most beautiful way."

I listened, but did not find any trace of the malice that used to accompany her description of my eyes. Either she had concluded that I really wasn't the spawn of faeries, or common sense bid her restraint before her queen. I actually believed that she was sincere in what she said.

"Thank you," I told them both with a warm smile. "It's so wonderful that you came. Is Madame here? My father?"

The two exchanged a significant look. Maybelle started fiddling with her dress, so it was left to Calliope to be the brave one. "Your father...no longer walks this world," Calliope delicately said, in a way that was also a careful question of how I could not know. "He passed a little while after you moved to the palace, and we buried him next to your mother, per his wishes. Iris, well, he let the bird free just days after you moved out."

I kept my face a careful mask as I digested her words. My father dead these past three years and no one had deemed fit to tell me? And what had happened to Iris? Why not let me care for him if Father would not? Like my ignorance of the people's CinderElla, surely the prince had seen to it that this information was kept from me. Why? Was he afraid of how I'd react, knowing about my father's indifference which had allowed Madame's mistreatment of me? What was the prince afraid of? What kind of bubble of deluded happiness was he trying to shelter me in?

"Of course," I finally replied smoothly. "I just wish so much that he could be here."

My stepsisters nodded, accepting my explanation because it was mine. Thank Heaven I was then saved by Princess Lyla's timely arrival. The princess, dressed in a ruby red dress as daring as always, sauntered over and took me by the arm, leading me away from my stepsisters without a backward glance.

"Don't tell me those are—" she began.

"They absolutely are," I confirmed.

Princess Lyla gave an exaggerated roll of her eyes and giggled in a way that made me question if she'd had too much to drink. My suspicion was proven correct as in the short time it took her to walk me from one waiter to another, she downed two glasses of champagne, as if intent on sampling from every tray to ensure the quality was all the same.

As we circled the party, the drink loosened Princess Lyla's tongue and I received her usual rundown on everyone there, but with spicier commentary.

"See those two," she pointed at a young, stiff, but flawless looking boy sitting with a kind looking man. "That's Geppetto and his son, Pinocchio."

I studied them from where we stood. "They don't look related," I observed.

"They're not really," the princess laughed, "Pinocchio wasn't a real child either till a short while ago." She scrunched her nose at him. "He has a nasty habit of stomping on any bug he finds. Especially crickets."

Before I could respond, she was already sweeping me off to the next waiter, and the next guest.

It wasn't unusual for Princess Lyla to take control of my attentions at balls and other official occasions. I didn't mind it either, because I usually felt safe enough with her to outshine me in looks, wit, and brazenness. That day, as ever, there was a recklessness about her, a daring to all present to openly question her behavior. Yet this was the first time I felt it didn't come from passion or rage, but sadness. Unfortunately, I didn't know how to ask her about it without fearing I'd open the floodgates.

"See him?" she soon asked, pointing across the fields to an attractive prince in green who was chasing after a boy and girl close enough in age to be twins.

"Yes," I replied.

"Handsome, isn't he?" she pressed.

"He is," I agreed.

The princess took a sip of her drink, then squinted her eyes in disgust. "He's really nice, too," she told me. "A good person, with a good heart. Unfortunately, he has the pleasure of being married to Princess Rampion."

"Princess Rampion?" I queried. "I don't think I've met her."

"You probably haven't," Princess Lyla replied. "After being cooped up in a tower most of her life, she can't stay in one place for too long. She's always traveling, leaving her handsome prince to run after their kids. Poor sod's too enamored with her to say anything, though you can't really blame him. She is beautiful," Princess Lyla conceded. She finished her drink and left the empty glass on a nearby table. "Want to see?"

"Sure," I agreed.

The magic mirror materialized in Lyla's hand. "Mirror, Mirror, answer me this one, whose hair shines beautiful as the sun?"

The silver face of the mirror melted and swirled, eventually reforming to show the image of a very beautiful woman. Her thick blond hair was short and unruly, which oddly accentuated her beauty. Even short, her hair glimmered in the light.

I studied the image. "Isn't she supposed to have long hair?"

Princess Lyla put the mirror away. "She hasn't let it grow out since it was all cut off," she explained.

A somewhat lovely woman with an adorable little boy in tow appeared before us, the silver circlet in her hair marking her as a queen. Unlike the princesses whose beauty paid homage to celestial beings, her beauty was far earthier. It made her seem less polished, which was its own kind of pretty. Her hair hung loosely behind her back, glittering like gold whenever it caught the sun.

She reached out her hand to take mine. "My most sincere congratulations, Queen Ella," she said in a warm, honeyed voice.

"Thank you," I managed to reply.

"We really haven't spent much time together," she continued in her sweet way. "We should take care to change that."

"I would like that," I replied honestly.

"As would I," the queen replied, then she turned away abruptly, her little son wobbling unsteadily to keep up with her.

I had been smiling after her, until I turned to see Princess Lyla glaring daggers at her back.

"What?"

"Do not trust that one," she hissed.

"Why not? She seems nice."

Lyla shook her head. "She's always telling stories and not one of them is true."

"How would you know?"

Lyla raised her eyebrows, questioning why I would challenge her on something she spoke as fact.

I raised my eyebrows back. It did seem rather extreme for a

person to be so evasive with the truth. "Who is she?" I asked, intending to later ask my prince about her.

The princess's mouth turned upward into something so unpleasant it couldn't be called a smile. "That's the thing," she replied. "She doesn't call herself by the name she grew up with, wherever that was."

"If you'd ask my stepfamily, then neither do I."

Lyla shrugged. "We know where you're from. Anyway, we just call her 'Mistress Miller' behind her back and 'Your Majesty' to her face."

"Miller?"

"She used to be the daughter of a miller. Became queen because she could spin straw into gold." The princess narrowed her eyes. "Or so *she* says!"

"King Rainn has a high regard for magic," I countered, finally realizing who she was talking about, "he studies it diligently and has all kinds of schools for magicals. Isn't that why magic is so strong in his kingdom? He would know if she spoke the truth."

Lyla shook her head, unconvinced. "No one knows how she pulled one over on the king," she replied, "but look at her eyes, there's no magic there. If anything, she keeps a thick wall between herself and everyone else. What does she have to hide?" Lyla shook her head. "She was unheard of before she married the king, and a magical unknown in Farthington...Something doesn't add up."

I thought of how I was once nameless, how the first step in Madame's dominance over me began with stripping away my identity by calling me something she wanted me to be.

With a jolt I realized that the prince had a habit of never calling anyone by their name, though I'm sure he knew them well enough. He simply called someone over with a gesture or "you," "guard," "valet." "Captain." "My love." The captain had a name once, before it was taken from him so he could be what he was expected to be. I thought of what Alaryx had told me about his brother in parting. Perhaps this had something to do with it.

As for me, I'd been called Ella with love, Cinderwench with malice, and CinderElla without knowing. I thought of the pride that name brought me, of the way it connected me to my people, a sacred trust, a shared dream. I thought of how each name had shaped me, had spoken to who I was or was expected to be.

"Why wouldn't she want anyone to know about her?" I wondered out loud.

The princess's smile turned triumphant. "Exactly!" She took another drink from a passing tray. "So, how are you enjoying your big day?" she asked offhandedly, not really expecting an answer.

"I still can't believe it's real," I told her anyway.

My gaze moved to my prince—my *king*—sitting proud and regal on the dais. Even from this distance, his nearness nearly overwhelmed me. I let my gaze linger on him.

Princess Lyla followed my line of sight and watched her cousin with me for a while. Finally, she dropped some of her bluster and commented, "Married almost four years and still in love with him as from the start."

I blushed despite myself. "Yes," I confirmed simply.

The princess shifted her gaze to study me. "You're really lucky, you know that?"

"Pardon?" I asked dumbly.

What was she talking about? I knew she didn't envy my crown, she would get hers in time, and I had nothing by way of looks or personality to rival hers. Considering that we'd all been through some thing or other until we'd found our princes, it didn't seem that my story would make me luckier than any other. True, Madame had never tried to kill me physically, but she had tried to reduce me to a level that could be worse than death because she had stripped away every last bit of my dignity until I was hardly even a no one. That was why I took nothing at the palace for granted, why I appreciated everyone and everything, why I rarely disagreed with the prince. Who was I to reject the privilege he'd given me? And weren't we all lucky, living as we were in our happily ever afters?

"Rampion and her hair, Alaina and her sleep, the list goes on," Princess Lyla elaborated. "Do you know I haven't eaten an apple in over five years, that I have a fear of wearing combs in my hair?" Her black eyes blazed like burning coals. "Our curses were broken, but the magic left deep scars. Yet we are not allowed to be anything but happy in our perceived faerytale endings."

I struggled to say something, anything to sweeten the bitterness, but I had no words of comfort to give. I was fairly new to this myself, but my relationship with the prince didn't sound like what she was describing. Wasn't she happy with her handsome Prince Daimyon? They certainly looked like a wonderful couple, and he was always cordial and genial whenever I saw him.

"It isn't like that for you," she continued, tugging up the layers of my dress to reveal the new pair of Castarrean glass slippers made special for this day. "And then there's your Prince Charming," she concluded, and she actually sounded jealous.

She *was* jealous, I suddenly realized. Not just of me, but of all those she mocked in our ever afters. Her life didn't appear that different from any of ours, that any one of us had something that she didn't. I couldn't tell if her jealousy was part of who she was or if there was something else about "ever after" that I was still unaware of.

Neither of us knew then what I know now, but it doesn't really matter. That my ever after was soon to be shattered didn't take away from the dark green envy snaking like poisonous vines over Lyla's heart.

"Didn't Prince Daimyon awaken you with true love's kiss?" I asked her incredulously.

The princess turned her gaze on me, and it seemed then that the fire in her eyes had dimmed. "Did he?" she questioned. "It's what they say, but either way what good does that do me?"

"What do you mean?" I countered.

"If we already know this is true love," she explained, "then where's the mystery? Where's the courtship? Where's the passion of pursuit?"

I stared at her dumbly. What was she saying?

"Why try at all, if we already know we're supposed to be together?" she sounded out slowly. "How strong can anything not cared for, not forged, really be?"

And then I understood. Princess Lyla had found her true love, but she was not happy. Why should she be if the man took advantage of what they already knew? Why should she be if he didn't notice her for who she was, as anyone but this physical manifestation of his destined true love? Once they were bound together, why check again to make sure she was still there at all? In many ways, I knew exactly how she felt. I knew what it was to be overlooked, ignored, forgotten, but that had been before. It never happened here at the palace. Did it?

I put a sympathetic arm around her, and she leaned into me for a short minute.

"Prince Daimyon is a fool," I whispered to her.

"I know it," she whispered back, "but that doesn't change anything. Or how I feel about him."

Very quickly, she pulled herself together, and the blaze of fire and defiance returned to her black eyes. We continued to meander around the celebration, but I was soon slipping away from her, needing more than ever to seek a few minutes of quiet to sort out my tangle of thoughts.

I had been so safely enveloped in my ever after that I had never once thought about what came next. But isn't that what happily ever after is about? That there's no need to worry about what happens next? I brooded under my pear tree a while, somber but not down, thoughtfully plying the pond water to play with my goldfish. I wished so much that Marie was there.

And then there she was, hovering before me like she'd been there all along.

"Grandmère!" I greeted her excitedly.

"Ella, dear, you look lovely," she said, her eyes shining with the pride of a real grandmother. And why not, hadn't she been responsible for raising me up to where I was today?

"Please, sit with me, Grandmère," I begged. "It's so good to see you again."

Marie's eyes darted around the garden nervously. Surely, she didn't think the king was lurking somewhere in the shadows, waiting for her feet to touch the ground so he could pounce? The very notion was absurd, from all angles.

"I cannot stay," Marie said. "I only wanted to see how you were."

I raised my hand to the gold crown that adorned my head. It was one of my favorites from the new ones, the gold a curlicue of vines sprouting small purple diamond flowers all the way around.

"Do you like it?" I asked shyly.

"I love it," Marie assured me with a warm smile.

"Grandmère," I asked slowly, "did you know the people call me CinderElla?"

Marie's eyes danced as if set in motion by the magic sparks in her wand. "It's a lovely name, isn't it?" She took my hand in hers and a magical warmth spread from her body throughout mine. "I hope it gives you strength," she continued too seriously, "for what lies ahead."

Before I could respond or ask about her odd mood, something caught her attention and her head shot up. She shimmered, as if ready to disappear. Seconds later, the captain came into view.

He stopped short when he saw her. "Good afternoon,

Grandmère," he said, his expression guarded, but his voice respectful and sincere.

"It's nice to see you again, Captain," Marie replied, glancing from him to me, then back again.

"The king is asking after his queen," the captain explained.

Marie nodded, and I stood to follow after him, not quite ready to let her go just yet. If my husband's fear of magic was true, then how long would it be before I saw her again?

"Take care of yourself, Ella," Marie told me. "Take care to be yourself," she added. Then with a look at the captain, "And you, keep her safe."

The captain nodded soberly. "Always," he promised.

With one last look, she was gone, and there was nothing left for me to do but follow the captain back to my life.

That night, or rather, sometime around dawn when the party finally tapered off, the king came into my room with two glasses of wine and a large smile.

I dutifully took one sip and almost spat it across the room. "What is this?" I asked.

The king smiled and took his time carefully tasting from his cup. "It's a bottle I found from the year my parents were married," he explained. "I thought it appropriate for tonight."

I took another drink and couldn't help from screwing my face up in disgust. It tasted horrible, even worse than whatever he'd been bringing me until now. "It's not my favorite," I said carefully.

The king pouted adorably. "Don't say that." He drank his wine slowly, rolling it around his tongue. "I'm tasting cherries," he said thoughtfully, "are you tasting cherries?" He made a show of swallowing and licking his lips.

Raising the glass to mine, I thought his mention of cherries ridiculous, but I didn't want to say so. I took another small sip and almost gagged, but I managed to keep it together and nod in agreement. The wine didn't taste like cherries. Frankly, it was even more terrible than the others he'd brought, like something bitter hidden beneath the taste of too much cinnamon and spice, as if trying to cover up for something rotten. But who was I to say that about a wine bottled in such a significant year. None of the past few years would have been possible without it.

Alexander was enjoying his wine, and if he wanted it to taste like cherries, then so be it. I nodded, and forced myself to sip along beside him, until the glass was drained and we went to bed.

THE SECOND CLUE

The next morning, I woke up feeling woozy. I could not hope that the nausea and dizziness were from pregnancy, for my body had recently let me know otherwise. Instead, I credited it to the day of nonstop feasting, the cartwheeling emotions, and the whirl of changes and preparations that had consumed our lives the past month. I would have liked to stay in bed until late afternoon, taking my breakfast quietly in my room while I watched the sun shift and play with shadows as the day went on.

However, I was now a queen, and the palace and kingdom were still celebrating my new crown. Javotte had told me that all shops in the city were closed for a full week to mirror the seven days of festivals and revelry within the palace. Thanks to the money I'd given her, she and the captain had been able to persuade a physician to travel regularly to tend to her mother. She was doing much better, and her daughter, now in training, could do much more for her.

All this, and more, she reported to me that morning as I

determinedly focused on standing while she dressed me in one of the gowns we'd altered. I tried to shake out my feet, tried to focus my vision as the room teetered around me.

"Is everything all right, Your Majesty?" Javotte's concerned face suddenly swam into view. "Your skin is very pale."

I tried to give her my most reassuring smile. "Yes, thank you," I replied. "I'm just tired, that's all."

Javotte frowned at me. "No one would mind if Her Majesty missed—"

"Absolutely not, Javotte," I countered. "The king expects me by his side and I will be there. I just need to sit a few minutes. A nice tea would help as well."

A chair appeared behind me and the hot drink was in my hands before I even sat down. I took my time, mainly because I was feeling so dizzy I didn't trust myself to drink without spilling all over my dress. I finally forced the rest of the liquid down and did feel better enough to stand and join everyone else.

The day's entertainment was going to take place on the wide lawns of the palace. The sport arena had been rebuilt in the grass along with the stands for onlookers. A special box placed front and center was draped with the king's standard. From there, we had a perfect, unblocked view of the field below, where feats of strength and courage were set to take place, just as they had on that fateful festival over four years ago. After almost a handful of years at the palace, I knew what to expect, though this would be the first time that the prince, now a king, would be unable to compete as it was deemed unseemly.

What I didn't know, and was only to find out too late, was that there was something else planned for that day. Something special for the king's coronation. Something I wouldn't like very much.

I had never seen a dragon before, especially not up close, though I'd heard enough about them from the prince whenever he chose to regale me about the years before we married when he had cut his teeth as protector of the kingdom slaying dragons, ogres, gargoyles, and all other sorts of fearsome beasts. My imagination wasn't keen on horror stories, but when the prince told them, they inevitably left me smiling because he always came out the dashing hero. No matter that I had a magical faery sword, if a dragon ever snuck into the palace, I'd immediately dive behind my brave and valiant prince. Or the captain. I could trust him to keep me alive. He'd promised as much to Marie.

The dragon was saved for the end, a fitting conclusion for an already spectacular display of valor. The crowd murmured appreciatively as the shiny cage bearing a mid-size dragon creaked into the arena. Keeping silver spears level at the beast, a pack of knights opened the cage and roughly guided the dragon out. The crowd fell suddenly silent and I clutched my husband's hand tightly.

"Don't be afraid, love," he said without moving his gaze from the dragon, his eyes gleaming in anticipation. "I won't let him near you."

"I know," I replied, forcing myself to lighten my grip.

"The metal's anyway enchanted," he continued, his lips curling at the distasteful word, "the silver's just for show."

"Yes, of course," I agreed.

I wasn't really afraid, but a sudden wave of nausea made me feel ready to throw up. That was the only reason I'd grabbed his hand. I turned my focus inward and, by order of the queen, commanded my stomach to behave. Good thing I hadn't eaten anything that morning or it may not have.

On the other side of the arena, five knights, armor gleaming, weapons glinting, rode in on fearsome black stallions. Seeing the dragon, the horses didn't run, but pawed angrily at the dirt as if they too were ready to fight the beast now tied to the ground with enchanted silver coated chains, restricting its movement so it couldn't fly or attack the hushed, expectant crowd.

For some reason, I couldn't take my eyes off that dragon. It was a beautiful creature, deep blue and purple, with soulful orange eyes clearly visible from our raised box in the stands. I didn't pay attention to anything else going on in the arena, my gaze transfixed on that poor creature's eyes.

I knew what dragons could do. I'd heard of the villages they'd burned down, of the men they'd eaten, but I couldn't reconcile stories from the war with the supposed beast before me. This dragon seemed sad and lonely, its bright, sun-colored gaze curious and confused at its treatment.

"Why are its wings so small?" I whispered to my husband.

"Not much room to grow in a cage," he whispered back.

So this dragon had been raised in captivity. For how long? It had to be four or five years old at least. Did the prince order its capture as a baby so it could be part of the celebrations today? Someone had to anticipate this day if the dragon had been caged before its wings fully developed. Spots appeared before my eyes, and I had to focus my attention to keep them away.

Without realizing when, the fight started between the knights and the dragon. The king leaned forward in unabashed excitement at the scene below. Surely for him, this was a return and salute to his glory days, when the kingdom sang his praises not for the laws he'd pass, but for the might of his will and the aim of his sword. His face gleamed with a vicious, anticipatory light as the five knights battled the flightless dragon on the trampled grass.

A silver chain wrapped multiple times around its jaw kept the dragon from breathing fire, but that didn't stop it from using its spiked tail to whack the knights against the walls of the arena. Despite the numbers, it really wasn't a fair fight, and it was only a matter of time before the knights had the dragon pinned down and cowering before the points of their lances.

The lead knight raised a sword in victory, then turned toward our box and kneeled to the king. The crowd took up a chant, which I only realized too late as a call to behead the dragon. I looked again at his large orange eyes and pity overwhelmed me. Maybe the dragon wouldn't have burned villages or eaten men if we had shown it a little kindness. Maybe it would have. There was no way to know.

The king stood and spread his arms, silencing the crowd as he gazed with triumph at his brave knights below. After a moment's hesitation, he raised his arms in the air and the crowd erupted in cheers. This being my first dragon fight, I had no idea what any of this meant.

I found out rather quickly.

The knight who'd raised his sword to the king bowed and turned back to the dragon, walking carefully toward it to keep the crowd at the edge of its seat. Then, with exaggerated slowness, he raised his silver sword, his blade catching the sun's rays in a flicker of light, before he brought it swiftly down and removed the dragon's head.

I had seen blood before. I had seen animals die. I had killed chickens myself when I was enslaved to Madame. But I had never seen such a beautiful creature needlessly robbed of life, and I was unprepared for the muffled, almost human cry that emerged from its smoky throat when it realized its days were over. I was unprepared for the deep hurt in its eyes, for the feeling of betrayal.

Without thinking, I stood too quickly. I swayed against my husband's chair as I tried to steady myself. The king threw me a quick glance, assessing my pale face, my unfocused eyes, and lazily raised a hand to make sure I wouldn't fall on him.

He beckoned the captain over. "The queen is unwell," he said without any discernible emotion. "Pleases see her to her rooms."

I searched blindly for the captain's arm before suddenly feeling his strength holding me up. "I'm here, Your Majesty," he whispered, as he helped me walk down from the stands and away from the bloody arena.

We had hardly reached the stone walls of the palace before I had to stop. I leaned against the wall, breathing heavily. The captain frowned at me, concerned.

"I could—" he began, but I cut him off.

"I can walk," I insisted. "In a minute."

The captain's frown only deepened. "What happened now, in the arena, it upset Her Majesty?"

Anger flared strong enough to fill my lungs with breath. "How can we allow such a terrible thing?"

"Does the queen wish for the dragon to live so it can be caged for another fight? The king acted mercifully in choosing to kill it."

"Mercy would be never knowing the inside of a cage," I retorted.

The captain tilted his head and eyed me with undisguised amusement. "Dragons are not entirely innocent," he reminded me, as if I could forget the scars I'd seen them cause, "they destroy crops and villages, harm people..."

"I know, I know," I said shortly. "But I am curious, how many villages did *this* dragon burn? How many people did *he* eat?"

A short pause.

"None, Your Majesty."

"And yet we killed it, for sport." My breath was running out too quickly. "We shackle its jaw and stunt its beautiful wings, all for sport."

The captain furrowed his brow, narrowing his gaze as he assessed my words. He didn't seem pleased with them, and I could guess why. He'd been with the prince when he'd slayed dragons and ogres and gargoyles in protection of the kingdom. His whole life, he'd been trained to attack first and never doubt it later. Why should he have any pity now, especially as he knew and saw much more than I had what kind of damage a dragon could do?

"Her Majesty is unwell," he concluded finally, as if that was the only reason for my whitened face, my tumbling stomach, my unexpectedly noncompliant behavior today.

My hand shot to steady myself against the wall as another wave of dizziness washed over me. I clenched my teeth, forcing my mind to fight against my rebelling body. "I may be unwell, Captain," I squeezed out, "but I am not entirely wrong."

I'm sure he replied with something, but I didn't hear him. I was only conscious long enough to see him spring toward me, before I collapsed.

I awoke in my bed some hours later, and caught a glimpse of stars brightening the sky through my window. I stirred quietly, turning enough to see Javotte sitting in a chair beside my bed. She looked frazzled, unkempt, so unlike the Javotte who'd served me faithfully all these years.

"Your Majesty," she exclaimed upon seeing my half-opened eyes. "You're awake!"

I worked my tongue around my parched mouth and Javotte gently lifted my head to bring it closer to the cup of cool water she was raising to me. I took in a few drops then closed my lips. It hurt to swallow. It hurt to raise my head.

"The king?" I rasped out, more a shape than a sound.

"His Majesty was here, but he's since gone to see after your guests," Javotte explained. "The king held your hand the entire time he was here, as if his strength would be enough to heal you."

A small smile tugged at my lips, but I was too weak to set it free. My husband, my king, ever my Prince Charming. I hoped I hadn't scared him too much. I hoped I hadn't ruined the day for him. I closed my eyes and pictured him sitting beside me. As I drifted back to sleep, I hoped his face would be the first I'd see in the morning.

~

His face was not the first I saw when I next woke up; rather, it was the worried, haggard expression commanding the captain's face. Although he'd kept his beard from that day when we snuck into the capital, it looked overgrown now, as if he hadn't cared for it in days.

The sky was just beginning to lighten through the windows behind him. If it was just morning, then I'd only been asleep a few hours. It felt like much longer. My body was tired still.

He sprang to the side of my bed when he saw my eyes open and took my hand in his without asking. I knew, somewhere in the darkness of my consciousness, that something wasn't right if he was clutching my hand so desperately, as if he were my final lifeline between this world and the next.

I wanted to say something to him, to ask after my king and for forgiveness for fainting, for the fright I must have given him. I wanted to reassure him that I would be all right. That though I was small, I was not too weak to fight back. To remind him how much I'd survived until now. But I felt too tired to speak.

Nothing was said as I drifted back to sleep, against his urgings for me to stay awake.

~

A familiar warmth burning steadily through my veins pried my eyes open.

My mind felt stuffed, my body heavy, but as the warmth spread throughout my body those feelings slowly began to dissipate the way a thick morning fog flees the sun.

Someone was holding my hand. The captain? I turned my head. Marie!

"Grandmère," I mouthed.

"Ella, dear," she replied in a hush, raising one of her hands to stroke my sun burnt hair away from my face.

Something didn't feel right, and it took me some time to realize that it was Marie. There wasn't anything wrong with her, but she'd been rather adamant about avoiding the palace, and now she was here with me, in my very room. She must have seen the confused look on my face.

"Matteus called for me," she explained. "You were unconscious for three days, and the physicians couldn't figure out what was wrong."

Who's Matteus? I wanted to know. But though I was already feeling better, my throat didn't yet have the power to speak. I relaxed into my pillows, and lay quietly as Marie held my hand and hummed something that sounded like a lullaby I should have known, but didn't.

Finally, I felt strong enough to sit up and did so with Marie's help.

My bedchamber was empty, save Marie. The fire was well fed, the room was tidy and warm, a tray of food had been optimistically left for me on a nearby table.

"Where...is...every...one?" I scratched out.

"The captain sent them off to bed when he knew I was coming," Marie explained as she prepared me a hot drink from the tray. "Though Heaven knows he's barely slept in days."

I could only imagine how things must have been if the captain had been forced to call for Marie. How did he feel greeting her under my pear tree, not long after he'd been charged with looking after me in that very spot? How should I feel knowing Marie had to come, even after I'd promised to look after myself?

"I'm sorry," I told her.

"Don't be," she said sadly. "This wasn't your doing."

"I was sick," I protested. "Over three days."

Marie shook her head. "Something evil was attacking your blood," she explained. "Your body needed time to fight it."

With that, she rubbed my hand again, and I suspected that the magic in her touch deserved most of the credit. It didn't seem likely that a frail, tiny girl such as myself could fight this supposed evil alone. Our talk was cut short when a figure silently appeared in my room.

"The queen's awake," the captain said, glancing uneasily at Marie as if to confirm this was lasting.

"She's awake," Marie confirmed, and even I could feel the relief flooding through him.

"When you—at the wall—then you fell—" he stammered. He stopped himself short and I could see him pulling himself together, could see the control and discipline returning to his frame. "Thank Heaven Her Majesty is well."

I reached out my hand to him, and after a moment of confused hesitation, he stepped forward to take it, his strong, reliable hand quickly swallowing my little one.

"Thank you, Captain," I said. "You are a worthy friend."

The captain blushed and took his hand back. "I was only doing my duty to Her Majesty," he said modestly.

"Don't belittle what you've done, Captain," I admonished. "How is the king?"

"The king sleeps," the captain replied, keeping his features carefully composed. "He's been very worried," he added, after too long a pause. "I will hurry to tell him the good news."

Marie jumped up before the captain had a chance to make it to the door. "Walk me out, Captain?" she requested.

The captain didn't seem eager to let her leave so soon, but he nodded his assent.

"Don't go, Grandmère," I said to her, though I knew she was

trying to avoid the king. Surely, he wouldn't be upset with her for bringing me back to life. Surely, she'd now be able to visit whenever she pleased.

"I must," Marie replied. "But we'll see each again, soon. Javotte sleeps in a chair just outside the door, we'll wake her as we leave."

It was mere seconds later that Javotte rushed into my room, and without thought for propriety grabbed my hand, kissed it, and raised it to her tear stained face.

"Your Majesty, I was so worried," she blubbered. "Praise Heaven! What a wonderful day! What a blessed day! I'm so glad. So very, very glad!"

I let her carry on, caring even less about propriety in the face of such concern over my wellbeing. I could have died under Madame's watch and no one would have noticed. Well, perhaps they would have caught on once their tea hadn't been served on time, or their baths weren't drawn. Even then, I wasn't sure my stepfamily would have bothered to give me a proper burial. They would have either left me to the scavenging animals, or carelessly laid me to rest atop my mother.

Four years at the palace, and I was still getting used to what it felt like to be loved by someone who wasn't my mother, to be cared for by someone who didn't share my blood. Only now do I fully understand how my stepmother had beaten me in ways that went far deeper than physical bruising. Thinking on it, I'm certain that's why I chose to be so blind to reality for so long.

Javotte only pulled herself together once we heard the door click open, followed by the blur of my husband rushing to my bed. He stared down at me, his face a whirlwind of emotions, I thought were shock, relief, and gratitude. As it turned out, I was only right about one of those.

Within minutes, he had climbed onto my bed and pulled my head to his chest where I could hear the strong beating of his heart. I settled in against him, gaining strength from his love. And so we let the morning pass, me resting against him, him holding me tight.

I spent the rest of the day in bed, though Javotte did make me get up briefly a few times, to "get my land legs back under me." The celebrations for the coronation carried on without me, and I could almost hear the revelry of the assembled guests reverberating through the stone walls. It was only later in the day that I was finally able to convince Javotte to throw open the windows and let the fresh air in.

I had visitors all throughout the day, which would have been tiring, but each friendly face gave me a much-needed boost of energy and determination to get better. First from all was Princess Lyla, who rushed in with pure and untainted joy all over her face. After she left with a promise to later return, Javotte sat some more by my side.

"Don't you have things to take care of?" I urged her, feeling guilty that she was wasting so much time with me, making small talk, running about the room trying to guess in advance what I might wish for.

"Her Majesty is here, where else would I be?" she asked.

"Somewhere, anywhere," I replied vaguely.

Javotte clicked her tongue in tune with the clip of her scissors as she continued to dissect more of my unnecessary dresses.

Alexander came by again for a short while in between a hunt and dinner, laughing merrily at the idea that he would not have time to change his clothes and everyone would have to accept it because he was the king. He brought with him a cup of wine, to "toast my good health," but when he raised it to my lips, my stomach recoiled at the too-familiar smell and I just couldn't force myself to drink it.

The corners of his mouth tugged downward, but he kept his smile intact, throwing back his own glass of wine with a hearty toast to the future.

It was quiet for a while after he left, then Princess Lyla returned with Queen Alaina and Princess Kiara in tow, all three insisting that, "We'd rather be here, because it's no fun there without you."

With them came servants wheeling trays overflowing with food from the banquet downstairs, and though I couldn't eat much, I enjoyed our dinner together.

After they left, the king came again to bid me goodnight, then Javotte sat with me a while more until I ordered her off to bed. Oddly enough, being sick yielded one of my best days in the palace, if only because it proved to me that I finally had people in my life who cared.

Although my day had been full of visitors, I wasn't tired, and even felt my strength returning with each passing hour. So it was that late at night, alone and with nothing else to do, I found myself bent over one of the dresses I had insisted in helping Javotte alter, humming the pixie flower tune to myself in rhythm with my needle.

"Surely someone here knows how to do that, Your Majesty," a deep voice rumbled at me, surprising me enough to jerk the needle out of line.

I looked up to see the captain watching me from the other end of the room. How long had he been standing there?

"Captain, you scared me," I said unnecessarily.

"I apologize, Your Majesty," he said. "I only stopped in to see how you were faring."

"Is this still part of your duty?" I teased, glad to see his face flush a deep red in response.

The captain cleared his throat. "I was hoping, Your Majesty, if it's not too forward," he bumbled. "I wanted to visit as a friend," he finally admitted.

I didn't hesitate at all. I waved him over to a chair near me, motioning him to sit. "Of course, Cap," I said easily. "It's been a while."

Even with his bold request, the captain hesitated, not sitting until I insisted he take the chair or leave. He sat uneasily, suddenly unsure of what to say or where to look.

I figured it was only right that I help my friend relax. "I used to do this all the time," I told him, gesturing to the dress in my hands. "There's something soothing about letting my hands take over. Helps clear the mind."

The captain shrugged, conceding the point. "I'm sure it will look nice, however you fix it."

That brought me up short. "How did you know?" I asked.

"It's my duty to know," he replied with a smile.

"No, it isn't," I insisted.

His smile only grew. "It isn't," he agreed. "But from the second day of the celebrations, there's been something familiar about your wardrobe. You've done a good job changing them," he hastily reassured, "but I wouldn't be very good at my job if I didn't notice the finer details. There's also the matter of Javotte's sudden ability to overpay a doctor to see after her ailing mother, and her sister's new apprenticeship."

"I'm sure there's a reasonable explanation for all of it," I said, though there was no purpose in denying his knowledge of the truth.

Rather, it seemed I would never be able to hide much from the captain. I would only understand later that it wasn't because I was careless around him, but because he was extra careful when it came to me.

"I don't see anything unreasonable about the conclusions I've made so far. If anything, it's important for a queen to think bigger than a princess," the captain said, and I had to duck my head to hide my pleased expression.

Regaining myself, I looked back over at him. "Tell me, Cap,

what's been going on around the palace while I've been confined to my rooms?"

The captain shrugged my question away. "I can't say you've missed anything you haven't seen before," he replied.

"I'm glad the festivities could carry on without me," I joked.

"Not entirely," the captain replied seriously. "All have been singing your praises and toasting your new crown. The people rejoice at their good fortune and thank Heaven for their new monarchs."

"Alexander will make a great king," I agreed.

"*You* will make a great queen," the captain fiercely insisted.

"You flatter me," I said, taken aback by his surety.

"You don't believe me," he said matter-of-factly.

"*You* wrote those notes," I shrugged in reply, but the gesture said as much as any words could.

Madame and her daughters never missed a chance to remind me of how unremarkable I was. Despite all I'd been blessed with, I didn't think a crown could change that. Sure, there were things I could do in my position, but there was nothing to distinguish me above anyone else. My mother, for example, would always be the kindest person I ever knew.

The captain frowned and fell silent a moment, so I feared he wouldn't speak anymore. Then the deep rumble of his voice rose up through his throat as he unfurled one of his stories.

"Once a mother duck found an oddly large egg near her pond," he began. "She pushed it next to the others in her nest, and when they hatched first, she sat on it still."

I raised my eyebrows at the captain, unsure if he was serious or not in telling me this child's tale. But the captain wasn't looking at me, not exactly.

"Finally, the egg cracked, but something was different. This duckling's body was covered in darkened scales. His eyes were red, his feet taloned, he hadn't a bill but a snout."

"Captain, don't mock me," I interrupted as soon as I realized he was talking about a dragon.

The captain blinked at me, recalling his focus from some other place. "My mother used to tell me this story," he said seriously, "and I thought to share it with you, as a friend."

He seemed genuine, so I nodded my permission and went back to my work.

"Though the mother duck tried to show the odd duckling much love, it didn't protect him from the mockery of others. Soon, he grew ashamed of all that made him different."

As the story unfolded, the captain's voice deepened. It was warm and comforting, a thick wool blanket for a cold, sleet filled day. I listened closely, the needle idle in my hand.

"Fearing the danger, he posed her ducklings, the mother duck sent him away. The dragon left with a heavy heart, and soon stumbled upon a beaver, gnawing and shouting angrily at a stubborn tree trunk that had fallen over him. The dragon smashed up the trunk with his spiked tail and the beaver escaped. Then promptly dove into a hole.

"'I only wanted to help,' the dragon spoke to the ground. 'On my honor as a duck.'

"A muffled giggle, then the beaver dared raise his furry brown head. He scurried out and stretched to his full height, tall as the dragon's knees.

"'No one thinks I can build a dam,' he confessed. He glanced ruefully at the splintered trunk. 'It seems they were right.'

"The dragon knew what it was to be teased for not being able to do things like the others.

"'Do you really believe you can build a dam?' he asked the beaver.

"The beaver nodded his head fiercely.

"'I believe it, too, so I will help you,' the dragon announced.

"'Only beavers can build dams,' the beaver replied, 'but

because you freed me and believed in me, I will be there for you if you ever need help.'

"They parted ways, and the dragon walked in the forest until night came. He stopped when he suddenly heard a small cry. He rummaged through the foliage until he saw a small baby robin cowering on a rock.

"'What worries you, little robin?' the dragon asked.

"'I fell out of the tree and hurt my wing,' the frightened robin told the dragon. 'I can't fly and I'm afraid I will be eaten.'

"'Rest on my back,' the dragon said. 'Tomorrow, we will look for your mother.'

"'Is this a trick?' the robin asked suspiciously.

"'No trick,' the dragon replied. 'On my honor as a duck.'

"The robin giggled. 'That's an odd thing to say.' But he hopped upon the dragon's back, and slept in the safety of his wings. The next morning, the dragon helped the little bird find his tree, then lifted him up to his mother.

"'Thank you, thank you,' came the chorus of chirps from the robin's family. 'If we can ever help you, then you need only call.'

"The dragon went merrily on his way, lost in thought about his new friends and all the things he could do with his silly-looking body. Thusly, he was distracted when a thick net fell on him from above and trapped him to the forest floor. His efforts to get out only entangled him further. He roared and roared, and in his cries were a call to the beaver and a call to the robins. It wasn't very long before they came to him.

"The beaver immediately gnawed the rope that kept the dragon pinned to the ground. Then the robins took the ends in their feet and flew upward, lifting it off the dragon.

"'Thank you for saving me,' the dragon said to each of his friends.

"'Why didn't you use your fire to burn through the rope?' the beaver wanted to know.

"'Why didn't you use your wings to lift up from under the net?' asked the robins.

"'Because my fire is too dangerous to breathe, and my wings are too long. It is why I am such an ugly duckling,' the dragon explained.

"The beaver started to laugh. 'You're not an ugly duckling!' he called.

"'You're a dragon!' the robins exclaimed.

"The beaver took the dragon to the river, where he showed him the reflection he had avoided looking at most of his life. Once the dragon understood that he was not a duck, he didn't seem so ugly after all. Heartened, he stretched out his long black wings and took off into the sky, rising higher and higher, straight through the clouds. Up there, he saw the biggest surprise of all, a whole flock of dragons just like him!

"Finally, he found his place, and he was happy."

The captain's voice faded out and the room fell silent save for the low crackle of the fire. I finally looked up and noticed him studying me, his dark brown eyes searching for something. It was only after he left that I understood what he wanted me to know but couldn't properly say.

The captain never saw me as a Cinderwench. Being queen was something he always believed I could be, and what's more than that, he believed I could be a good queen. He was reminding me that I can see hunger and suffering in others, because I have known it myself. I care about the sick, because I have known loss. I could be generous with my kindness and compassion, even though it was scarcely afforded me. I was in my rightful place at the palace.

But what about all those other things? Did I have the fiery heart of a dragon? Wings large enough to soar above the clouds?

He seemed to think so.

He seemed to think that those, among other things, would give me strength enough to raise up others beside me.

But I didn't understand that until later. At the time, however loath I was to break the spell the captain's voice had woven, I raised my still full glass of wine to him. "A toast to your story, Cap," I said. "Though forgive me for not drinking, for I don't think I can stomach this right now."

The captain gently took the glass from my hand. "It would be a shame to let a good toast go to waste," he said. He took a brief sip, then his face curdled and he spat the wine back into the cup.

"You don't taste cherries either?" I giggled, feeling strangely validated that the captain had done to the wine what I'd so often wanted to do.

"What is this?" the captain asked, furiously wiping the back of his mouth with his hand.

"Wine," I replied.

"This isn't wine," the captain countered.

"Of course it is," I retorted. "It's a bottle from the year the king's parents were married."

"His parents were married," the captain echoed distantly. He shook his head definitively. "His Majesty would never drink anything that tasted like this."

I shrugged. "He brought it here himself, and drank a glass here himself. He says it tastes like cherries, but I think it too bitter and over spiced."

A flurry of conflicting thoughts warred across the captain's face. "Like cherries?" he repeated slowly. Suddenly, he snapped to attention and his eyes narrowed at the cup. He picked it up and sniffed suspiciously. "Was this cup by your side the entire day, Your Majesty?" he demanded to know.

"No," I replied, "My husband brought it, I couldn't drink it, so it was left here."

"And there were a number of visitors here today?" the captain thundered, holding court as if he were judge, jury, and executioner.

"Yes," I confirmed.

"So any number of people could have touched this cup from when it was brought until now!" he concluded triumphantly.

I shook my head. "I don't think so."

"But can you be sure, Your Majesty?"

I nodded. "The first time His Majesty brought me this vintage was the night of the coronation. It tasted bitter then, too. He always brings wine with him, though none nearly as bitter as this."

This brought the captain up short. He looked dumbfounded, then upset. Though he was careful to keep his face impassive, it was obvious that his mind was whirring.

"Cap? Captain?" I asked tentatively, when the silence had gone on too long.

He snapped his attention back to me. "Are you all right?" he sighed. "I hope I didn't upset you."

"Not at all," I waved away his apology, "though I would like to know what that was all about."

The captain nodded his head. "You shall soon enough, Your Majesty."

Then he walked over to my night table and took the cup beside the pitcher of water. He poured over some wine from the glass, then strode purposefully over to the fireplace where he poured out the wine, before dashing the actual glass against the inner bricks and leaving the pieces to burn. There was a flash of green when the wine hit the fire, so quick it was easy to doubt if it had really been there at all.

He came back over to me and knelt before my chair, hesitating before taking each of my hands in his. I wasn't sure if this gesture was still as a friend, or not. I wasn't sure if, as queen, I should be allowing such liberties. I was sure that I was too confused to know just what to do.

"Ella—Your Majesty," he corrected. "If ever you don't taste the cherries, don't drink the wine."

I nodded at him, still befuddled. He raised one hand, as if to touch my face, then seemed to remember himself. He jumped back and resumed his regular, impeccable posture.

"Sleep well, my queen," he said, snapping out a perfect bow.

He pivoted and left the room, leaving me to wonder about his thoroughly confusing behavior.

THE THIRD CLUE

I rejoined the coronation celebrations on the last day, just in time to see most of our guests off.

Just before that, however, my life shattered.

It seemed that all the time I was forced to spend in my chambers recovering did my mind some good, because no sooner had I emerged, ready to rejoin the ceremonies that last evening, then an idea hit and I redirected my course from the banquet hall to Sir Percival's office, knowing he'd still be there, because he almost always was.

I waltzed in without bothering to be announced. "Trade schools," I declared with triumph.

"Pardon, Your Majesty?" Sir Percival asked.

He rushed up to bow but kept one eye on the papers on his desk. I wondered briefly if he dared treat Alexander with the impertinence of divided attention.

"Eyes here, Sir Percival," I commanded. Only after he quickly obeyed did I continue. "The solution to our problem with the poor. We establish trade schools for them to attend."

I didn't have to demand Sir Percival's attention now, though it was plain he wasn't entirely sold on the idea. Yet.

"I'm not sure I understand, Your Majesty," he said as delicately as he could.

Spurred on by my idea, I paced the room to keep control of my sudden rush of energy. "There are poor villages without craftsmen enough," I began, "and there are poor men without craft enough. There are men without work. There is work without anyone to do it. The simple solution is to train those men and women so both issues will be resolved. Bridges will be fixed, the sick will get their care, anyone else, their families and towns must look after them."

Sir Percival shook his head. "Perhaps Her Majesty isn't considering the cost to the Crown in setting up such fine schools," he said.

"Fiddlesticks the cost!" I exclaimed in exasperation. "Must I do all the thinking for you?"

"Your Majesty, just the coronation alone..." Sir Percival left his sentence to finish itself. "Where do you think the money comes from? Even for the gown you're wearing now?"

I pulled up short midstep. "I'll have you know, good sir, that while this dress is new, the materials to make it are not."

"I'm not sure I understand Her Majesty," Sir Percival stuttered again.

I really hadn't meant to tell anyone else, Javotte and the Captain were already enough. With each person that knew, I risked the king eventually finding out. I didn't think he'd take to the news well, as he'd been most decidedly set on my designing of a new wardrobe. But once I let it slip, I had to explain. If only so Sir Percival wouldn't muddle things up by asking around about it.

I sighed. "When we moved quarters, I realized just how many dresses I have. So I took apart the better ones and remade them instead of ordering up brand new ones."

Sir Percival didn't answer. He simply stared at me in shock.

"Back to these trade schools," I resumed my pacing, hoping my enthusiasm would help pull him back on topic. "There must be something we can figure out. If the Crown must build them and not the villages and cities themselves, then the Crown must get something in return to make it worthwhile. Don't you agree?"

Sir Percival nodded dumbly. I had never said so many words to him, and probably not to anyone else around here either. He must have been amazed that I had a voice, let alone that I knew how to use it. For my part, I thought most of this was just pent up energy from spending too many days in my rooms. With time, I would recognize this energy as a positive force to fuel worthy goals. I did have a dragon in me somewhere.

"As we are speaking of poor people, they will not have money for tuitions," I continued, not even giving him a chance to comment. "So we must demand what they can give, which will be the very skills we teach them." I stopped having hit upon the real solution. "One month of service to the Crown for every month spent in the Crown's school. That can mean a significant portion of income, free assignments for the Crown, whatever we deem appropriate. Roads from stonemasons, windows from glassmakers, whatever the service may be. At the same time, the now educated craftsman will be given leave to return home and practice his trade according to the laws of the land."

I finished in the center of the room, planting myself there with a flourish. Sir Percival, for his part, had not yet moved from the side of his desk. I would like to think the astonishment in his eyes was shaded with respect.

"Well?" I demanded.

Sir Percival's lips worked to let words out. "Your Majesty, I must confess, when the queen originally spoke about finding an answer to the problem with the poor, I was not expecting," he waved his arm over the length of my pacing, "this."

"Didn't expect this?" I titled my head, energy still coursing through me, which is the only explanation I could give for my newfound boldness. "Didn't expect that a peasant Cinderwench could have any idea about running a kingdom?"

Sir Percival kept mute.

"Answer me!"

He flinched. "Yes—no, Your Majesty," he floundered.

I sighed and tried to recapture the anger that had snuck out of me. "Well, maybe I don't," I conceded, much calmer now, "but I do know about hard work, about poverty and the indignity of charity." I tried to hide my wince in thinking of the flash of a gold coin in an idyllic piazza, tossed without care to a lowly servant girl at a well. I forced myself to think of wings cutting above the clouds. "Let us train these men and we will help them believe in themselves again," I advised him. "No matter the initial cost, it will be for the ultimate good of the kingdom. The king will be proud of what we've done when he sees what comes of it."

To his credit, Sir Percival didn't respond immediately, the furrow in his brow proof that he was seriously contemplating what I'd said. Finally, he refocused on me and asked, "May I speak openly, Your Majesty?"

"I would appreciate it," I replied in earnest.

"I truly believe that much good can be accomplished with this plan. It has been a while since any royalty came in here with such a sound idea," he admitted.

I frowned at him. "What is that supposed to mean?"

Didn't my husband meet with Sir Percival often? What had they been wasting time on if this was the most sensible idea he'd heard from the family in a while?

As if reading my thoughts, Sir Percival's gaze flitted, but only for a second before he yanked it back, to two particular stacks of papers on his desk. Neatly lined up side by side, the first was significantly higher than the second.

"What are those?" I began to ask, then darted forward and snatched up a paper when I saw Sir Percival shift to block them.

I quickly skimmed through the contents of the page. "What is this?" I demanded, shaking the parchment in his face.

"One of the king's proposed edicts," Sir Percival answered me straight.

"To lock up anyone caught throwing a gold coin? What for?" I cried.

He answered through tight lips. "Because his image is engraved upon it."

I stared at him long enough to see that he wasn't joking. "That is a terrible decree," I decided.

"I agree, Your Majesty, it is foolish," Sir Percival dared to say.

"Sir Percival, you forget yourself!" I snapped.

He bent his head slightly. "Forgive me, Your Majesty. I only intended to be open with you."

That stopped me short and I nodded vigorously. "Yes, you are right. You must be open with me. But these, these are vexing." I grabbed the next page from the pile. "This is to hereby decree that the Crown has full right, without warning or reason, to annex any man's property, according to the king's judgement, in the interest of the kingdom.

"According to the king's judgement?" How much had Madame taken from me according to *her* judgement? I looked up with wild eyes. "Are they all like this?"

Sir Percival nodded and indicated the taller stack of papers. "Those are." He pointed to the smaller stack. "These I could alter to better versions of His Majesty's original ideas."

I reeled from this newest revelation. How could it be that I had married a man so perfect, yet still so vain, so... thoughtless? Something didn't make sense here, and I was determined to get to the bottom of it. Sir Percival must have seen the look on my face, must have understood my shock, because he respectfully offered me his hand so he could walk me out.

I shook my head and stepped away from him, though I didn't want to be there anymore. I didn't want to see those papers, that proof of Alexander's inability to understand those he ruled. This had to be a mistake. Being married to me *had* to have taught him something about the common people. *I* was of the common people and he loved me!

Before I left, I stopped abruptly. Heaven knows why, but suddenly the day the prince came to me with the slipper I'd left behind flitted before my eyes. I saw it then with undiluted clarity, as clearly as if I was looking through a freshly shined, clear glass window. The scene replayed, not the way the stories remembered, but the way it had truly happened. I saw the moment when I had come down the steps, the moment when the prince had hesitated to try the shoe on me, though there was hardly any doubt it would be mine. Then came the moment Sir Percival had reached out for the prince and a sick feeling washed over me.

I lifted up my ribs as Madame had taught me, lifting up my tiny frame as high as I could raise it and looked into Sir Percival's eyes, holding his gaze determinedly so he couldn't look away. "If you didn't think I would be much of a ruler," I asked, my voice low as if the volume would soften the blow for me, "then why did you let the prince find me? Why not choose someone who at least had the title to cover up her inabilities?"

Sir Percival gave me a small smile, and through it I could feel the pressure building against the glass bubble of my life. "First, let me humbly admit that I underestimated Her Majesty, and I am glad of it," he said simply. "Second, as to the question," he shrugged, "rumors about the mystery woman were catching the interest of people across realms. Then we found you, and you were just a servant girl, just one of the people, yet you had the chance to become a princess!" Sir

Percival's eyes shone as he relived the drama that was my life. I thought then that Alexander may have been wrong in his assessment of Sir Percival's ability to have fun. "No lady with a title stood a chance after that. And why should she? You made for a much better story."

As each word left his mouth, I felt the pressure increase. The moment he was done, the glass bubble of my life splintered to bits around me.

"Thank you," I managed to say, then turned on my heel and left.

I stormed down the hall, my mind both furious and numb. I hated what he said, hated what that said about my life and the love I thought I shared with my husband. However, I had to admit that I appreciated his honesty. Rather, I appreciated that he respected me enough to be honest with me.

My night would only get worse from there.

The energy I unleashed in Sir Percival's office followed me the rest of the night, setting me down a warpath on which I was intent on deciphering every piece of fantasy lodging in my skin like glass the moment my bubble had burst.

Some I had to find on my own, others came straight to me. Some would come immediately, others would take a while. But all would be found eventually.

I joined the banquet when it was already well under way, but the moment I stepped through the doors, I no longer wanted to be there. I didn't want to be with those people celebrating our coronation, didn't want to be with those people celebrating the farce that had been so meticulously maintained.

Truth be told, at that point, I was still certain the prince loved me, that I was very deeply in love with him. I was wrong.

I stayed long enough to be noticed, greeted the right people so word that I was well and attending the celebrations again would get around on the rapid gossip vine present in all courts. From the raised dais at the head of the room, the new king caught my eye and indicated the empty seat beside him. I forced myself to give him a special smile, then shook my head and pointed to my stomach, as if the rich smells had proven too much. The king nodded in understanding then raised his glass toward me. It took everything I had to answer him with an innocently flirtatious smile and wave. I didn't want to see him then, didn't want to be held by the hands that had signaled death, didn't want to drown in the deep pools of his eyes. I wanted to be alone. I wanted to breathe.

Someone came up from behind and diverted the king's attention, so I diverted mine to find Princess Lyla.

"Ella!" she exclaimed upon seeing me, as usual not caring a whit about propriety as she flung her arms around me and pulled me into a tight hug. "I'm so glad you're well."

"Lyla, I must talk with you," I said into her ear.

At the tone of my voice, the princess pulled away and gave me a worried look. "What is it?" she asked.

I shook my head, not here, not now. "Later, after midnight," I whispered, "under my pear tree."

Princess Lyla nodded, and I turned away, pressing myself through the crowded room so I could press out of it completely. The truth was, I wasn't yet sure what I was going to say to her, but I knew I had to speak with someone about this. As cousins of sorts, the princess knew the prince fairly well, and as my friend I trusted her to steer me right. The captain, as a friend to us both, was another option. I hurried down the hall back to my chambers where I could think in peace. I wasn't keen on seeing him right now. He'd been there that fateful day. He'd been the one to find me in my attic cell.

Apparently, he couldn't read my thoughts, because no sooner

had I left the revelry behind, then he materialized out of a shadowy alcove and caught my hand so I'd follow after him.

"Please, Captain," I begged, taking my hand back.

"I'm afraid it's rather important, Your Majesty," he rumbled, not budging a foot.

I sighed and ducked into the alcove behind him, whereupon we came across a small man who, upon seeing me, let out a small yelp and threw himself at my feet.

"What is this?" I demanded of the captain.

"This man," the captain explained, "is one of the royal food tasters."

"Rise," I commanded the man impatiently.

On shaky legs, the man eventually managed to get off the floor, but he stood hunched and trembling, trying his best to shrink into the stones at my feet.

I really wanted to get back to my rooms. This man was wearing on my patience. "Speak," I encouraged.

A string of indecipherable syllables escaped the man's chattering teeth.

I glanced at the captain, who rolled his eyes in exasperation. "Go on," he told the taster, "tell the queen what you told me."

Still, nothing coherent came out.

"This is very important," the captain growled. "You'll not be harmed for anything you say." He gave me a meaningful look.

"You'll not be harmed for anything you say," I echoed, and finally the man peeked out from under his scrunched frame.

"Good. Now, tell the queen what you tasted in the drink I gave you," the captain said, holding up the cup he'd taken from my room, in case I still had any doubts of what this was about.

"Bloodapple," the man dutifully replied.

"And what is bloodapple?" the captain asked in a tone used for reviewing lessons with children.

"Poison," the man explained. "Very powerful poison."

"How powerful?" the captain pressed.

"Near untraceable once consumed. Causes temporary sterility in small doses. Can kill a man in large ones," he recited. "Or an animal. Like a horse," he unnecessarily added.

The captain concluded his interrogation with one more question. "And what does bloodapple taste like?"

The man scrunched his brow in response. "Bitter. Acidic. Rotted fruit. Some try to hide it with strong spices, like cinnamon."

"Thank you, you are dismissed," the captain said, and the taster scurried away as fast as he could.

The captain turned to me and even he couldn't hide the pain, hurt, and fear etched in his eyes. Or maybe I was only seeing a reflection of my own. I didn't have anything to say, I simply shook my head at him slowly, right to left, left to right, as if doing that enough times would undo all that I'd just heard. Facts I knew too well to be true.

The captain clenched the cup in his fist, and I expected it to crack any second. "I will find out who is behind this," he vowed. "On my life, Ella, I will protect you."

I didn't respond to his improper use of my proper name, or the ferocity with which he made his vow. In succession, the night had taken an ax to my foundation and disinterestedly observed as I lost ground each time it swung. I shook my head again and walked back to my chambers.

I hated the thought that came next. Hated that it could even exist in what was still supposed to be the enviable faery tale of my life. Which may be why I didn't walk straight for the palace doors and leave my ruined dream behind. In its own way, magic had made me weak, too, so though my heart remained delusional and firm, my rational mind fought for every step it could take toward the truth.

And that mind knew exactly what it would ask of Princess Lyla.

~

But I never spoke to her that night. Restless in my chambers, I went down to the garden early, hoping to find the peace I sought in that one quiet corner of the palace.

The moonlight shone into the little pond, glinting off my goldfish's shiny scales. He was swimming sluggishly, as if even he didn't have the energy to endure this night with grace. Glancing up at my pear tree, I frowned, noting in the moonlight that the tips of its leaves were yellowing.

It didn't make any sense. The tree hadn't been yellow for years, not since I'd first planted the branch, which had grown up yellow before permanently turning green. Once it had taken root, regardless of the weather, the leaves had always been full and verdant, the only notice of seasons in whether or not they were also weighed down by wonderfully green, succulent pears.

I gently ran a finger over a leaf which felt coarse and brittle to my touch. I frowned. The leaves had always been healthy and oddly soft. Something was wrong.

I climbed into the tree and tucked myself away, wrongly thinking that my weak frame was strong enough to give it life. Princess Lyla came and called for me, I could hear her circling the garden looking for me, but I suddenly didn't want to talk anymore. I held my breath until she left. I'd explain another time. She'd understand.

I stayed by myself in the garden, hidden in the boughs of my wilting pear tree, watching my fish take too much time to drift across the small pond. My heart felt empty, my mind couldn't think. I simply had no idea what to do with myself anymore.

And then I felt a warm glow and there she was beside me, her warm touch an instant comfort to my sorry, broken state.

"Grandmère," I whispered.

"Hush, Ella," she said, cradling me against her. "It will be all right."

I shook my head against her embrace. "How can it ever be?" I asked. I shook my head again. "Everything is different, even my husband. I can never, will never be able to look at him the same way ever again."

"Good," Marie said.

"Why is that good?" I demanded to know, momentarily upset enough to pull away from her. "Everything is ruined!"

"You never really saw him," Marie explained gently. "You romanticized him, you idealized him, I suppose the magic dresses didn't help either," she admitted with a shrug. "You didn't see him, and perhaps for that reason, he never really saw you."

"What are you saying?" I asked, trying to stop up the bottomless well of tears flowing from my eyes.

Marie stroked my hair. "I want you to remember that the magic may have given you dresses, footmen, and a carriage, but you made yourself a queen. And with kindness, with humility, with an eye that seeks out the good in others, you will be a great queen."

I was used to Marie's non sequiturs, but there was something else going on here, something deeper running beneath the words she was actually saying out loud.

"What is it, Grandmère?" I asked warily. "What aren't you telling me?"

Marie didn't answer right away. She simply continued to stroke my hair, study my face, memorize it, it seemed.

When she finally spoke, I wish she hadn't. "I'm going away for a while, away from this kingdom," she clarified. "Magicals are being driven out and magic is receding deep underground. We need to find somewhere more welcoming."

I was shaking my head even before the words could tumble out of my mouth. "No, no," I pleaded. "You can't leave me here. You can't leave me alone."

"You're not alone, Ella, dear," Marie said, putting a finger under my chin to keep my head still. "You have friends, people who care about you." With that she fell silent a moment seeing something, sensing something I could not. "I cannot stay here," she said softly.

"Take me with you, then," I begged, nearly sobbing. "Please, just don't leave me!"

As much as I didn't really want to leave the palace, I would have gone with Marie. Because running away seemed like a viable option over facing down the truth I was sensing I wouldn't avoid for long.

And just when I thought the night couldn't get any worse, just when I thought I had no tears left to cry, both thoughts were simultaneously upended.

Marie tried to brush away my tears. "Things may be hard now, but remember you've been given a tremendous gift."

I didn't let her finish. "You can take it back; I don't want it."

"Ella, dear, you can't return Heaven's gift, not when there's still so much you can do with it," Marie said. "Whatever has been your whole life, I never doubted you or how strong you really are." Pride tinged her face and voice. "Think of the bit of good you've done in your position until now, think of how much more you could do."

I didn't want to hear what she was saying. Didn't want my rational mind to know and make sense of the parting words of comfort I was refusing. I embraced her fiercely, hoping I could hold her back with strength of will alone.

For a short, wonderful time, Marie hugged me back, pulling

me close to her before she released me and faded away before I could stop her, the warm smile on her face seeming to linger even after she'd disappeared.

I never made it to bed that night. I stayed in the garden until dawn, perched on a wilting branch in a trance-like state, my mind too shocked, too broken to work at all. It was there that Sir Percival found me the next morning, while ostensibly out for an early morning walk.

"Your Majesty," he called up to me.

I gave him a distant smile.

"What brings you out here so early?" he asked.

"Thinking." I stretched the truth.

Sir Percival smiled in approval of my use of time. He had no idea of how my life had been drowned then wrung out to dry in the few hours since I left his office yesterday evening.

"Thinking about what?" he inquired, inclining his head toward me. The whole scene was really quite ridiculous.

"Life," I answered vaguely. "Laurendale. Responsibility."

If I stretched the truth any further, would I hear it break?

"Very wise," Sir Percival agreed, his eyes taking on the distant color of reminiscence. "When His Majesty, who was rather annoyed with his father and me, suggested we invite everyone to the masquerade, no one actually thought anything would come of it." He smiled up at me. "But I hope we can agree it was the beginning of quite a wonderful story."

I made a choking sound he somehow took as assent. What was it with palace people and their stories? Couldn't he see I didn't want any more of his honesty?

"We really needed something at the time," he blithely continued, unaware of how uncomfortable his words made me. "The prince was in a dark place coming off the battlefield. He was protecting the kingdom, but it does something to a man's soul, all that bloodshed. Then Her Majesty came along, and the people had something to sing about other than wars and rivers of blood. Love makes for much nicer lyrics, doesn't it?" he questioned, without really asking at all.

Sir Percival, dull as he was, could make anything dramatic. What was he doing here as advisor if he could be spinning tales for eager villagers across the realm? He'd also struck something in me by suggesting that I had stepped forward to save the prince, that my purity and innocence should have been enough to diffuse the blackness fighting for his soul. Why was this my responsibility? How could I help someone who didn't even know he needed help? And what about the toll something like that could take on me?

Sir Percival astutely caught on to the change in my expression. He made a show of checking the time on his pocket watch before bowing low and turning toward the palace. "I interrupted the queen's thoughts and made matters worse by blathering on and on. Forgive me, Your Majesty. I hope you'll visit again soon with further ideas for Laurendale."

He scuttled away, and I stared after him for a time. Then I roused myself and returned to my rooms, sure Javotte would be in hysterics if she noticed I hadn't returned last night. I slipped in and slid under the covers quietly as I could. At some point, I fell asleep and didn't care that I only woke up early afternoon.

I changed after that, lost my faith in magic and the faery tales my mother had spun for me. I became disconsolate, and someone, noticing my mood, decided it would be best to get me away from the palace for a while, somewhere with a friend who could uplift me. So it was early that fall, mere months after being crowned and around our fourth wedding anniversary, the king and I set sail for Calladium.

We'd visited Lyla about a handful of times in the past few years and each time the trips had been pleasant and enjoyable. There was a closeness between Alexander and Lyla, even as they teased each other like the siblings they never had, so Lyla's palace soon had a feeling of a second home. Additionally, the men got along very well, and I knew how much my husband looked forward to hunting with hers.

"It's difficult to pin down," he paused, searching for words as he tried to explain it to me, "the way he moves, the way he senses things that can't be touched or seen. A truly marvelous huntsman," he concluded, shaking his head in wonder.

To me, Calladium had a hushed peacefulness about it this time of year, possibly because their winters started earlier, and lasted longer, then ours. One of the first times I was there, the princess showed me the legendary room where her mother had sat, looking out a black ebony window frame as her red blood dripped onto the very white snow inspiring her to pray for a baby girl of such colors. It was actually rather simple, rather unremarkable compared to almost everything else there was to see. Lyla had laughed when she'd seen that understanding on my face, knowing full well what a faery tale telling could do to even the smallest detail of reality.

I didn't say anything to Lyla about my current state when I saw her, but she was a good enough friend to know that something wasn't right. Still, she didn't press, biding her time until I would be ready to talk.

"Little Snow White!" the king greeted his cousin as we stepped out of our carriage.

"Ella, I'm so glad you came," Princess Lyla ran to me, ignoring him.

"Where's the man of the house?" Alexander wanted to know.

Lyla waved across the courtyard to the stables where Prince

Daimyon was talking to the stable master. The king went off after him and caught his attention with a hearty "Halloo!"

Daimyon waved back with a warm smile, then shook the stable master's hand before turning to welcome his guest.

"He really is a good man," Lyla said beside me, watching her husband with me. "Compassionate, caring, I should know; he spared my life, then saved it. But at times it feels he reserves those things for those on the outside."

"Perhaps he's still adjusting to his position at court?" I suggested.

Lyla let out a quick, derisive laugh. "How many years does one man need to adjust?" she questioned.

I shrugged in response. I still struggled at times.

The princess shook her head and tried to dispel her thoughts with it. "Come see who's inside," she said, pulling me along.

Interestingly, Kiara was there, and though it took me a day to realize it, she was wearing her hair differently, in a way that hugged one side of her face. It wouldn't have been odd, except for a few things.

For one, it didn't seem she could see very well like that.

For two, if possible, it was less flattering than her other hairstyles.

For three, Kiara was there without her husband.

For four, later that day, when Kiara, Lyla, and I were enjoying the cool fall afternoon outdoors, the wind lifted Kiara's hair away from her face long enough for me to see what she was hiding underneath. An ugly bruise, already turning green, under her eye and covering much of her high cheekbone. She tried to block it quickly, and I didn't say anything because it didn't seem she wanted to talk about it. Still, it was a rather curious thing.

The day after we arrived, the men decided to spend their hours hunting, which I knew Alexander would be ecstatic about. It was a clear, crisp day, warm enough to be out, but not enough to stay out for long. So the women chose to stay home. We ended up in one of the drawing rooms on the main floor of the palace. It was fitted with a small terrace that Lyla liked to take tea on during the warmer months as it opened into her gardens. Kiara took up a seat at the harp and Lyla and I had chairs pulled up close. Sitting down, I almost squashed a small handheld mirror that had been left on the seat. I jumped up, and noticing what it was, picked it up and handed it to Lyla.

"That one's not mine," she said with a smile.

I looked at her quizzically.

"It's Kiara's," she explained.

I offered Kiara her mirror and she took it from me with a sad smile.

"Is this—can this—is your mirror like Lyla's?" I asked.

Kiara shook her head. "Not entirely. In mine you see whatever is most beloved to you."

"May I try?" I asked, though unsure if, with all that had happened, what I would see. My maps? My tree? My charming prince? Who was most beloved to me after him? Lyla? Javotte? Marie?

Kiara placed the mirror in my hand and it wasn't long before the silver began to warble, twisting and turning until it showed Alexander exulting in the thrill of the hunt, racing his horse past thick forest trees, his loyal captain not two strides behind. I smiled and stroked the mirror's surface. There was something so young, so free about him, the way I'd always imagined, always wanted him to be. Before I remembered the truth from that day with the slipper. Before the wine lacked the flavor of cherries. Before Marie was forced away.

I was about to hand the mirror back to Kiara, the thank you already on my lips, when I pulled the mirror back for one more look. The image was still there. I peered closer. Over his hunting clothes, Alexander was wearing a fine black cloak embroidered with blue stitching I'd never seen before. The blue against the black was rather startling, rather distinctive.

"What is it?" Kiara asked.

"Just another peek," I replied.

She grinned in understanding and took the mirror as the image dissolved back into silver. She glanced at it once, as if debating looking in herself, before hurriedly tucking it away.

The next two days were rather nice, nice enough to drag me out of my darkened mood enough to enjoy the time I had with my friends. It also helped that we didn't see much of the men, who were either busy with sports or other diplomatic business.

One afternoon, we were taking tea in the drawing room, when a messenger was presented to us. The man was tall and thin, with a heavy accent and dusty clothes that spoke of hard riding.

Once in, the man immediately rushed forward and bowed before Princess Kiara.

"Forgive my appearance, Highness, but I've strict orders not to stop until I give this to you," he announced, presenting her with a beautiful, long stemmed red rose.

Kiara smiled warmly and took the proffered rose. She dipped her face to it and inhaled deeply. When she lifted her head again, the light sparkled off the tears in her eyes.

"Rise, Kellan," she said kindly. "We must hurry to pack my things, there isn't a moment to lose."

The rider scampered out of the room to relay instructions for her belongings. Still clutching the rose, Kiara turned to us with a glittering smile.

She hugged Lyla first, tightly. "Thank you so much," she whispered in her ear. "Thank you for everything, always."

"I hope we'll see each other again soon," Lyla replied. "Under better circumstances," she added under her breath.

Kiara hugged me, too. "It'll be all right," she told me, though I didn't know then if she was talking to me or herself. I suppose it didn't much matter. Encouraging words are always welcome.

Kiara swept out of the room, the added glow in her heart igniting her inner beauty so her face took on a heavenly sheen. It was only after I was sure her footsteps had completely receded that I turned to Lyla with a confused look on my face.

"Why—" I began to ask, lifting my hand to the part of my face that Kiara was trying to cover on hers.

Lyla pursed her lips then answered carefully, "There are days he still struggles to be rid of the beast."

I nodded in understanding, an understanding I would become too familiar with. Except I don't think my husband ever struggled at all.

For a moment, I saw us in the room as if I was a butterfly flying through on a wrong turn to the garden. Kiara, myself, and Lyla, who had created a safe haven for us in her incomplete happiness. Regardless of how bitter she was, how jealous, how daring, how unrelenting, I had never, nor would ever, have a friend like her. It was better than being cousins of a sort, because friends are a chosen loyalty. I decided then that I would not leave until I had done something good for her, if only to show her how much I valued all that she'd done for me. I just had to figure out what would be good enough.

Then my mind took a sharp turn and I remembered that image of my husband in the mirror. I thought of Kiara and her patience for a man who was still fighting to regain his humanity. Then I thought of the story I'd been made into and the rancidness in my wine that the king never seemed to taste.

Tonight, I would have that talk with Lyla.

～

I tiptoed into her room well after dark. The men were still

downstairs amiably trading jokes and stories before the fire, so it was only a matter of time before we excused ourselves to go to sleep. But I couldn't sleep. Not yet.

"Ella!" Lyla warmly welcomed me when I knocked. She was already in her nightclothes, wrapped in a dressing gown, her finger holding the place of the book in her hand. "What brings you here so late?"

"I've been thinking," I stuttered, then decided to plunge right in. "We never spoke when you last visited."

"Ella, first sit," Lyla insisted. She didn't check the page as she set aside her book and filled a cup of water for me. It was only when some dripped onto my clothes that I realized my hands were shaking. The princess studied me with her sharp eyes. "You are not yourself," she said simply.

I shook my head, unwilling to go into too much detail. "I—I would like your help with something," I said.

"Whatever I can do for you, I will," the princess promised immediately, and I suspected she was about to regret her eagerness to help.

"Your mirror," I asked, "do you have it with you?"

"Always," she replied, reaching for it then abruptly stopping herself as realization slowly dawned. She narrowed her gaze at me. "It only answers one type of question."

"I know."

Lyla's eyes widened. "You are not happy," she said.

I shook my head, not trusting myself to answer.

"Why?" Lyla questioned, but not of me. "You were to have been so good for him," she added softly.

"He doesn't seem to agree," I countered.

Here was the second person admitting that they thought I could have done more for the prince, and I didn't like it. They knew the prince was less than perfect, Lyla had even hinted at it the first time we met, but I had chosen to ignore everything that would have let me know it, too. The difference between us was that they still had hope for him; I didn't, not anymore. Perhaps I had once been innocent and pure, but like all things pure and white, I had been stained by the blackness I was fighting against. And I was only beginning to glimpse it now.

"Ella—"

"Please, just ask."

Lyla shook her head at me. "Please, Ella, please don't do this to yourself."

I rubbed my temples in a fruitless attempt to quell the growing headache beating mercilessly behind my forehead. The choice was so simple, really. Either I could ask for an answer I didn't want to receive, or I could keep living in my blinding faery tale. Considering what Sir Percival had said in the garden, considering what the captain had weaned out of the taster, it seemed everyone acknowledged something dark was lurking in the palace but me. I really just wanted to go back to the way things used to be. Really, really wanted to go back to the simpler life when we were just a prince and princess with a love bright enough to illuminate darker times. But I couldn't. And now it seemed life had never been that way at all.

"I need to know," I said simply. "Please."

Lyla still shook her head sadly, but she took out the mirror and held it to me.

"No," I pushed it back to her. "You ask."

The princess blanched as she looked down at her mirror, building up the courage to do what I had unfairly requested of her.

"Mirror, Mirror, in my hand," she chanted, throwing me a look to tell me it wasn't too late. I shook my head; I wasn't backing down from this now.

"Mirror, Mirror, in my hand, who does King Alex think fairest in his land?"

The face of the mirror swirled ominously, like a thick, blinding fog lurking over a dark swamp. The princess had the good sense to angle the mirror's face away from me so I couldn't see the answer taking shape. I waited as the image formed, waited as her eyes studied the face it showed her, waited as her expression turned to shock, then anger, then sadness. She looked up at me and slowly shook her head.

"Do I know her?"

"She is known in your court," she said carefully.

"Let me see," I demanded.

Lyla shook her head and held the mirror away from me. "It is better if you do not."

I felt like someone had violently ripped out my insides.

I had asked the question because my rational mind had demanded it, but my heart never believed that the face that would appear would be anyone's but mine. And even if my husband thought someone else more fair, that didn't mean he didn't love me. Did it? But asking the question and receiving the answer had slammed the door shut on that possibility forever.

Tears streamed unchecked down Lyla's cheeks, and though I was too numb to feel them, I was certain they matched my own. After living so long in the clouds, I'd suddenly, viciously, learned that they weren't strong enough to hold me. It was as if reality was waging war with my conceived fantasy, as if, after being neglected for so long, each truth had decided to ambush me one after the other with their undeniable existence. The first one had shattered my protective bubble, the last one would sweep every last bit away altogether.

"Stupid, stupid mirror," Lyla's sadness turned to rage, sparking her brilliant, intelligent, always caring black eyes.

And then she was gathering me in her arms, and I could hear her heart breaking for me, the one person she was sure had the happily ever after promised to us all. If even I didn't have it, then what hope did anyone else have? We would all be locked forever within the image of what was supposed to be, no one daring to look past the illusion to the way ever after had really turned out.

Her tears, and I suppose mine as well, dried up after a while. I pulled away from her with a promise that I would come to her if I needed someone to talk to, that I would not act without thinking twice. She seemed to understand that I needed time to process what I hadn't seen, but still seemed loath to let me go on alone. She ended up walking me back to my rooms, clutching my hand in a greater display of emotion than what I was then feeling.

Because at that point, it all added up. It finally made sense. The dragon, the wine, the taster, Sir Percival. The darkness had been gaining on me all this time, and I'd only looked up once the impending shadows completely blotted out my sun. The only thing left to wonder was whether I had enough light left in me to chase it away.

Before anything else, however, I entered my rooms and ordered Javotte to draw me a very hot bath. Then I soaked in the water and scrubbed my skin over and over again, as if I could actually remove any lingering sensation from wherever my prince had once touched me.

Our visit wound down three days later, but the evening before we were off, I was able to make good on my fervent desire to do something for Lyla.

I was wandering the gardens without much heed for the time, knowing it was dinner soon, but not caring. I ended up walking to the edge of the gardens where a layered stone ledge marked the end of the palace grounds, which overlooked the villages nestled in the plains below.

A figure stood at the top of the ledge, unrecognizable at first because the setting sun was turning everything black as it sucked all color into its burst of orange flame. Stepping closer, I recognized Prince Daimyon, and the opportunity Heaven had sent my way.

Daimyon motioned for me to join him, though I'm sure he doubted I actually would. His fearsome pet bat circled the air above him, but that didn't stop me from accepting his invitation. I tried my best to climb the tall step-like ledges. He had to help me up toward the top, but I made it. The view spread out below us was magnificent, so I had no question as to what he was doing up there by himself.

As for myself, I never would have done anything like this just months before, but I had faced death, and I had faced hatred, and I was still standing. There really wasn't much that could bring me down now. Not even a fall off a steep palace ledge.

A lone wolf howled in the distance, and Prince Daimyon's head rose up, as if ready to return the call. Instead, he turned to me and said, "Whenever a wolf calls, I think on what once was. I suppose a part of us will never really let go of the things we left behind."

"No, stop," I shook my head, my newfound clarity finally allowing me to understand so many things I had been told all along. I would not commiserate. I would take away his self-pity. "We were given a gift," I told him firmly, pointing up toward the darkening sky, "because of what we can do with it. There is purpose in all this, and we have to make it real. We were raised up to royalty, commoners among princes and kings, princes and kings who know the hearts of commoners."

Prince Daimyon shook his head at me. "I never asked for this," he said. "I don't want it either."

"Which is why you live in a palace, yet yearn to roam with wolves," I said sharply. "Did you know that my people call me CinderElla?" I added for good measure.

Daimyon shook his head wordlessly.

"Alexander kept it from me, but I found out." There was a note of defiance in my voice now that I wasn't bothering to keep out. "They gave it to me, because I mean something to them, because I was one of them. Don't you understand: our good fortune is their good fortune, too?"

"How can you say that?" Prince Daimyon whispered, still shaking his head. "True love gave me a princess; a glass slipper gave you a prince. That's not—Then what—" his voice tapered off as he fumbled to put into words what he was feeling.

We don't make a difference.

Don't give the people reason to hope in what will never be.

There is no happily ever after.

Haven't you learned that yet?

I caught his gaze and held it so he couldn't look away. "There is so much we can do," I insisted.

"They don't need us," he disagreed.

"Yes, they do. They know much, but they don't know that feeling of disappearing without anyone noticing you've gone. This is our life now, and we have to believe in what we can do. Your wife is one of the best people I've ever been blessed to know," I added. "She is fierce and loyal, and though she tries to hide it, her heart is warm, caring, and filled with more love than she has people to share it with. And she wants to share it with you."

The prince listened quietly, and though he still held my gaze, his dark gray eyes took on a distant hue. His voice was low when he finally spoke. "At thirteen, I became the queen's youngest huntsman, a title that didn't come easy."

His voice trailed off into memory and I waited for him to come back. I knew most of Lyla's story by now, but it was different hearing it from him.

"Two years later, I disobeyed my first direct order from the queen. I had never been near the young princess before, but once

I had, I couldn't go through with it. How could I kill such magnificent beauty? I would not be responsible for taking it from the world, and I paid a heavy price for refusing."

The prince smiled sadly at something only he could see. "Four years later, there she was, so still, so serene in that glass casket the dwarves built for her." He looked up at me suddenly. "Did you know that one third of the king's council is made up of dwarves because of what they did for her?"

I shook my head no. I didn't know, but it didn't surprise me either. Lyla, driven and passionate, fierce and daring, would never forget to repay people who were so good to her. He was only proving my point in saying so.

"When I saw her there, I couldn't control myself," he ended with a shrug. "I just never—I did not anticipate this."

"Those used to being unseen rarely do," I said, repeating the captain's words from what felt like a lifetime ago. "You don't really have anything against her," I added, speaking to myself as much as to him, "you're more upset with yourself."

I studied him in the fading light, studied the good man before me and looked at him through Lyla's eyes, through my eyes, through my king's eyes, through his own eyes. I saw that though he was brave, he was still frightened of the beauty he'd been given, still unsure of how he'd risen so high, because when he looked in the mirror, he still only saw a simple huntsman. I was sure Lyla would show him otherwise, if he would only let her.

"Do you know what Lyla's favorite color is?" I finally asked.

My heart hurt when he shook his head no.

"Yellow," I supplied. "Do you know why?"

"No."

"Because she loves the way the sun brightens everything with a single touch," I explained.

A short pause.

Then the prince lowered his head. "I've been a fool," he said simply.

"You have," I agreed. "The shadows you hid in are long gone. You may as well leave a mark to be seen."

Now it was Prince Daimyon's turn to study me, and though I wasn't sure if he had accepted what I'd said, at least I could be sure that he'd listened. He seemed then to notice that night had fallen and there was somewhere we both needed to be. He stepped down from the ledge first so he could offer me his hand to help me after him.

"Her favorite flowers are lilies, by the way," I added on our way back to the palace.

He stopped. "Lilies? They're funereal."

I smiled. "Just like a certain significant moment in her life."

We stepped into the dining hall together and went straight to our places, ignoring the curious looks from the others who were already there. When I lowered myself into my seat beside Lyla, she barely leaned over to quietly whisper, "What were you and the prince talking about?"

"Commoner stuff," I answered simply.

"Ella!" she hissed sharply.

"You'll find out soon enough," I reassured her, and refused to say anymore.

Silently, I prayed I was right.

I knew my work was done when I passed Prince Daimyon that night as I was leaving Lyla's rooms. He held a modest bouquet of orange-streaked yellow lilies. Honestly, he looked a little scared, and I gave him a warm smile of encouragement. He returned it very tentatively.

I shouldn't have, but I couldn't help myself from pressing into the wall around the corner and hiding in the shadows while he knocked on Lyla's door. Having just seen me out, she was the one to answer his knock.

"Daimyon?"

The confusion was plain in her voice.

"Lyla," he replied. "I was hoping...I was thinking...we're always so busy...we need to make time for each other."

I didn't hear her response, but that was because she had pulled him into her rooms and closed the door firmly behind him.

I didn't eat much in the months that followed. My small frame rapidly grew even smaller, my eyes sunk in, my skin turned unnaturally pale. I was stuck in a bog of darkness, thick enough to keep my appetite at bay, plus there was also the idea of being poisoned again. At the rate I was going, I would finish the job my unknown assassin had begun.

I stopped fencing with the captain. Stopped thinking about what I wore. Stopped caring about what my prince thought or how I could make him happy. I became listless, and Princess Lyla tried to help with a constant barrage of letters that ranged from the sympathetic to the outrageous. Javotte was beside herself, ever on the lookout for something, anything that would make me smile. Even the good captain, whenever he could, went out of his way to bring me food from outside the palace, because only he knew the truth about the wine. He'd bring freshly baked rolls and little pastries from the market, anything to coax my appetite back to life. I would eat a little then push the rest away, which did nothing for the worry lines embedding themselves around his eyes.

Alexander tried to make me laugh, tried to bring me treats and bring me back to myself with his attentions, but it was too late. I hadn't seen it, but I had known what the mirror had to tell. What did it matter to him if I lived or died?

Even Sir Percival took to stopping by to ask me about matters of state. I tried my best to engage with him, to continue to prove his newfound trust in me that I may know something about the people I was supposed to rule.

He once came with an influential individual he introduced as Sir Archivalle, who was "interested in the idea of using the students from our trade school to repair broken roads and bridges throughout the kingdom." He saw the potential in how this idea could be expanded to all the needs of Laurendale, Sir Percival explained.

I pulled myself together enough to speak with them about it, a brief spark of energy returning as we spoke of the positive changes we could make. And when they left, I knew that I had finally made my first real ally at court, the beginnings of a network of support that could help me help others.

After that, and despite Alexander's protests, I insisted on visiting the building site of the first school about half a day's ride from the capital multiple times a week. The captain came along to watch over me, but he didn't hide the disapproving slant of his lips. Perhaps he knew I would have walked on foot if no one had prepared the carriage, because standing before the slowly rising structure was the only time I felt anything but despondent, the only time I didn't mind being small only because I was a piece of something bigger.

I became obsessed with my maps, scouring the towns and topography for ideal school locations, furiously circling the parts of any road that needed strengthened bridges or regular repair. Over and over, I drew thick lines of possible trade routes, pressing so hard my quill often ripped through the paper. Sir Percival had my maps redone on canvas and gave me charcoal to write with instead.

Most of my information came from Sir Archivalle, who sent me a steady stream of letters about the physical conditions of Laurendale, which he gathered from the vast network of friends he had across the kingdom. He wrote about towns in need of specific craftsmen, about craftsmen who needed new places to work. I reread his letters until the pages wore thin enough to be translucent, and when my husband would try to pry them from me, "You're driving yourself mad," I would defiantly tuck them into my pocket, keeping them close, intending to read them again once he'd left.

Perhaps I really had gone mad, or perhaps the schools were the only things saving me from complete madness. Either way, I needed them desperately, needed to know that I could make a difference in someone else's life even as mine was falling apart around me. Because I couldn't think about that fact either, for if I stopped long enough the truth knocked me back, shook my confidence, and drew out rivers of tears for all the things I'd lost.

Outside in the garden below me, my pear tree continued to wither away. My goldfish bellied up and died.

I was almost unsurprised when the captain appeared white-faced in my rooms one night, knowing I wouldn't be asleep, even at this late hour. I was wrapped in a blanket, sitting in a heavily cushioned chair that was so large I always felt it swallowed me up. Buried as such, Sir Archivalle's letters clenched in my hand, I stared at the fire, entranced by the giddiness with which the flames danced and burned. How could something so destructive, so beneficial be so at peace with itself? Did it never question its own duality?

Yes, that is exactly how muddled my thoughts were during that time.

"Your Majesty," the captain began, and his usually clipped, confident voice betrayed him by cracking. "I have news I wish I did not have to share but know that I must for your safety."

I studied him disinterestedly. "Do you come to me as a friend, or as captain of the royal guard?"

The captain considered a moment. "Both," he finally said.

"Then pull up a seat and speak plainly," I commanded.

The captain pulled up a chair, but as soon as he sat, he sprang back up again. He paced the floor a few times, before he came to kneel before me.

"Ella—Princess—Your Majesty," he bumbled. "I have made inquiries about the wine from your room."

I raised an eyebrow questioningly at him. This could be interesting. If not, it certainly couldn't make my life any worse than it already was.

I was so, so incredibly wrong.

"It seems, Your Majesty," the captain braved on, without quite looking at me, "the night of his coronation, His Majesty requested a special bottle of wine be brought to his rooms. The wine arrived unopened and the king commanded it stay as such."

The captain searched my eyes nervously before going on.

"From when it was delivered, the king was in possession of the wine until he brought it here. The only man I could find selling bloodapple, long outlawed in Laurendale by the way, within a few hours ride from here, was persuaded to admit to having sold it to a finely dressed gentleman who kept his face hidden throughout their transaction. He mentioned that the man, most definitely a man, had a particularly educated manner of speaking."

The blood ran cold in my veins and I shivered despite the blanket.

"He also mentioned a black cloak with startling blue embroidery," the captain unnecessarily added.

He paused before he said anymore, as if even he couldn't believe the words about to leave his mouth.

"I have searched part of the king's private chambers but have yet to find anything resembling the packet with the dealer's green seal upon it. I will continue searching," the captain finished, with a resolve at odds with his desire to fail.

I stared at him with unseeing eyes. Did some part of me already know what he said? Is that why I had demanded Lyla use her mirror for me that wretched night in her room? Or was I truly shocked at this admission?

I didn't know. I didn't know what I felt anymore. I didn't know that I could feel anymore.

I only remembered the captain was still there, kneeling before me, because I heard his breath catch on an inhale. I refocused on him and watched two silent tears trickle down his suddenly aged face. His eyes weren't brown as the earth I thought, but brown like hot chocolate, rich and comforting, too.

"Should I leave the palace?" I asked.

"Where will you go?" he wanted to know.

"Alaryx?"

The captain arched an eyebrow at me. Bad enough he was tangled in this mess, I couldn't involve his brothers, too.

"He'll find me anywhere," I added for him.

I reached out my hand and pressed it lightly to the captain's stubbly cheek. He stilled at my touch.

"It will be all right, Captain," I reassured him, seeking strength so I would have some to lend him. "We'll figure something out."

A bitter, muffled laugh escaped him. What was there to figure out? His best friend, the man he had grown up with, fought beasts with, had sworn fealty to, had just been found out as the intended assassin of his new friend, his best friend's own wife. Betrayed by his monarch, betrayed by his friend. And for what reason?

The captain stood hurriedly, but not before I caught his hand and squeezed it. "Thank you, Captain," I told him in earnest. "I'm glad you told me."

"I'm not. I need to think," was all the captain replied as he turned toward the door. I watched him go, struggling to withstand the weight of the secret on his shoulders. I was hardly the one strong enough to bear the burden with him.

Yet, oddly, as he left, some sort of resolve started flooding back into me. It came on the tail end of the same sort of relief I felt when Madame finally admitted just how much she hated me.

This was it. This was the final moment of my old life, the point at which a decision had to be made that would decide what my future, if I had any future left, would be. I could no longer be in denial of what was going on, for that is how I'd already fallen so low. I sat in that chair and thought a long while, slowly stirring up my first set of options.

For one, I could confront Alexander with what I knew and work out a solution that benefitted us both. I would gladly move out of the palace to a country estate, or even abdicate the throne, if that meant he would let me live. Considering his malice, I didn't really think he would allow that.

For two, I could live in fear and paranoia the rest of my life, either hoping to outlive the king through sheer will or for some peaceful death that would end this all. That really wasn't much more of a life than I had now.

For three, I could flee to a neighboring kingdom. Princess Lyla would surely grant me asylum, but it wouldn't be long before too many questions were asked. I would either be forced back to the palace or forced to wage war against my own people. I did not think I could bring myself to that.

For four, I could accept the king's dissatisfaction with me and patiently bear his disappointment as I had once before in a previous life. My life would be the schools, but how would that save me in the long run? Hadn't similar behavior cast me down before?

If there was a way, we'd live separate lives in the palace, so the people would never know of the irreparable rift between us. For my kingdom, I could pretend to turn a blind eye to whatever he chose to do next, to whomever he chose to love next. But could the king really accept a life without the promise of an heir? Could I really accept a life that would force me back into my own little corner, no longer a shelter for my imagination, but from the deception of it? Why must I always be the one to bow before those wishing me harm?

I knew I had a choice to make, that I had to find a solution before my life got any worse than it already was. This realization had been slow in coming, because I still stubbornly held onto the last remnants of the dream, refusing to accept it was but a mirage that only I could see.

But not anymore.

TO WALTZ ON BURNING STARS

*L*ife took on a new normal for the next few weeks, something akin to an unspoken truce, a calm before the final, most destructive storm. My pear tree soon followed my goldfish to its death, the magic slowly retreating, untapped, deep into the land as more and more magicals left. I would stare at it for long hours through my window, taking in its naked limbs and downtrodden boughs, wondering if I was projecting my misery onto it or it onto me.

I don't know now if I should have acted sooner, knowing my life was in danger, knowing that I was to have no life the way I was living, but I was too confused, too unsure of what to do. I doubted myself and my decisions, I berated myself for not gathering the courage for a final stand. As miserable as I was with Madame, at least she never hid how she felt about me. That I always thought I might one day make her happy was my own foolishness; she'd never said anything to make me believe it to be true. But with the prince, I never knew for sure. His mouth said one thing, his heart another. Were he a prince from my childhood faery tales, the one I still believed in when I first came here, there never would have been any doubt. That one would have given me a life full of happiness, this one was chipping away at my very life.

These were the thoughts that kept me from sleep. However ill, however gaunt I'd been until then, further exhaustion only made things worse. All color drained from my skin, even my hair dulled. Javotte was beside herself with worry, but I couldn't bring myself to tell her that there was nothing she could do for me. I would've sent her away, but that would only have broken her heart completely.

One spring morning, I awoke to the news that there would be an execution the following day. The courts had just convicted a man, and it was only notable because it was to be the first capital punishment administered under the rule of the new king. For that reason, the king and I were expected to be there, to help instill fear of the Crown in the people's hearts, to accept the convict's pleas for forgiveness, and a lot of other things I didn't have the heart to do. Not much outside of the school and my maps interested me in those days as it was.

There was an odd buzz in the air the rest of the day, as if an execution was all it took to validate a king's crown. As if the people were actually looking forward to watching a man die.

As the spectacle was to take place in Camallea's main square, the king and I would have to ride in to witness the event. The captain was beside himself with only one day to scope out the area and set up proper security, so it wasn't any surprise that a nervous hum soon found its way to my ears. Knowing we'd be leaving the palace and riding into the center, the first thing I did was pull out my maps and trace our route.

The next morning, I dressed in an appropriately somber, modest dress. I suppressed a flinch from my husband's touch as he handed me into the carriage. Whereas I had become thin and pale, he was bursting with life, his sandy hair glossier, his eyes brighter, his skin practically glowing. He couldn't even keep a serious expression, his lips twitching up to show the tips of his shiny white teeth. Considering the charges, the convicted man deserved to die, but did the king really have to be so thrilled about it?

The king kept up a merry stream of conversation as we rode, and I responded as best I could. Surely, he'd seen a change come over me, but perhaps he thought to overcompensate by being extra cheery. Perhaps he thought he could infect me with his own tumbling abundance of happiness.

Sick man.

When we crossed the bridge, I was surprised the carriage didn't turn right onto the promenade, but rather continued onto the main road. I knew from studying the maps that this wasn't the most direct route for us to take. I glanced up at Alexander questioningly, but he innocently pretended nothing was amiss. I turned to look out the carriage window and caught a passing glimpse of a sculpture embedded with glass pieces catching the light from the sun.

I looked forward again, also pretending I hadn't noticed, my mind racing to deny the obvious explanation that we hadn't turned right because my charming prince didn't want me to see the shoe and the CinderElla inscription. Maybe he didn't want to see it either. Maybe he didn't want to be reminded of those heady days when we lived in storybook love.

But half seeing it shook something inside of me anyway. The thought of that monument, a kaleidoscope of hope, a celebration of overcoming circumstances was a reminder that whatever was going on between me and my prince was bigger and more important than the two of us. Our happiness, our joys, our successes were our people's, too. Hadn't I recently said as much to Prince Daimyon? Whatever was broken, we had to fix it, for them. Even if a shattered glass slipper cannot be put back together again.

The carriage soon turned off the main road onto a wide street that cut through Camallea. The king finally looked out the window, and from the set of his jaw and the steel in his eyes, I knew he'd mapped this route on purpose. He wanted to ride down the main road, wanted the citizens to see their monarch, wanted them to know he was fearless. It was the kind of thing Lyla would do.

When we arrived at the square, the carriage was forced to deviate from the planned route as foot traffic thickened the road, not allowing anything wider than a person to fit through. The coachman led the horses around the crowd and parked behind the square, in line with a set of wooden steps leading up to the hastily erected platform from where we would watch the Crown's justice done.

A red carpet covered the steps and the small square of platform, showing some effort had been put forth in consideration of the king and queen. Two large cushioned chairs stood side by side overlooking the executioner's platform and the surging crowd beyond it. All around, like little purple wildflowers popping up for spring, stood the king's soldiers, attentive and wary, their eyes roaming the crowd without ever really leaving their monarchs.

As we walked up the steps, a low rumble that turned into a cheer rose up from the crowd at the sight of us. The people whistled, they clapped, stomped their feet, and raised their fists in the air, raising up their monarchs on the work-worn backs of their fealty. The king stepped forward and beamed down at his subjects, an image of beauty and power, opening his arms to them in a show of acceptance and love, belief and pride in his people. I managed a small wave from my place, just so they wouldn't think I had rejected them. Still, it was enough to raise the noise from the crowd even more.

The king lowered his arms and with them fell the cheers. He sat in the seat beside me just as the low staccato of drums announcing the prisoner rose to a dramatic crescendo. As one, the crowd held its breath and the manacled prisoner was yanked forward and brought to his knees to hear the verdict against him.

Usually, the court's justice was clear, but as part of the ceremony of this day, the king would choose the man's death; a slow, painful beheading or a swift, merciful hanging.

The prisoner was pushed forward, to his right the noose, to his left the chopping block. The executioner looked to his king. Alexander didn't hesitate, he pointed to the block.

"Please," I gasped, "some mercy."

Alexander glanced down at me and shook his head. "A lesson must be taught," he said simply.

"There is another lesson you could teach," I reminded him with a nod to the noose.

He simply shook his head at me, disappointed at the weakness he thought he saw in me.

The executioner grabbed the prisoner by his neck and kicked his knees from behind so he was kneeling before the block. He grabbed his neck and shoved his head down, then towered over him, his blunt blade gleaming with anticipation. The onlookers responded in kind, leaning forward to better see the oncoming punishment.

Suddenly, from the back of the crowd, someone cried out. From my seat, I could see a man exiting a narrow alley and throwing himself against the mass of people as he attempted to push his way through the crowd. I looked around to see if anyone else had heard him, if anyone was seeing the man frantically waving papers above his head to attract someone's, anyone's attention.

His behavior could really mean only one of two things. Either the man before us had been pardoned, which was highly unlikely because the only one who could pardon him was sitting beside me, waiting for him to die. The second option was that new evidence had been uncovered, evidence strong enough to stay the execution and send the case back to court.

Either way, the man needed to get through. But no one seemed to know he was there.

"Alexander?" I questioned softly but received no response.

Realizing it was up to me, I half rose from my seat, lifting my hand to indicate to the nearest guard that he should help the man through. At almost the same time, I saw a guard step forward, but instead of helping the man, the guard pushed him back, essentially silencing him and the content of his papers.

I turned to look at the king, only to catch him looking away from what I had just seen. Without blinking, the king caught the eye of the executioner and nodded. My hand jumped to his arm, just as the executioner's sword began to saw at the man's neck.

The king glanced down at my grip and looked at me curiously.

"But that man with the paper," I whispered.

I received a blank look in return, the lack of question, the lack of curiosity evidence of feigned innocence. My hand left his arm to cover my mouth.

"The king's justice was decreed, so it had to be done," he said simply, and even after all my years of living with Madame's madness, I had never heard such cold words.

A possibly innocent man had to die, so cruelly, just so the king could prove the power of his crown.

What about the love, the justice, it was supposed to represent? What about the protection it was supposed to offer the people? The security? The compassion?

I saw something then in my prince's gaze which caused my stomach to curdle. Were I to live one thousand years, I would never forget that moment when I looked into his crystal blue eyes and no longer saw the depths of the ocean, no longer saw the clarity of a cloudless sky. The eyes that looked back at me were icy glaciers and I was only seeing the tip of their cruelty.

I knew what he'd done to me, but now I knew the problem ran deeper. It wasn't about lost love, or that this man hadn't lost the war with the evil inside; rather, he'd never fought it at all. It even seemed there were times, like now, that he willingly embraced it.

I felt like I had been suddenly skewered on a knight's lance. Whatever I thought about myself, I knew that I had accomplished something meaningful during my time at the palace. Maybe it wasn't anything great, maybe it wasn't enough, but it would be if I kept at it. Perhaps I hadn't found my happily ever after, but I had what I could do, and I would not let him take it away from me. I wouldn't let anyone take anymore from me.

I stood up and stumbled away from the king, who didn't even bother to call after me. He turned his focus back to the execution and I forced myself not to tumble down the stairs. Ignoring the carriage and the beckoning coachman, I began to run, removing the crown from my head and clutching it so tightly in my hand, I was certain it would draw blood.

My footsteps followed the map in my mind and I didn't stop until I could no longer hear the bloodthirsty crowd. I rested in a small piazza with a single well at its center. I could hear irony's maniacal life bouncing off the stones as I recognized it as the piazza where I had first met the prince and his captain all those years ago.

I studied it now with new eyes and realized that it was actually quite small and simple. Not the sunlit slice of paradise I'd once believed it to be, but just an ordinary piazza with a well whose screechy chain echoed annoyingly against the stones of surrounding homes.

I don't know how long I stayed there. I don't know if the king cared I was gone, if the carriage awaited my return, or if he'd given the nod, this time to turn the horses home regardless that the queen was missing. The shadows shifted in the piazza, afternoon dwindled, but it was still light when I heard the familiar clip of a royal horse.

It was no shock to me when it was the captain of all people who stepped into view.

"Won't you come home, Your Majesty?" he asked, offering me his hand.

I glanced up at the single horse, and it took a moment for the captain to realize his presumption.

"I can walk," he assured me quickly.

I shook my head at him. "No need," I said.

I gave him my hand, forgetting about the crown in it until he carefully released it from my grasp. He polished it with the corner of his tunic, and I was glad I couldn't see the narrow streaks of blood he lifted off the sharper points. The pain inside me then was too great to feel what the crown had done to cause that.

"Please help me up."

The captain complied. He knelt as I raised my foot to the stirrup, his hands ready to boost me, to steady me as I gave a little hop and somehow managed to swing my tiny frame onto his huge horse. The captain was seconds behind me, softly resetting the crown upon my head once he was set. As I sat uncomfortably sidesaddle, I could see the blush bloom in his cheeks when he had to reach around me for the reins, essentially holding me to him.

I didn't even blink.

The captain turned his horse toward home and keeping an eye on the first few streets we passed, I knew he was choosing the quickest and safest way back.

It didn't matter much to me at that point.

All I could think was that the last time I had ridden to the palace on the same horse as a man was when my charming prince had swept me into his arms and carried me off to a life brimming with hope and promise.

This time, there was no promise awaiting me. Only the scattered pieces of one.

~

I made straight for my little garden as soon as we arrived, the captain close on my heels, holding back his stride to keep pace with me. Once there, he tried to reach out to me, but I didn't want to speak with him. I needed time to think.

"Leave me," I commanded.

He hesitated, torn in his loyalty between doing my bidding as queen and fighting it as a friend. I had to pity him then, but I still didn't want him there.

"Please?" I asked again, much softer.

The captain nodded and left me to myself, and though I heard his footsteps retreat, I knew he wouldn't be far away.

Caring little about my clothes at that moment, I hiked up my skirts and clumsily clambered onto the decayed limbs of my once beautiful pear tree. It wouldn't be much longer before the bark would shrivel, the trunk crack from thirst, and the gardeners would drag it away and turn it into kindling, because a dead tree did not belong in the queen's garden. Or so they would think.

I still had it for now, and though it was a shadow of its former self, I pulled leaves and pears from my imagination and tenderly draped them along the branches in my mind. Thusly settled, I began to think. After some time, I finally forced myself to accept the uncensored, unvarnished truth, going all the way back to the beginning of my life in the palace.

Because of the situation he had lifted me from, I was grateful to the prince for every little thing I had. Therefore, I only wanted to make him happy, only wanted to do what he wanted, only wanted what he wanted. But while focusing on his perfection, I had missed the bigger picture. The prince hadn't brought us together. Heaven had given us an opportunity and we had taken it, Heaven had given us options and we'd chosen, just as the prince was doing now.

It really wasn't that different from when I lived with Madame. I was so grateful for any glance, any attention she'd give me, that I had allowed myself to become enslaved to her because I thought that if I would only do one more thing for her, if I could only make her happy, then she would be happy with me. But Madame never wanted to find any good in me. She never wanted whatever happiness I could bring her.

Then I thought how because of all that, I had only ever seen myself as too small, as too little, as not worth all that I'd been given. But there were those who had believed in me. My mother. Marie. Princess Lyla, Javotte, the captain, even Queen Alaina and Princess Kiara. So why had I never believed in myself? Why did I need the prince's approval to validate who I was?

So what if I hadn't been raised in court? So what if I had the body of an overgrown faery child and no magic despite my purple eyes? So what if I'd scrubbed the skin off my hands again and again with hard work and unwarranted labor? Did that mean I wasn't worthy? That my best wouldn't be something to be proud of, at least? Why did I need to wait for others to tell me what I could do? Why was I once more sliding into submission instead of rearing up in defiance?

What had I done with all the faith that had been placed in me?

I saw clearly then, as I'd never seen before, the map of my life from Heaven's eye, laid so plainly before me that I wondered how I could have mistaken the route I'd been pushed along, the route that had brought me here. I saw as well the paths that lay before me, the offshoots of roads that could have ended differently. I didn't want to be pushed along anymore. I needed to make changes, and I had to take a leap, do something big to make that happen. I would choose my way, and my eyes would be wide open to see where that road would take me.

Thusly, I came to a number of simple conclusions.

For one, this was my kingdom too, and therefore it was my duty to protect it and its citizens from all harm, including any stemming from the king himself. The king who would execute a possibly innocent man.

For two, the people had raised me up, had called me their CinderElla and I would regain my strength for them. I would raise them up with hope, even if I had none left for myself. In the same vein, I could let no harm happen to that CinderElla, or the people's hope would shatter as surely as that other glass slipper had on the steps of my old home.

For three, there were many people who had done much good for me and I could only repay them by showing that their faith and kindness had not been misplaced.

For four, I really, really, really did not like being poisoned.

I had tried to be kind to Madame, and she had belittled me, took all I owned, and locked me in my attic. I had given my entire self to the prince, and he had rejected it, wanting nothing more than to be rid of me. I was done with being kind to those who had been so cruel to me. It was time I made a definitive move to protect myself from cruelty and not just think about kindness for others, especially those who jeopardized me body or soul.

I didn't know how my mother would have reacted to such an assessment. She'd given me so much, brought me much farther than anyone would think possible from beyond the grave, but this was my life, my decision, my move.

So it was that I returned to my rooms invigorated by the new course I'd mapped for myself. A few days later, I snuck into the king's private quarters alone.

Although I'd been in my husband's rooms before, it hadn't been often, because he usually came to me. Standing in his rooms, everything felt distant and familiar all at once. All things here belonged to the man I had married and lived with almost five years, and yet I was only now getting his full measure. If I didn't know his mannerisms so well, every flicker of his eyes, every quirk of his lips, he could very well be a stranger for all I had known of the heart that beat inside.

I had timed my visit so the rooms were quiet when I came, and I didn't expect the king back for a while still. I had begged away in middle of dinner, my declined health excuse enough to allow me to leave without question, though there were always those who would talk. No one yet knew of my new resolve to live, and to live well.

I wandered around the king's rooms, taking everything in, looking at nothing in particular Finally, I made my way into his bedchamber and stood for some time in the doorway thinking about the man who slept there. His room, as I expected, was neat and orderly, a perfect mirror of the outwardly perfect man it sheltered. The bedspread was a royal purple etched with gold brocade, the curtains were purple with gold tassels, the colors successfully declaring how noble and wealthy the occupant was. With so much purple, I was surprised that the fire had been allowed to maintain its orange and blue glow. All the purple could not hide how similar those colors were to the captive dragon he hadn't hesitated to order slain.

I wandered over to a window and looked down at the grounds below. It was only after a few minutes that I realized the view from these rooms included an angle of the queen's gardens, but from a different side. The way this floor was built, my rooms were located at one end of the palace, and the king's rooms took up the center, so although his view was more expansive, it still shared some of mine. From where I stood now, I could just catch the glint of moonlight off the goldfish pond, but more important, I had a clear view of the encased glass slipper.

For a moment, I imagined myself as the king staring down at the blasted slipper that derailed my life. I could feel his annoyance, his anger, percolate each time he saw the singular reminder of his misguided actions. If I stood like this long enough, I would begin to hate myself, too.

So I turned away from the window, turned completely away and came face-to-face with my reflection, framed by the blasted window overlooking that blasted shoe. I studied myself curiously, studied the degeneration that was surely a secret source of pride for my husband. Standing there, scrutinizing myself, my eye caught onto something out of place in the window frame. I squinted, then turned around to closer examine what looked like a chip in the wood.

Bending down I ran my fingers along it and was surprised not to find it uneven because it sank in, but because it pushed out. I tapped my finger against it and soon decided it wasn't wood I was feeling. Sliding my tiny fingers along the height of the white piece, I dipped over with it as it crested the top of the frame and found my finger could get behind it as well. I pushed and wiggled and after some effort, popped up part of the frame so a flattened square of parchment could fall through.

Even before I picked it up I knew I would see a dealer's green seal. Even before I opened it, I knew I would smell the acrid, bitter bloodapple poison. Even before I had seen how little was left, I knew the prince had used the rest on me.

Once I confirmed all this, I knew the choice I would make.

My current way of life would not last. I could live in fear forever or do something to stop the force working against me. I could coax, persuade, cajole my husband, but it would be to no avail. Even his father, in his odd way, had warned me about him, warned me about the poison in his blood. I had been foolish enough to think my love would make a difference. I had seen the darkness of his cruelty manifest in different ways since I met him. My devotion would do nothing but continue to make me weak.

For too long I had been too kind to my prince. I had loved him, I had excused him, I had forgiven him, and I had turned a blind eye to his most grievous faults. And I had been given poisoned wine in return. My next act of kindness would not be for my prince, but for my people. I could no longer be kind to the cruel, allowing him to be cruel to the kind, the unfortunate, the innocent, the struggling, day after day. I had to withhold kindness if I wanted there to be anything left to hold onto.

Even so, I didn't really expect the night to turn out the way it did. Even then, I held onto the invisible strands of a thin, battered belief that maybe, just maybe, there was still something left between us, something worth saving. Even then, I thought one small kindness would be enough to reawaken the prince's heart, even if I would never fully hold it again.

I quietly left the king's room and waited in my own for the night to darken.

I returned to the king's chambers a few hours later, when the palace was so quiet that even the swish of my dress seemed too loud. I had wanted to wear the grand purple dress from our coronation, but I needed help putting it on and didn't want to alert Javotte about what I was about to do. Instead, I wore a simple gold dress, without jewels or beading, without extra stitching or embroidery. I though it appropriately understated.

I had to be careful slipping back in unnoticed. It wasn't easy but considering how many years I'd snuck around unnoticed before, I managed.

Stepping into the king's chambers, I stopped long enough to grab a half full decanter of wine from a small table. I was sure it tasted like cherries. Then I quietly crossed the threshold into my husband's room and gave my eyes time to adjust to the dark.

Once ready, I stepped toward the window and set down the wine so I could pour two glasses. I still wasn't convinced that I would have need for them, but I wasn't convinced that I wouldn't. I didn't bother to wipe up the few crimson drops my shaking hands spilled.

I drew open the curtains so the dim light from outside filtered in, illuminating my handsome, charming prince where he slept. The noise stirred him, and he began to roll over when he must have sensed something was not right. He noticed me there, standing with a glass of wine in one hand, my faery sword, void of magic but still lethal, in the other, my own balance of justice for the man who'd betrayed his kingdom.

His face worked through surprise, curiosity, anger, and finally settled on amusement. I studied the way the moonlight played across his once breathtaking features. He looked like an angel, illuminated as he was by the ethereal glow from outside. And wasn't it right to think he'd fallen from the sky? To return me to my once-lost Paradise? For so long, I had felt we were dancing on stars, but stars are made of fire after all. Dance there too long and someone will get burned.

"Hello, Ella," he finally said, devoid of any expression, despite using my real name for the first time in years.

"Hello, Prince Charming," I replied.

We watched each other a moment, a moment long enough for him to realize that I came with one intent. His amusement turned back to anger in the same flash that he lunged for me, hands flailing to grab my face, my hair, my dress, the hilt of my sword, anything. His fingers managed to swipe just above my wrist, leaving a trail of scratches that made it look like I'd tried to pet a tiger.

The sword in my other hand shot up and dug its point into his neck, drawing out a few thick beads of blood to match the spilled wine. I had to force my hands to remain strong and steady, force my eyes to stay clear so he wouldn't read any uncertainty, any crack in my resolve. Inside, my heart trembled with every nick of the sword. Five years ago, I could never, ever imagine the day when I would hold a sword to my beloved prince's neck. I was seeing it and I still couldn't believe it.

"Don't bother calling for the Captain," I hissed at him. "He let me in."

It wasn't true, but it could have been. I felt no regret at adding one more lie on top of the many that were already between us. I only thought then of keeping the upper hand.

"What are you doing?" the king growled, his voice a faded refrain of the melody it once carried.

"I'm here to say goodbye," I said simply.

Alexander actually smiled. "So you figured it out," he said.

I only nodded in reply.

He leaned back languidly, haughtiness overtaking his expression, a sneer overtaking his lips. Having preyed on my kind and willing nature for so long, he probably didn't think that night would be any different. Obviously, he was wrong.

"I tried to love you once, I really did, but whatever folly encouraged that silly notion is gone, long gone," he said, his words jabbing me like his own invisible sword. "I finally realized it wasn't worth it anymore. Rather, *you* weren't worth it anymore."

Through sheer and stubborn will, I kept my face blank. I wouldn't even give him the satisfaction of reacting. Inside, my thoughts roiled. I came here to give him a chance to prove my suspicions wrong, but he was only making things worse, much, much worse.

"Did you know that we knew who you were after the grand ball?" he asked suddenly. "Maybe we didn't know your exact identity, but the good captain trailed you on foot from the streets of Camallea, after your pumpkin exploded on the promenade. He spotted you in the alley, you and your blasted goose, and followed you home. Of course, then he only thought your dress was torn because you'd have taken quite a tumble from your mysteriously vanished carriage."

Actually, I hadn't known any of that, but I wasn't about to tell him.

"Imagine, while we took the shoe all over the kingdom, you were anxiously waiting for your prince to show up, and I was taking my time. That's why your house was one of the last ones we visited. Sir Percival may not have much sense of fun, but he certainly has a flair for the dramatic." He paused in his memory, then his face puckered like he'd unintentionally tasted wine meant for me. "Of course, you pulled one over on us when we came to your house and found out what you really were. A Cinderwench dressed by magic." He had to stop and swallow down the bile that came up with those words and I couldn't tell which one was more hateful to him. "Sir Percival had to convince me to put the shoe on you. He knew it would make for a good story, would rally the kingdom around me and all that; necessary, but loathsome nonetheless. I will admit to feeling like a hero for a while for having rescued you from that pitiful place. Even if you did deceive me," he added with a glare.

"You fell in love with a dress," I countered, "not the person within."

"I was as weak as my father," the king admitted bitterly. He smirked. "Though, the same could be said of you."

I didn't answer him. He was right after all, and more perceptive then he'd ever shown himself to be. We could have saved a lot of heartache if we'd only had this conversation a little earlier. Before he'd started to poison me.

"Once I saw the real you and knew what you'd done to trick

me, I couldn't ever let you bear my heir. I would never taint the royal lines with your blood. You crossed the line, Ella."

"You never gave me a chance," I protested.

"You didn't deserve one," he spat back.

"I would have earned it!" I snapped at him, temporarily losing the cool I was forcing myself to maintain. "I have earned it," I added much softer.

"How? What could *you* have possibly done?" the prince rolled his eyes disdainfully. "Anyway, once I was set on that I thought to get rid of you altogether, but there was no way to do so without angering the people. I could have lived with my decision until I'd figured something out, but the people just wouldn't let it go. All that CinderElla nonsense, and those monuments to you—"

"—that you never told me about," I cut in.

"I wouldn't give you the satisfaction," the king retorted. "And they had to be stopped. The people believed that if it could happen to you, it could happen to any one of them, and that's dangerous thinking, because most of them will never know anything other than their petty, little lives. I began to resent you, and it surprised me how quickly that can turn into hatred. I just didn't want you to live anymore."

"You would have made a martyr of me," I told him.

The prince shrugged. "Maybe. But *I* would have made such a tragic figure, mourning my true love taken from me, ever after cut short before we had the chance to grow old together. No one would question me or anything I did next." He gave me a devilish grin I would have once thought irresistible. "Even Sir Percival couldn't write a better story."

"Sir Percival would never try to kill me," I rejoined.

He waved away my comment as if it didn't make a difference. "I got the bloodapple and mixed some with wine so you wouldn't be able to fall pregnant. The idea was always there, but I never dared take the next step until the coronation, when I would have to make some important decisions for my kingdom. And you, you see, were a bad decision that needed fixing. A constant reminder of my weakness." He eyed me carefully, seeing me not as a person, but as a specimen for him to dissect.

"What did she do to you?" I whispered in horror.

"My mother?" The prince snorted. "She really was something. Never loved anyone but herself, not even my father who would do anything for her. She loved the crown and the powers that came with it, though I could believe she wanted the best for me." He paused a moment before continuing, his voice laced with scorn. "It was her idea to send me to the Academy, her idea to pull me out and stick me on the frontlines when those blasted wars began. Perhaps she feared I would be as weak as my father. Well, she wanted her son to be a man, and she got one, one she carved from stone herself."

It was right then, that look on his face that told me all I needed to know. I actually had the urge to vomit thinking of how well he'd hidden his true self from all of us, his wife, his captain, his cousin. I hadn't truly believed I would have to go through with my last resort until that very moment.

"Anyway, when your faery godmother stepped in with her magic again, she slowed my progress for a while. Of course, when she left, you were so distraught, you almost finished the job for me yourself," the man ended with a smug smile.

"Did you know that I was the servant girl who gave you water from the well the day the masquerade was announced?" I asked.

He blinked. He didn't know. Worse, he didn't remember. He never cared to. The moment that had meant so much to me could just as well have not happened for him.

"We can't go on like this," I said. "It isn't good for the kingdom either."

Alexander sneered again. "*We* most certainly will not go on at all. And I'll take care of Laurendale. It's not your concern."

I knew he only meant one thing by that. Despite the calm I'd maintained until then, at that point, I could hardly see him clearly as I fought away the tears threatening to blur my vision.

"So this is it?" It wasn't really a question.

"This is it," he confirmed.

I thought of the man he'd ordered executed, even when possible salvation was just footsteps away. I thought of the malice in his eyes, the compassion he'd decisively pushed away. I couldn't leave him the kingdom. This was no longer just about me.

I handed my once charming prince the glass of wine. "It's only right we toast the future together," I suggested.

He seemed to hesitate in putting the wine to his lips, but I shifted my grip on the still raised sword and he complied.

"To the future," I repeated, taking a sip of wine, twirling it around my tongue, finally tasting the cherries, which were delicious.

The prince's eyes widened as he drank from the glass I'd given him. From the first sip, he knew what I'd done, especially as I had no cinnamon to hide it with. He sputtered and tried to spit it out, but my sword was at his hand, pushing into it as it pushed the cup back to his lips.

"Finish it," I commanded, looking him straight in the eyes. "It's quicker and less painful."

As he slowly choked down the wine, I stood as tall as I could manage, but by then I understood that I didn't need height to raise myself up.

"Do you know what year this wine is from?" I asked calmly, forcing myself not to drop my sword, forcing myself to be brave, for my people. "It's from the year that *my* kingdom was reborn. Do you taste the hope? The tingle of promise?"

The prince didn't answer. His face had already paled with the knowledge of what was about to happen to him. He leaned back into his pillows heaving shallow breaths.

I pressed closer to the bed and peered into his terrified face. "You made a mistake not having an heir with me," I told him, my heart breaking from his deception. "For now I will start a new line of kings, untainted by your evil blood."

The prince choked in response. I didn't know anything about measurements. I had simply dumped the rest of the packet into his cup and prayed it really was strong enough to kill an animal. I couldn't let him live after this. And slitting his throat would raise too many questions.

I watched over him as he lay back and closed his eyes, but only because no man should die alone. I watched the hours tick toward dawn and watched still as the life drained from his beautiful face, as the swell of the sea left his enrapturing blue eyes, as the glint of gold faded from his sandy hair.

And when it was done, and he had breathed his last, I took the glass from his lifeless hand, smashed it into the fire, and left the room.

I still don't know if I made the right decision, but even now I can think of no other way out of the corner I was forced into. The prince hated me enough to kill me, and there was nowhere I could go to be safe from him.

I tried to leave that night behind me as I walked away from his rooms, but I couldn't. It would be a long, long time before I could think of his final moments in their entirety without dissolving into gut-wrenching tears.

AFTER EVER AFTER

*N*o one ever found out the truth of what had happened to the king in his final hours, and no one was ever meant to. Honestly, no one even bothered to ask, and I realized then how easy it would have been for the prince to get rid of me as the kingdom rallied around me in my sorrow. He was right: My supposed despair at true love cut short made for a story that even Sir Percival couldn't have written any better.

There were two full weeks of mourning leading up to his burial to allow nobility, dignitaries, and commoners to pay their respects to him and the grieving widow he left behind. Only once it was all over could I finally begin to fix the kingdom.

Princess Lyla came for a few days to say farewell to her cousin, and to make sure I was really recovering.

"Did you ever make peace with Alex, before he—" She choked in middle of her question, unable to get the rest of the words out.

I thought back to that last night together, of the cruel honesty of a conversation that had come too late to save either of us from what came next.

"Yes," I told her. "Yes, I did."

She smiled and squeezed my hand, not understanding, never to know all that was held in my answer.

Despite her sorrow, Lyla looked wonderful, much better than I'd ever seen her since the day we met almost five years ago. What's more, she seemed almost content. I found out why the day she left, when after we'd said our goodbyes, she caught my hand and placed it on her stomach.

"If it's a girl, we'll name her Ella."

She laughed when my lips floundered soundlessly as every word escaped me. She then left a thick paper in my hand, in which was pressed a large orange-and-yellow lily. It made me smile to think that perhaps, with enough time, with enough work, with enough perseverance, she'd finally find real happiness in her ever after.

I genuinely mourned the king with the rest of the kingdom, and not just because he had done some good for me after all.

For one, he'd given me a new life.

For two, he'd given me a crown.

For three, he'd given me a kingdom.

For four, he'd forced me to take control of my life for the first time since my mother died.

In addition to all that, I mourned a man who'd turned his heart to stone. I mourned even more for what could have been.

There came one day when the captain found me in my newly planted garden, the pear tree having been dug up and replaced, the pond filled with new fish, the glass slipper remaining untouched. I was sitting on a bench I'd requested installed as I would not climb the new tree to sit in. By my leave, the captain sat beside me and placed something in the space between us.

I glanced down and saw a small bundle of dead flowers. I didn't understand its meaning until I looked closer and recognized it for the small bouquet of yellow flowers my stepsisters had given me on that long-ago night when I thought I would never see the palace again. The same bouquet I left with the captain when I had collided with then spun away from him in my final retreat from the prince.

There were a number of things he could have been saying by showing me he still had it after all these years. I wondered if it had anything to do with his brother's enigmatic remarks from the afternoon we spent at his family's estate, when he'd told me how his brother had changed in the time since I'd come to the palace. I wondered if it had anything to do with how I'd been given an invitation to the masquerade that had started all this.

Unsure, I didn't say anything, waiting for the captain to speak first.

He broke the silence with, "I would have done it."

I never doubted that he would figure it out. "I know," is all I replied.

"I would have accepted the punishment for my crime," he added.

"I know," I said again. "But it had to be me."

He nodded and without looking, as if not wanting to bear witness to what his body was about to do, his hand reached out to take mine and I gave it a small squeeze in return, so he'd know I'd be all right. I was scared of what lay ahead, but I was ready, too. He should know that. He never thought I was too small for anything Heaven sent my way.

I can't say that everything suddenly changed now that I was the only one sitting on the throne. It wasn't easy trying to rule a kingdom as I was still so fairly new to a title that others trained for from birth. I also began to understand Alexander's view that there were times that harsher lessons had to be taught, though I always, always tried to temper mine with some compassion.

I tried my best to work with Sir Percival and from his mutterings it seemed I had some ideas that were worthwhile. I wasn't deterred, though. With enough time, with enough work, with enough perseverance, I would become a queen worthy of the gift of my kingdom.

Magic was warmly welcomed again, but it trickled back slowly, the faery folk hesitant to come back right away. That was all right by me. I didn't need someone else's magic anymore. And I wouldn't let it rule me either. I would create my own, in the kindnesses I did for others, in the kindnesses they would do for someone else in turn. And when I did have children, there would be magic in their smiles, in our shared joys, in the good things they accomplished, in our lives together.

About half a year after Alexander was buried and my kingdom began to take form, a new normal began to take over our lives. One quiet afternoon, I was leaning over my maps, now pleasantly dotted with multiple spots for new schools, when the captain was announced to my rooms.

"Your Majesty," he kneeled before me.

I studied him there a moment, not yet giving him permission to rise.

"CinderElla," I decided. "From now, I shall be called Queen CinderElla."

The captain peeked up at me and his cheeks rose in a smile. "I think it a wonderful idea, Your Highness."

"And do you think, Captain, when they tell CinderElla's story, when they tell tales of my kingdom, will they remember everything that was? Not just the faery tale clouding the beginning, but the truth of what occurred?"

"They will, Your Majesty," he replied confidently.

"You don't know that," I said, "but your faith is encouraging."

A twinkle shone in his eyes, and all at once I saw him clearly, saw the man he'd always been and not just the parts I'd never bothered to piece together. From that first day at the well, a succession of images flashed before my mind, the basket of bread he'd bought me to give the poor, the time he'd dried my tears, the afternoons he'd sat with me in the tree, the nights he'd stayed by my side when I was sick, the moment he set my rejected crown back upon my head.

I had long thought the stars danced in the prince's eyes, but all this time there was a guiding North Star burning much brighter, more constant before me.

"Rise, Captain," I finally allowed, and as he stood I held my hand out to him.

We'd been through a lot and we had a way still to go, but I knew, somehow, we would get there together. I thought of what my life was, of what my life had been. I clearly saw every piece that had made me, the parts of goodness I'd received from my mother and Marie, the pieces charred by pain from Madame, the prince's blackness I fought to keep from tainting others.

I thought I had tumbled out of paradise, but it was never really mine. However, I could build my own, every day I lived for my people, every day I ruled with a kind and fair hand. I could not see the future, could not see what my life would become, but I did know what I did not want it to be. I didn't want my life to be dark, I didn't want it to be bleak no matter who tried to block the sunlight from streaming in. I never wanted to stop seeking happiness, hoping that one day, somehow, someway, I would find it, create it, again. I needed to heal, but before me was someone who would help me along the path I'd choose, someone who encouraged a caged girl with stunted wings to fly.

"You needn't bow before me anymore, Matteus," I added, returning his name to him.

He smiled knowingly, and the twinkle that began in his eye

sparked, as sharp and potent as the magic from a faery godmother's wand.

In that one instant, that flash of time when dream and reality, hope and ambition, potential and possibility converge, in that one moment, however fragile, however brief, I believed once more in happily ever after.

THE END

The faery tales continue in
Lies of Golden Straw
Available November 27, 2018

Turn the page for a sneak peek.

Don't miss your next favorite book!

Join the Fire & Ice mailing list
www.fireandiceya.com/mail.html

LIES OF GOLDEN STRAW

SNEAK PEEK

Ever After

Once upon a time, I was naught but the miller's daughter. That time is over and no one will ever call me such again. I have a new name now, a name I took the day I left my past at the mill and agreed to a future with the king.

Since then, I have seen much of the world, not just the lives of my citizens, but the kingdoms across the realms. I have met queens and princesses far more beautiful than I, met men with tales far taller than the ones Father used to tell, and I have seen magic far greater than any a young magical I once knew could yield.

Was it worth it?

When once the glint of my future was only bright enough to light the forest around the mill, the present shine is dazzling enough to illuminate an entire kingdom. I don't think much on the life that could have been, of the possibilities I refused the day I stepped into my new name. Yet there is a man, once a boy with a bright, lavender gaze that lit up when he saw me, who would say the cost was not worth the gain, no matter that jewels instead of straw now adorn my hair. No matter that the price for such riches was but a few simple words to shade the truth.

For the story of how I came here unfolded in ways that prove truth is much stranger, much more dizzying, much more dangerous than fiction. For unlike others, I wasn't made queen for my beauty, my courage, my wisdom, or my lands and title. Rather, ludicrous as it may seem, I became queen because of my magical ability to spin straw into gold.

Except I can't.

I became queen on a lie, and it wasn't even the biggest or grandest one ever told. It was simply the one that changed my life for good.

ACKNOWLEDGMENTS

For this book, and for the rest to follow, I must acknowledge all the fairy tales, fables, and even Biblical stories and Talmudic teachings that were the inspiration for, and have been woven into, each telling in this series.

Fairy tales aren't real but they could have been when Caroline said yes! to this whole series. Many thanks to you and to all at Fire and Ice YA.

Magic, on the other hand, isn't really so hard to find with Miryam as an editor. I am so grateful and thrilled to be working with you again. Thank you for your patience as I searched for those elusive Rumpelstiltskin-like names.

Thank you Cousin Andrea, my brother Levi, and Disney acolyte Emily for reading and critiquing when this was just a rough-and-tumble draft.

Special shout out to my family and friends for never locking me in the attic with a crazy macaw.

And to you, the reader, thank you.

THANK YOU FOR READING

Did you enjoy this book?

We invite you to leave a review at the website of your choice, such as Goodreads, Amazon, Barnes & Noble, etc.

DID YOU KNOW THAT LEAVING A REVIEW...

- Helps other readers find books they may enjoy.
- Gives you a chance to let your voice be heard.
- Gives authors recognition for their hard work.
- Doesn't have to be long. A sentence or two about why you liked the book will do.

ABOUT THE AUTHOR

E.L. Tenenbaum is fairly certain a bookstore is really the happiest place on earth. In addition to being an author, her love for stories in different shapes and sizes has led to a degree in journalism, a stint as a script reader, and a few runs as writer/director for community musical theater. When she's not reading, or writing, she enjoys speaking at middle/high schools as a visiting author.

For more information about previous/current/upcoming work follow her on social media or visit :

www.ELTenenbaum.com

www.facebook.com/ELTenenbaum
www.twitter.com/ELTenenbaum
www.goodreads.com/ELTenenbaum

ALSO BY E. L. TENENBAUM

WITH FIRE & ICE YOUNG ADULT BOOKS

End of Ever After Novels

End of Ever After

Lies of Golden Straw (November 27, 2018)

Beautiful to Me (January 2019)

Human Again (2019)

Heart of a Hunter (2019)

Novels

The Sapphire Legend, Part I

The Sapphire Legend, Part II

Silhouettes

CPSIA information can be obtained
at www.ICGtesting.com
Printed in the USA
LVHW091740221019
634989LV00002B/163/P

9 781680 466898